The
UNEXPECTED
JOURNEYS
of
Lawrence Tyrone

The

UNEXPECTED
JOURNEYS

of

Lawrence Tyrone

A NOVEL

A.K. BLACKMAN

LIFESTYLE
ENTREPRENEURS
PRESS
LAS VEGAS, NV

ISBN: 978-1-948787-2-08

Published by:
Lifestyle Entrepreneurs Press
Las Vegas, NV

If you are interested in publishing through Lifestyle Entrepreneurs Press, write to: *Publishing@LifestyleEntrepreneursPress.com*

To learn more about our publications or about foreign rights acquisitions of our catalogue books, please visit: *www.LifestyleEntrepreneursPress.com*

Printed in the USA

For Jo – a bright, shining light
and for my mother – always

The
UNEXPECTED
JOURNEYS
of
Lawrence Tyrone

Part One

[1] The Bartered Bride

On a bright morning in August, Lawrence Tyrone walked down the street with a newspaper under his arm and thoughts of revenge. Trees loomed over his head, shading him from the sun while a sporadic breeze disturbed his grey silk tie. He did not notice these things. He was fully aware that revenge was a double-edged sword, satisfying yet fraught with potential disaster. He could point to men and women in prison who let their thirst for revenge lead them to ruin.

"Let's talk about deviant behavior," he'd said to his students during his lecture the week before. "How do you think it contributes to an understanding of ethics and ethical conduct?" Some of them left the class still debating the issue, but the general consensus was that criminals and criminal behavior were not templates for what not to do in real life. It was a very old philosophical question in legal debate.

He considered himself to be a good professor, willing to push them further than they might be willing to push themselves. The fact that his law faculty branded him as a maverick, or a loose cannon, depending on who was at the table, was a badge of honor in his opinion. And yet his personal life was a different matter.

On one of the backstreets leading towards his office he stopped, diverted. A little boy was playing by himself on the paved driveway in front of his house, oblivious to his surroundings. He was humming quietly as he pushed around a bright red toy truck. The child's self-sufficiency and total absorption made Tyrone forget his ill feelings for an instant. Then the boy spun the wheels faster and faster on the pavement until the truck flew down the driveway towards the street. Tyrone reacted quickly as the boy watched his escaping toy.

"Here you go," Tyrone said, almost certain the tyke had done it on purpose. He'd been tempted to let the truck go and watch what happened but thought better of it when he heard the sound of a car engine as it drove by.

The boy looked up with a serious expression. "My truck," he said.

"Yes, yes, your truck," Tyrone was saying when a woman he presumed was the mother, appeared at the door. "Just rescuing the truck from the street," he said quickly before she had a chance to react.

"Oh, yes," she was distracted. "He came out here by himself when my back was turned."

"Yes, well," Tyrone said, aware of her uneasiness. "Good day."

"Thank you," she called out after him before herding her son into the house.

As he continued on his way, his thoughts took a detour. Perhaps he should continue to concentrate on what to do about his own son — a boy he had never met — before he tackled world peace.

He pushed the thought away. It made no difference to his desire for revenge.

Once seated at his office desk, he unfolded the newspaper he was carrying and stared at an announcement.

He'd assumed he was numb. His first wife, after all, meant nothing to him. Not from the time she left him. Why should he even care after all she had done and all that had passed between them? He was convinced he had obliterated his longing to touch her body one last time; buried his regrets and his memories of her dark hair and milky skin.

Strangely, the announcement in the paper did not include his colleague down the hall. This deceitful character he had been so sure was her lover was not the man she was engaged to. What she was doing was far worse.

He crumpled the paper and threw it across the floor, then went after it. The words stayed the same. The two names were outlined in bold.

Damn it all to hell, you conniving rat, he thought, staring out through the ancient panes of his office window. He struck his desk with a clenched fist.

Once he calmed down he was shocked he could feel so bereft while everything outside remained the same. The grass stayed green, the sky blue, the boy and girl under the farthest oak were still necking when they should have been studying.

Worst of all, the memory of his final hours with his faithless ex-wife had not left him.

He could still see her, sitting at the kitchen table, her glossy lips moving, her voice sounding further and further away. Trying to buy time, he said, "There's no *coffee*." She stared at him. "Arrogant bastard, didn't you hear me?" she said. "No matter what I say you don't listen." Her eyes were narrowed, full of an emotion he couldn't bear to see.

And now, five years later, with the afternoon sun shining in strips on his office floor, he was suddenly back in that same dark place he'd plunged into just after she was gone. He crossed the room and extracted a hip flask from the bookshelf on the right, which was stuffed with legal precedents and journals. The flask was jammed behind the 2000 and 2001 volumes of *The Journal of Criminal Law*. He wanted to avenge himself. But wait, he thought, there was another way. There were many things he couldn't — and wouldn't — do. But what he had in mind was perfectly justified. A faultless, if unoriginal, plan.

He reached for the phone.

"Spenser, you lying bastard," he hissed into the receiver the moment he heard the voice at the other end.

"Have you been drinking?" Spenser said. "Call me when you're sober."

"I'm sober enough, you lying shit. You said you weren't seeing her."

"I'm hanging up now."

"Don't you dare hang up. It says you're engaged. I'm coming to the wedding and you can't stop me."

"Listen to me, Lawrence," Spenser said. "Just listen — okay, okay — I swear it's for the best. Can we get together and talk? I'm there. Just tell me what I have to do."

Tyrone could hear the urgency in Spenser's voice that signaled he was getting ready to negotiate. "I'm your brother," he said. "Did you think you could just go ahead and plan to marry my wife?"

"Your ex-wife," Spenser broke in. "She's not —"

"The hell with you," Tyrone said, slamming the phone down.

On the day of the wedding, a Sunday in early September, Lawrence Tyrone got up at six in the morning and removed his tux from the garment bag in the guest-room closet. He brushed it off and laid it on his side of the bed along with a starched white shirt and his cummerbund. He placed his gold cufflinks on the dresser, polished his Italian leather shoes and put on his black wool socks, thin as silk.

Stepping back, he surveyed the room and the laid-out clothes. The morning light shone on everything he wore to his own first wedding, an occasion where he had been confident and, he was sure, happy. He remembered overhearing a wedding guest, a curvy blonde, describing him as magnetic and surprisingly attractive. A backhanded compliment if he ever heard one. At the time it made him smile.

He dressed with attention to detail, ran a wet comb through his salt-and-pepper hair and sank into the living-room sofa. His apartment was on the fifth floor facing south and the rising light was beginning to hurt his eyes. Permitting himself a half glass of single malt with just a splash of water, he waited, keeping the bottle handy on the rosewood table at his left hand.

In the hazy light made real by the effects of grain alcohol, he dreamt.

"Bastard," she says. He hears the word more than once. "Leah," he calls out to her on that morning long ago, as he feels a searing pain in his gut and falls to the kitchen floor clutching his stomach.

"You never listen, you just don't want to know," he remembers her whispering as she looks down at him. Before he passes out, writhing in pain, he also remembers wondering if she has poisoned him and is suddenly feeling remorse and a belated affection.

At one in the afternoon, more than a little mellow, he congratulated himself on making a wise decision and called a cab. For good measure, just before he left the house, he slipped a mickey into his inside pocket. From here on the trajectory of his life would change, but he didn't yet know it.

He had pried the location and date of the wedding, which was not mentioned in the engagement announcement, from Leah's grandmother, the one who never liked him, the one who used to stare at him darkly when he came to visit and mutter heavily accented observations in Leah's ear. He learned through the grapevine that the old bat was now hard of hearing and tended to get confused. It was fitting that she should be the one to help him.

"Hallo? Anatoly, that you? Tawk to me!" she had shouted into the receiver in her deep whiskey voice, mistaking him for one of her nephews.

"I lost the wedding invitation," he shouted in turn, wondering if he was wasting time. After fifteen minutes of verbal maneuvering, while the old woman coughed and introduced seemingly irrelevant topics, he hung up the phone smiling. For just a moment he felt uneasy, as if there was something in the interchange he should have paid attention to but had missed. When nothing came to mind he decided he was just imagining things and put his misgivings aside.

The cab ride to a golf and country club overlooking the immensity of Lake Ontario from the Scarborough Bluffs was a bumpy one. He noticed the bumps especially when he was trying to take a surreptitious swig. The place used to be a former hunt club, but fox hunting was no longer in style. Instead, it was often used as a meeting place where Bay Street lawyers and investment managers hatched plots and brokered deals while ordering liquid lunches and dinners that were exorbitantly overpriced. Tyrone was pleased to see the number of cars in the parking lot. They spilled over onto the brilliant, perfectly manicured grass along the private road leading to the front entrance: Rolls Royces, Bentleys, Jaguars, BMWs, even a Lamborghini parked sideways, taking up two spaces.

While the valet was pretending not to notice the arrival of the battered cab, Tyrone handed the driver a bill. "Keep the change," he said.

"What change?" the cabbie said. "You owe me another twenty."

Tyrone frowned. The cabbie was waving five dollars in his face. The man must have palmed the fifty. Then he noticed the fifty lying at his feet. Not wanting to admit his mistake he took a closer look at the meter. The amount was $24.95. He pocketed the fifty and pulled out a twenty from his wallet. "*Now* you can keep the change," he said.

Out on the curb, he negotiated the steps at the entrance to the club with great care and made it to the top in what he considered to be a calm and elegant manner. He smoothed his tux jacket and was pleased to note he was no longer angry or vengeful, just another ordinary wedding guest showing up at his ex-wife's marriage to his brother. What could be simpler? And besides, he was looking forward to the occasion. He was too upset to think of the pleasure beforehand, but his anticipation had grown on the cab ride down.

Past the imposing green copper doors of the club, there was a reception desk. A man and woman dressed in black-and-white formal attire were checking off names against a list printed on creamy vellum and handing out seating cards along with boutonnieres to the gentlemen and corsages to the ladies.

Tyrone jumped the queue and headed straight for the woman, a pretty redhead with translucent freckled skin, who was dressed in a strapless gown. In the afternoon light, her shoulders gleamed.

"I need to sit down," Tyrone said, holding a hand to his heart. He noted from her glance that she didn't believe it was his heart that was the problem, but he knew she couldn't afford to take the chance. "A chair if you will be so kind," he said, staring at the chair just behind her.

"Of course, sir," she said. "Will you need help?"

He supported himself against the table, wondering if she was being brash. He needed all his concentration to keep his eyes focused on the guest list. Just before he sat down he managed to glimpse a name he could use.

Once past the officious guards at the reception desk, he declined the glasses of wine on trays proffered by white-gloved waiters and headed straight for the bar. Holding a full glass of single malt, he wandered past unfamiliar guests who were gathered in hushed little groups and went outside past rows of chairs to the cloth-covered table under the white canopy facing the lake. The uneasy feeling nagged at him again, as if he were still overlooking something. Then he got it. Why didn't he know anyone? Shouldn't there at least be a few people he and Leah and Spenser had in common? He was looking forward to saying hello and giving them his unfiltered, yet perfectly objective, opinion about the wedding. But Spenser had lots of business connections Tyrone was not privy to. So, no need to worry.

The southernmost part of the Hunt Club's perfectly manicured lawn was poised on the edge of the Scarborough Bluffs. The tall cliffs of the escarpment towered 300 feet above Lake Ontario. A remnant of an ancient ice-bound lake carved out by glacial water flowing under immense ice floes, the deep blue waters of the great lake flashed and sparkled below the precipitous drop. It was a perfect day to get married.

His eyes began to ache from squinting into the bright light. For just a moment he allowed himself to remember Leah, the way she looked on their wedding day, how she smiled at him when he broke the glass to commemorate their vows, the softness of her warm, full lips when he kissed her. And then he thought about how she never visited him in the hospital after he collapsed on their last day together.

When he was discharged from the hospital, his ulcer more or less on the mend, her clothes were gone. What remained was a very faint scent imprinted on the unchanged sheets and pillows on her side of the bed. During his first night back in their bedroom he could have sworn her dark head, her warm skin, her generous ass, were still there beside him. He didn't wash her pillow case for a month after she was gone, holding on to his anger and her scent, resolving never to call her.

A jab on his ankle from a twig he stumbled against brought him back to the surroundings of her second wedding. He focused on two red foxes skulking around the edges of the lawn, secure in the knowledge they would no longer be shot or torn apart by hounds. Fishing two ice cubes out of his glass, he lobbed them and watched the foxes disappear into the bushes.

It occurred to him that the man whose name he'd borrowed would show up and cause trouble, so he made his way deeper into the trimmed bushes and tall trees surrounding the club, holding his liquid courage in one hand and the mickey he brought in the other. Observing from his woodsy hiding place, he watched two serving staff half-heartedly carry out what he took to be a search around the chairs set out in rows on the lawn. He wondered if the staff were looking for him, the rogue guest.

Leaning against a tree behind some tall bushes out of sight of the main event, he drained his glass and replenished it from his supply. A half hour later he opened his eyes, surprised to find himself sitting on the ground with his back pressed against the tree trunk. He stood up and brushed himself off.

Out on the lawn, everyone was filing to their places in the rows of outdoor chairs, ready for the action to begin. Taking his last sip, he left the glass under the tree and headed over to the last row.

The music started. A quartet, seated on a little platform at the rear of the assembly, launched into a quietly spirited rendition of the famous aria from "Carmen." It was a piece of music Leah loved, even belting it out in the shower at the beginning when they had been happy, her voice soaring on the high notes. "Oh, you faithless witch," Tyrone said under his breath, at a loss to understand how she had so easily transferred the things they shared to his brother. By the time the quartet started on Offenbach's "Barcarolle," he was already seated in the rearmost chair on the far right.

The sun was bright and the sky was brilliant. While the groom walked up the aisle, accompanied by his best man, Tyrone skulked down in his chair. The man in front of him was tall and wide and blocked his view of both the groom and the Chuppah, the covered canopy under which a bride and groom traditionally stand during a Jewish ceremony. The Chuppah was positioned closest to the lake facing south. To get a good look at his brother's back from where he was sitting, Tyrone would have had to stand and he wasn't prepared to do that just yet. In the end, he couldn't contain himself and, pressing towards the person sitting on his left, he peered around the behemoth sitting in front of him. On catching a glimpse of the best man's back, he was puzzled, but convinced himself this too was to be expected. Probably just as well he didn't recognize him. Were it not for his brother's lack of ethics, he would have been his brother's best man. *You bastard*, he thought, *you despicable traitor.*

At the first bombastic notes of the traditional "Wedding March," the guests stood up. Tyrone attempted to steady himself against his chair. He strained to catch a glimpse of the bride. She was covered up by her veil. For a moment he was surprised, having expected a more secular wedding or even one with more eclectic traditions in keeping with Leah's artistic sensibilities. The "Wedding March?" A veil? A female rabbi? Still, Spenser, although not particularly religious, usually liked to refer to the Torah, whether he knew what he was talking about or not. What a coward his brother turned out to be.

Tyrone cleared his throat. His vision was blurred and the elaborate white wedding dress gave him pause. But Leah's favorite aria had been so exuberantly played by the quartet just a few minutes earlier. He closed his eyes for a moment and then jerked awake as his head dropped forward. There was an anxious roaring in his ears. He told himself to wait. Not yet. Not yet. Finally, he could bear it no longer. The groom had just been instructed to kiss the bride.

"I object," Tyrone shouted, shooting up from his seat. "She is still married. This marriage is not legal."

The bride and groom looked back, their faces white and startled.

It was not Leah. It was not Spenser.

It was only then Tyrone realized what he should have guessed long ago had he not been so intent on drowning his anger all morning with a bottle. All those misgivings meant something he had been determined to ignore.

In the complete silence, he felt faint, his mind for once blank. The next minute, he was sprinting towards the empty, welcoming back entrance of the club. He was aware of blurred faces, arms and hot wind at his back as three ushers, plus the groom, ran after him. Even though he was older by far than all four of them, the duplicity of the evil grandmother propelled him. The crafty old bat hadn't forgotten or forgiven him his transgressions. She sucked him in proper. In the state he was in, all he could think of was how fast he could get away.

[2] Another Day Older

Back at his apartment, in the late afternoon, Tyrone fortified himself with a few more tumblers of Scotch, swirling it around with a splash of water and opening a second bottle at the kitchen counter in the early evening without spilling a drop. Then, in his study, watching the shadows cast by the light of a yellow desk lamp, he attempted to formulate his thoughts on the coming week's seminars. It was the best way he knew of to keep himself moving. He'd been planning to cover how laws and the consequences of breaking them continued to change with the times. It was a favorite thesis of his. But his circumstance was far from normal and he couldn't concentrate.

He imagined how his brother and Leah were laughing at his follies on their wedding night, how the bat of a grandmother was chuckling and rubbing her hands together.

For a moment, he was aware of the old familiar feeling of being alone and without purpose. Tyrone was eleven and Spenser was nine when their mother died. Their father, unable to hold up began to drink heavily. Spenser relied on Tyrone in those sad, intolerable days. It was Tyrone who took care of his younger brother, making sure he got to school on time, had his books and his lessons, ate breakfast, even though there was only two years between them. It was Tyrone who shouldered adult burdens and who left his boyhood behind. In his very darkest nights he wondered if he would ever recover from his mother's loss; it was not something he would have confessed to anyone. During the long period when he was feeling there was nowhere to turn, and no one to confide in, he turned to smoking dope — just a little here and there, nothing to worry about, enough to blunt what he didn't want to feel.

And now here was another long night with no relief or indication of what he could do to make it better. He kept sipping his single malt and putting his pen to the yellow legal pad, drawing circles and squares, willing himself to put together his next lecture.

But this intolerably long night defeated him. He could not think of a single word he wished to write.

He was still doodling, unable to start, when he noticed the bottle was empty, there was a water ring around the empty glass beside him and daylight was glinting off his pen.

Two hours later, he got out of a cab on the busy street in front of the Law Faculty and had the brilliant idea of confiscating a motorbike from one of his top students, who was removing his helmet after having parked in one of the few choice spots at the curb. Tyrone thought it would be a wonderful way to start his lecture. Show his students the difference between arguments of law necessary to maintain law and order as opposed to mere impolite behavior. In short, the difference between breaking the law in one form or another versus intentional rudeness, which generally had no legal consequences. He took a closer look at the student. Ah, it was Don somebody, or was it Dick? No matter, Tyrone felt magnanimous. "Come to my office later, there's a way to improve the paper you wrote," he told the disconcerted young man as he rode of on the motorbike in a roar of firing pistons.

Much later, whenever he could bear to think of this day, it was to try and recapture his convoluted reasoning so he would never repeat it. Still, on that day, riding that motorbike up the shallow concrete stairs and through the heavy faculty double doors into the hallway, he felt his reasoning was exceptionally sound and laughed when a few of his colleagues scattered to get out of his way. At the last two disciplinary committee meetings held in his honor, he showed up sober with explanations befitting an exceptional scholar of litigation. This time he cursed when the dean pulled out a cell phone to call 911.

He was aware of pandemonium and then deathly silence as he watched two policemen come towards him. When they got closer he let the bike fall to the ground and raised his arms. "I have a sugar imbalance," he said with composure, remembering an old case he could quote from. "I've just eaten a candy bar. I am now perfectly well."

"Steady there, sir, don't strike a match while you're breathing," the younger cop said. "You wouldn't want to start a fire." The man was obviously a boor who didn't know about professional courtesy.

Checking his anger with some difficulty, Tyrone stumbled towards the professor he once pegged as Leah's former lover. "Send them away," he said. "And I will behave, I promise."

He leaned against the wall while he watched his unexpected ally in conversation with the dean, who kept shaking his head. Finally, the dean took a long, hard look at Tyrone and walked towards the officers.

After the confusion subsided and the police were gone, Tyrone walked carefully into the nearest boardroom followed by the dean and some of the other faculty. He propped himself up in a chair, while his ersatz rival eyed him with pity from across the table. In a perverse way, Tyrone now decided he admired the man, even though he had once assaulted him.

The hearing was very brief. The previous two times he was hauled in front of the disciplinary committee he was not so outrageous in full public view. This time there was undeniable proof. Drunk and disorderedly conduct unbecoming. Given his previous history of flouting rules and teaching the curriculum with no thought of following standard texts, all five committee members said they had no choice. He was suspended immediately pending a full hearing.

"Now," the dean said, looking him in the eyes, "you are free to go home."

Tyrone got up. Leaning forward on the table, he said, "Suspended? I believe we need to see about that."

As he cautiously made his way towards the door, he noticed his colleague, the professor who had interceded on his behalf, standing there. He owed the man.

"Thank you," he said with as much dignity as he could muster. "I do apologize for — well — for everything." He couldn't bring himself to elaborate.

The man nodded. His face was unreadable but seemed to be void of judgement.

Ignoring all the students standing in the hallway looking at him with curiosity —maybe even pity — Tyrone made his way past them.

It was only when he was outside under the high sun that he realized he was still wearing his tux and his dress shirt needed tucking in.

[3] Palomino Sal

The formal hearing took place in the great hall of the Rheimann wing of the Osgoode Hall Law Faculty at the beginning of October, attended by some of Tyrone's former colleagues and three outside lawyers. The Law Faculty, an immense heritage building with myriad additions, corridors, nooks and crannies, occupied six acres of prime downtown real estate, situated on more than a full city block of land behind ornate nineteenth-century wrought-iron fencing.

Tyrone waived his right to a lawyer, determined to represent himself. One showed up anyway. He fired the man on the spot and another lawyer stepped up, smiling benignly. It was one of his old professors, a man who once told him he had promise and whom he admired. For the first time, Tyrone felt humbled. He sat back, concentrating on his self-appointed legal representative's white hair and mottled hands.

Listening to the proceedings, he grew increasingly indignant. They were talking about someone else, they had the wrong man. Each time he rose to interrupt, his old professor restrained him with a surprisingly strong hold. In the end, he could not articulate the cogent points that came so glibly to him in the past and kept silent.

Outside, looking tired after his few unsuccessful and, arguably, half-hearted arguments, his professor patted him on the back. "Come back to us, Lawrence," the old man said. "Come see me when you're ready."

Throwing himself into his car he drove straight to his brother's place in Barrie, exceeding the speed limit, itching for a confrontation. He hadn't wanted to face Leah, but now he was past caring and swerved into the driveway, then pounded on the solid door of his brother's house.

One of the neighbors came out to stare at him and then called over, "You're wasting your time. They're away."

He glanced over at the man, who was in shorts and flip-flops with a beer paunch filling out his AC/DC T-shirt. "Is that right? When will they be back?"

"Hard to say, they're away a lot."

"What, they're on vacation?"

"No — they're — say, who are you anyway?"

"Just a friend." Tyrone nearly choked on the word.

"Do you want me to tell them you came round?"

"No need. I'll be back!"

Nursing his hand, which was beginning to ache from the pounding he'd given the door, he got back in the car and drove to his apartment, simmering all the way.

Once he was seated on his sofa in his silent and empty apartment with his customary tumbler of oblivion, he was forced to listen to that insistent inner voice he'd been determined to ignore. His surroundings were so quiet, there was no way of disregarding what he knew. At the age of fifty-three, he was ejected from a profession that had given his life meaning and divorced by a second woman who left him long before his disgrace. They were married for less than a year. The divorce had been far less painful than the ejection.

He didn't like where these thoughts were leading him. He needed to refill his empty glass, not interested in examining the pitfalls and blind alleys of his life at the best of times. The hell with it, he decided, when his thoughts kept circling round and round, he'd figure out what to do in the morning, after he'd had a few more drinks.

He had one unlikely refuge. The circumstances of acquiring the property occurred at the tail end of his very brief second marriage. His blonde and very Canadian second wife, Irene, once dragged him north of Toronto to a social event he had no wish to attend. On the way he got lost and, seeking directions, he drove down a rutted lane off Guelph Line. He came to a comfortable farmhouse with gabled roof and a large spreading oak shading the drive.

There was a *For Sale* sign among the low bushes to the side of the front door. An interesting placement, given it could only be seen if you were standing directly in front of it. He got out of the car thinking it was the most half-hearted sales effort he had ever seen. Irene came up behind him.

"Don't be an idiot," she said. "You can't possibly be thinking of buying this place stuck in the middle of nowhere."

"Oh no?" He smiled ferociously. "I thought we were coming up here to see people you liked."

"It doesn't mean I want to live here!"

He knocked on the door. "But I do," he said, intent on goading her, digging himself deeper even though he knew how important it was for her to see and be seen.

There were no hidden layers to his second wife. He married her in a moment of foolishness with the mistaken belief she would reveal them to him. It was just after Leah put out a restraining order against him and he was a desperate man. Irene married him in the belief he would escort her to Brazilian balls, carry out all her wishes and only drink socially and in moderation. She also expected him to wholeheartedly endorse her taste in bric-a-brac. As these things usually worked out, neither of them got what they thought they wanted. His rough edges had never shocked Leah yet had always displeased his outwardly sophisticated second wife.

The farm was 200 acres located an hour and a half northwest of Toronto and the day he took possession was the day she moved out of their apartment. Sitting by himself in the dark, he felt neither regret nor surprise.

At the tail end of October, after much indecision and procrastination, he fled up north, to the place he bought in such a throwaway and confrontational manner.

For the rest of November and into the winter months he wandered aimlessly around his property during the day and kept sipping from a stash of booze he kept hidden in his 18th Century pine buffet at night. Sometimes he'd sip in the mornings with his coffee, but he tried to control himself whenever he thought of it. The ulcer he'd recovered from taught him a lesson. He knew how to pace himself to keep mellow but to never totally lose it. Even at his worst, he reassured himself, he'd always been more of a steady social drinker.

At Hanukah he drove to the local supermarket and bought some birthday candles to be inserted into the Hanukkiah he'd kept from the time his mother was still alive. On the eighth day he sipped his whisky and watched all eight candles burn. He wasn't up to making potato latkes or anything else having to do with the holiday. He remembered celebrating it with Leah the year they were first married. She'd overcooked the latkes and they bounced around the dinner plate each time he tried to cut them. Finally, they'd just picked them up with their fingers. He thought they were the best latkes he'd ever tasted.

When Christmas rolled around he drove to his local supermarket and wandered up and down the aisles impatiently. Sod it, he decided, heading for the freezer section. He added a frozen turkey dinner with mashed potatoes, stuffing and cranberry to his cart along with six cartons of Four Cheese Pizza Deluxe.

Christmas day, he turned on the CD player and inserted Stuart McLean. Spenser had given him the CD of McLean reading from his short story collection for his birthday a number of years ago. The story about Dave and the Christmas turkey was famously funny, Spenser said. "You have to listen to it." And so, sitting in his kitchen while a light snow fell outside, Tyrone listened, sipping his usual tumbler with a splash of water. He didn't feel much like laughing.

And there he might have ended, lost hopelessly amid aimless wandering and empty LCBO bottles, except for a fluke, a wild card that knocked him out of orbit and put him on a trajectory he could not at the time have possibly imagined.

Around noon one day, he opened the front door in baggy pajamas to bring in the paper. He'd been feeling despondent and had opened the bottle early. Not able to keep his balance, he fell over the front stoop headfirst into four feet of soft snow. It was February, and, according to the myth of the infuriating groundhog who failed to see his shadow yet again, at least another six weeks of winter were in store. It was clearly a lie. It looked to be at least another six months given the looming cold fronts. At first, face planted in snow, he felt nothing, not even the cold crystals working their way up his nose and into his mouth. He decided this might be a comfortable position to have a nap. Then, "Up, up," he heard a loud voice which he tried to ignore. "Up. Up."

"Shut up," he said, trying to get some peace. The voice persisted. Just as he was dozing off, it kept interfering with his sleep. It wasn't until he was enraged to the point of shouting at the rude intruder that he realized he was having a snow-filled yelling match with himself.

He crawled in the house, hanging on to the half-wet newspaper. Kicking the front door shut from a prone position, he lay there on the floor while his left eye stared at three words in the feature headline. He was shocked enough to sit up. The disciplinary committee gave his story to the paper. *Homeless and Drunk* was not an accurate description of his state.

Once he pushed the paper a little farther away, he saw with relief the stories were about other people. Slowly and carefully, he managed to read that not all of these men had been losers. One, Palomino Sal, used to be a high-powered financial executive who went on a binge after a disastrous merger which was further exacerbated by his fondness for horse racing. Now the man begged for booze money under the pretext of using it to buy Hungarian salami for his poor old mother. The lurid photographs got to Tyrone. He, who had always been so careful about his image and his clothes, now imagined himself among has-been lawyers and accountants, lying on a park bench covered in newspapers, snoring with an open mouth. The terrifying thought caused him to stagger around the house in a panicked fury, rooting out all his remaining bottles and pouring their contents down the sink.

When he awoke again, his face against the floor boards, the first thing he remembered was his lack of booze. With deepest remorse, he berated himself for his idiocy until he remembered the garish details of what he'd managed to read.

Head in hands at the kitchen table, he was unsure if he could go cold turkey. At the same time, he was terrified of being photographed in such a horribly compromising position as the men he'd just read about. The thought almost jarred him into instant sobriety. His terror included visions of his colleagues or his students or even ordinary dull citizens looking with pity at his morgue shots and shaking their heads. He could not bear the stigma of being labeled a filthy derelict who died covered in piss all alone in his filthy house. The image and the reality of it made him vomit. And then there was Spenser. Why should he give Spenser and Leah the satisfaction of seeing him so far gone?

Over the next few weeks, no matter how painful sobriety became, the thought of Spenser kept him focused. He reasoned he never really had a problem in the first place. Only an understandable lapse he would put behind him. He resolved to show his faithless wife and his conniving bastard of a brother who was the better man. His anger kept him alive but he wasn't sure how he was going to hold on to it and survive. There were nights he would walk around the farmhouse drinking water and aching for just a sip, holding his stomach, nights he would lie curled up on the floor, grateful no one could see him.

"Spenser, you bastard," he would yell throughout the silent rooms on those nights, "I'm not down yet, you miserable excuse of a brother."

One especially dark night of the soul, there was Leah. He had been supremely confident about his own articulate brilliance until Leah taped him late one afternoon when, in a nostalgic mood, he decided to come home early. She hid a small tape recorder somewhere under the cushions of the sofa or among the library of books or perhaps even behind the African violet and let him ramble on. Not knowing about the recorder, he tried to put his arms around her. She pushed him away, her soft full mouth tight and annoyed. The next morning, she turned on the tape and made him listen to it as he was trying to clear his head with a cup of bitter coffee. He was both angry and saddened at what he perceived to be her petulant rejection, so obvious in the taped exchange.

"It's not me," Leah shouted furiously when he pointed it out as it was playing. "It's you. Just listen to yourself. Why are you concentrating on me?" But what he was listening to and noticing was not something he could bring himself to talk about. What he was finally hearing was the loss of love.

One of the things he knew about himself was no matter how hard he tried to hide the rough edges of his own upbringing they would always be there. The other thing he knew was it would be his determination that saved him even if it killed him. Along with his determination to best and outlast Spenser, one of the surprising things keeping him going was the thought of his father who died of cirrhosis. Whenever the urge to get in the car and find a liquor store became overwhelming he would crawl into a corner, hold himself tight and remember his father. Then he would conjure up his vitriol against Spenser. There was a time the Tyrone boys were inseparable, which made Spenser's betrayal even more galling.

He couldn't bring himself to ask for help from anyone. And yet the two bastards, the living one and the dead one, seemed to be there beside him no matter how bad it got. At those times, Tyrone wanted to hold onto something solid, the sheets, the sofa cushions, a chair, anything to prove to himself he wasn't over the edge.

Once he even thought he felt his father's hand on his shoulder, holding him steady, giving him strength, even though it was impossible. His father was a long-dead drunk. He couldn't be there to help him. As usual, there was no one to count on but himself. But it was okay. More than okay. He could do it, would damn well do it — or die trying.

[4] The Great Harley Sale

A couple of months later, one very ordinary day in early April when the skies were covered in bright, scattered clouds, Tyrone was leaving his local supermarket with a case of bottled mineral water when he glanced at the bulletin board just outside the main doors. A snapshot of a long-haired woman standing beside a motorbike seemed to leap out at him from among all the other flyers. He walked closer to have a better look. She appeared irritated, although her hand, in a fingerless leather glove, was placed possessively on one of the bike's handle bars. In careful block letters she advertised a Harley in mint condition and promised a great sale. Under the phone number there was a request for references.

The request for references from a potential seller intrigued him. It was as if the bike was a pedigreed dog requiring a carefully vetted second home. On impulse, he wrested a pen out of his jacket pocket and copied the phone number on the water carton as he juggled it under his arm.

That evening, a crisp April twilight, he felt a wide-awake focused energy he hadn't felt since those teenage trysts in the back seat of a car. It was something to hope for, an adventure. An opening into what to do with his life and how to keep on living. He hated the feeling of drifting without purpose. He needed to get a grip, push himself to do something even if it was as far out as revving a Harley engine.

After reheating leftover pizza and gulping down a cup of instant coffee, he drove out to the phone booth at the variety store southeast of his farm. His fingers were tapping the steering wheel. Maybe the coming spring weather was stirring him alive, he thought, maybe it was because the days were getting longer, or maybe it was the energetic influx of field creatures suddenly awake and busy everywhere he looked.

From then on nothing went according to his expectations. The next day, on his way to the appointment to see the bike, he heard a strange rattle coming from the front of his '98 Audi and felt it momentarily losing power. He pulled over to the side of the road and, in a display of Oscar-worthy bravado, opened the hood, stared inside, and frowned. He closed the hood, drove two more kilometers and repeated the procedure, glaring at the exposed engine, afraid each time to turn the ignition.

Eventually he made it to the right street and number. The owner of the bike answered the door in bare feet and a long skirt. Her toenails were painted red. She had a full, soft face, framed by thick chestnut hair falling to her shoulders, not nearly as tough as she appeared in the photo. Her eyes were disconcertingly clear. Tyrone ran a hand over his short beard, a nervous habit he no longer noticed. "I'm here about —"

She stared up at him for a moment. A woman not given to much conversation.

"Back there," she said pointing the way through the house. He noticed how smooth her arms were and how her hips moved under the soft material of her skirt.

In the courtyard, the bike was shiny black, chrome and glitz, so well-polished even the black leather gleamed.

"What bike did you ride?" she asked, before he had a chance to compose himself.

He did not imagine a drunken ride through the wide hallway of the Law Faculty was what she was after. He pretended to cough into his hand. "Why are you selling?" he asked before she could repeat her question.

She lifted her skirt and showed him a red festering welt running down the length of her shin. It was shiny and puffy and made her leg appear twice its normal size. She regarded the welt for longer than he cared to look, then dropped the skirt and shrugged.

"Road burn," she said.

They started talking at the same time. "What kind of references —" he began.

"Let's see you ride," she said, pointing at the bike. "Right there."

He approached the big machine with care, his mouth dry, hoping to appear as the man he wanted to be. Once in the seat he smiled. The ignition turned instantly. He found the accelerator on the handle and revved it a few times feeling tense. He suddenly couldn't remember the location of gears, clutches and brakes. He hoped it would come back to him, or he could go at a snail's pace so braking wouldn't be necessary and he could drag his feet on the ground. Unsure, he switched the motor off and steadied the bike with his foot.

"Go on." She crossed her arms. "This bike deserves a good rider who'll take care of it."

"Well then, why aren't you keeping it?"

"Because —" she hesitated.

He got the distinct impression her reason for selling might not have been road burn. A love affair gone wrong? A need to run away and disappear owing to insurmountable credit card debts? A biker friend who became a stalker? Before he could formulate another nosy question, she said, "— it's not important. I just want to see you ride. Please. Will you do that?"

Okay then, no chance to delay the inevitable. He booted the kickstand, turned the ignition once again and revved the engine.

"Ha," he said as the bike accelerated. He hung on with white knuckles while surreptitiously trying to remember how to stop before he went too far.

He jiggled a lever on the left handlebar and the bike almost threw him. Sweat dripped into his eyes. As a young man, he rode a motorcycle so he wasn't totally inept, yet right then he couldn't remember a thing. The truth, he now realized, was he felt more at ease on a bike when drunk. Sober, he was afraid of the unleashed power of the damn machine. Frightened and dizzy, he lost his balance as the bike crashed into a post at the far end of the yard before he could react.

As he lay on the ground, his first emotion was anger. He imagined she planned revenge on the bike for her wounds by seeking out a novice rider. When he attempted to pull himself up she confused him.

"Are you all right?" she asked, holding out a helping hand smeared with dirt even though he couldn't recall her dragging the behemoth away from him.

Once in the house she insisted he sit. He thought it was ironic that a woman responsible for his injuries was offering to make him coffee.

"I'm Roxanne," she said. "Why on earth did you try to ride it?"

There were too many unspoken questions he wasn't prepared to answer let alone that one. He winced as he rubbed his elbow and left leg. "Well now," he said, "I believe the bike in question is damaged. Requires a price reduction, don't you think?"

Without a trace of mockery, she gave him a half smile. "On the contrary," she said. "It's now safety-tested and I have decided it's yours for the advertised price; no references required."

He reached down for his killer instinct but his aching bruises and her blood-red toenails conspired to make him lose focus. Instead, he nursed his car back home, wondering what he'd gotten himself into.

Later that night, in the pre-dawn country silence, on a farm surrounded by wolves, coyotes, wild bees and unknown neighbors with barking dogs, he saw what he'd come to. A change was needed, he was aware of it, couldn't help being aware of it despite his actions. It pissed him off that he'd done nothing so far. And yet, he'd gotten into the rut of coasting along.

Before he picked up the bike, he went shopping for a pair of black jeans and a black T-shirt, items he'd never owned, but which might be a good segue into the new life he was trying to imagine. He even had a brief fantasy about the soft look of Roxanne's breasts under her tank top and the slow way she lifted her skirt, daring him to look.

A week later, twice showered, trimmed, doused with his best aftershave and wearing his new black T-shirt and jeans, he faced her again.

"Well, I hope you still want to ride," she said the minute she opened the door. Her nose twitched and she turned away to sneeze.

He wondered if he'd overdone the aftershave.

She was wearing the same skirt she wore the last time he'd seen her. He noticed how tall she was in bare feet while imagining how both the cloth of her skirt and her warm skin would yield to his touch. It was a long time since he'd felt as nervous as a suitor.

He asked, "Will you ride again?" Unbearably tempted to reach out and touch her.

She smiled. "Oh, no. I have other plans."

He wasn't prepared for this disappointment and left her house right after handing over the check. The next day he hired a transport company to haul the bike to his barn. He assumed she would mock him for it but by then, eyeing the useless black T-shirt and jeans crumpled on the floor of his closet, he didn't care.

Once the bike was in the barn, he covered it with an old tarpaulin. The barn also served as his garage and he didn't want to see the bike every time he unloaded groceries, mineral water or pizzas out of his car. He wanted to see himself as a man for all seasons, an urbane and polished gentleman farmer, rather than the nervous and limping owner of a Harley in need of repair.

[5] Spanish Lessons

Two months after he felt obliged to buy the machine, he was listening to bees humming in the ruined apple orchard behind the barn. His bruises were healed but not forgotten. The day stretched out before him just like yesterday. On his right, the untamed clover wore a rich head of purple. On his left, the scraggly buckwheat ripened in the breeze. Tomorrow he knew would be another day without surprises unless those wild bees, come to torment him all season, decided to swarm and upset his closest neighbors. The neighbors who appeared to be harboring packs of rogue dogs.

On this dull June morning he entered the barn, approached the grey tarp, and tore it away from the machine with a sense of relief.

The bike was just as he remembered, black, dangerous, chromed and shiny except for the dented fender: a machine any ponytailed, tattooed, leather-vested biker would be proud to own. He pictured Willie Nelson riding and singing in the wind and almost lost his courage. And then he noticed something wedged between seat and fender. He pulled. A crumpled snapshot of the bike's former owner came away in his hands and fell to the ground face up. She appeared relaxed and smiling. He remembered his embarrassment at the fiasco in her backyard. Stooping to pick up her photo he noticed there was a bulletin board behind her displaying a blurred sign in a language he thought he recognized from his high school days.

He hurried out of the barn and headed straight for the house, startling a field rat who disappeared in a blur of tail. In his study nook, built into the bay window at the kitchen's north end, he scooped the supposedly feral cat out of the bottom desk drawer. The cat, who had gotten way too used to the comforts of home, let out a yowl and eyed him belligerently.

"You're not doing your job," he shook his finger at it. "Run out and grab your lunch. At least pretend to earn your keep."

Scattering papers and pens, he rummaged in the drawer until he found the magnifying glass.

Enlarged, her eyes looked too close together, he noted with satisfaction, but it was the sign behind her in the photo that interested him the most. *Se Vende — Propriedades — Los Arroyos*, the sign read in fuzzy bold letters. Properties for sale in Los Arroyos.

Los Arroyos. It sounded like Mexico — a dusty town where streams roared down from sharp mountains during the rains. He was sure it was where she came from, riding the big bike with her hair pinned up under a shiny helmet, hard boots on her feet, until the day she made the mistake of wearing a skirt and sandals and everything changed. Or perhaps it had already changed because of a troublesome lover or a strident collection agency.

Well, today, he thought, everything had changed for him too and he was ready to leap. He could see the twisted humor of trying to recoup respect and position by becoming an adventurer who roared into a Mexican town on a Harley, but the part of him that had always been impetuous, crashing through walls when doors were readily available just for the sheer thrill of doing something, nudged him further. He wanted to feel the excitement once more — the wakefulness that came when he was taking a chance.

Throwing her photo into the back of the desk drawer, he rooted around for a legal pad and carefully penned a note he intended to place in the local paper, no matter how outdated ads in a local paper might be. He liked being low tech. Or better still, he would post it on the bulletin board of his local supermarket. The only problem was they couldn't call him. They would have to send an answer in the mail.

> *Wanted: Motorcycle riding instructor — former professor of law wishes to hire an instructor with impeccable credentials.*

He squinted at what he'd written with dissatisfaction. Something was missing. It didn't make him feel the rare excitement he suddenly craved. He picked up his pen and added: *Double pay for Spanish lessons.* Now there was an adventure he could lose himself in. A plan for the future to ride all the way to Mexico and surprise Roxanne or someone just like her. For the first time in a long time, he almost forgave himself.

Over the next few weeks he examined Mexican road maps while making his plans. Impatient for his life to change, he checked the mail box daily for responses to his posting and then

A. K. Blackman

walked the farm boundaries, imagining the rough landscapes
he would travel under blue skies, a changed man, or at least
a man secure in the identity of his position — whatever that
position turned out to be.

One evening, he drove to the local library. After looking over
the nonfiction titles, he stood in line to check out a book he
remembered from a time he was interested in such things. On
the way home, his car seemed to be hesitating or losing power
on some of the hills and he wondered again if he should have
it checked but ignored the premonition.

Next to the Tiffany lamp in his living room he prepared
to settle into the life of El Cordobés, arguably Spain's greatest
bullfighter after Manolete. When Tyrone was young he used
to read Hemingway's expositions on what made a man a man.
He found the writer to be inspirational until the day he learned
Hemingway had committed suicide, after which he began to
question everything he thought he understood. What good was
the philosophy of a dead man who did not have the courage of
his beliefs? He turned to other writers, other biographies. Of
them all, El Cordobés, the story of a talented boy's rise from
poverty to adulation, the story of an emerging Spain, stuck with
him. The story used to move him, now he found it depressing. It
might have helped a lot, Tyrone thought sourly before snapping
the book shut, if bullfighting wasn't such a bloody useless sport.

The next morning, among the usual bills and flyers in his red
mailbox, he found three letters bunched together with an
elastic band.

Sitting at his kitchen nook by the bay window he leaned
back to take a breath. The insulated French doors to his right

were open to the air. The fields were ripe, the sun was climbing. He heard the wild bees as they journeyed about, sticky with pollen. Birds sang and small animals rustled in the high grasses out of his sight.

Looking around at all he possessed, he was having second thoughts, wondering if he should disturb himself for some crazy adventure. The brief glimpse into the life of El Cordobés had not inspired him. His life, though admittedly low-key, was safe and predictable and he was settling into it. Why launch himself into the unknown when there was no guarantee it would make him happy? In fact, he thought wryly, what is happiness? Is anybody ever happy or is it just pretense? From his own experience, he couldn't say what it was. He could only say he always felt he had to keep moving to try and catch it.

Shuffling through the letters, he was about to flip them into the garbage when he noticed one of the envelopes was from his brother. Spenser, the bastard, the big shot real-estate tycoon. He gripped the envelope until his fingers hurt.

What right did Spenser have to contact him after what he'd done? It wasn't enough his brother married Leah, he'd done something far more malicious. Even now, the thought of Spenser's continuing duplicity caused Tyrone's anger to simmer. His usual response had been to retreat to the comfort of single malt.

He hit the desk with the palm of his hand and flung Spenser's letter away. It slid across the floor like a rat and disappeared under the buffet.

Trying to calm himself, Tyrone ripped open one of the two remaining envelopes. The writer was greedy. Spanish lessons could be given immediately. How much was the double pay? No mention of riding. He threw the letter in the garbage and opened the last one. The writer claimed that he, Enrique Maís Barajador, was pleased to offer stupendous *motocicleta* lessons. When did the *señor* wish to start? A phone number was offered and requested.

It was what he had advertised for, but the sight of Spenser's letter took away whatever pleasure he might have gotten from it. He ran his fingers through his wiry hair and put on his suede jacket before driving the five kilometers to the phone booth outside the nearest variety store. It was at the junction of two roads crossing each other and winding deep into undeveloped government land.

A lithe brunette was leaving the booth just as he got there. She looked up at him with interest and gave him a wide smile. He rubbed his short beard and nodded. He hadn't smiled in a genuine way for so long he had no idea how to play the game anymore.

He listened to the phone ringing and ringing at the other end.

"Señor Maís?" he asked when a male voice answered.

"You have wrong number."

"Spanish lessons?" he said quickly. "Motorcycle instructor?"

"Ah." There was silence. "One moment, please."

He heard someone clearing their throat in the background and blowing their nose.

A voice came back on the line. "Yes?"

Tyrone was planning a quick dismissal. "Yes! *Habla Español?*"

"Of course," the man said and followed up with a staccato barrage, a surprising development for a man who had not recognized his own name.

"And motorcycle — the lessons?"

"Pues," the man said. *Well.* "We will meet."

"But you give lessons?" Tyrone persisted.

"Of course, of course." The man laughed loudly. "No problem."

They agreed to meet at the local diner in the next town — a greasy spoon diner serving French fries, fried eggs, spaghetti and hamburgers with fried onions on surprisingly fresh buns. Tyrone was swirling murky coffee in a mug when a stocky man walked through the door and headed straight for him.

Tyrone rose and extended his hand. *"Señor Maís?"* At five-eleven he felt both taller and thinner than the other man.

"You may call me Henryk," the man said. He was cocksure, his palms calloused. A fighter's nose and thin, almost white, hair down to his shoulders suggested a street fighter, even though the voice was deeper and more cultured than expected and the accent was definitely not Spanish. Tyrone needed to hear more to be sure.

"And you speak Spanish?" Tyrone asked.

"Please show me the *moto*?"

"First tell me about the Spanish," Tyrone interrupted, finally pinpointing the accent and trying to decide if this was an Eastern European scam.

Henryk turned and pointed to a sallow man in a blue suit with very dark, short hair, entering the diner. There was a scar running from his forehead to the middle of his cheek on the left side, making the eye appear strangely lopsided.

"My colleague, the Maestro," Henryk said.

The Maestro nodded his head as he approached their table. He was as tall as Tyrone, slim and sinewy, and would have been good looking in a shady, careless, easygoing sort of way, were it not for the washed-out complexion of someone who had not seen very much daylight in a long time. In spite of this, his handshake was steady and firm.

Tyrone looked from one man to the other, attempting to gauge which one was more trustworthy. He thought it was ironic that his advertisement, stating he was a professor of law, had attracted a possible tough from Eastern Europe as well as a probable recent graduate of the Ontario Peel County penal system. You could never predict anything these days.

"We are one," Henryk said, holding up two fingers crossed over each other.

Tyrone disliked him at once.

He fixed his attention on the Maestro, who was examining the room with one half-closed eye as if making note of all the exits. Tyrone cleared his throat. "I've had a change in circumstances," he said. "I will only require one of you."

The Maestro rose quickly. "No, no," Tyrone held him back. "I will be requiring your services. Thank you for your time," he said to Henryk, not bothering to conceal his animosity.

"You do not wish lessons with motorcycle?" Henryk asked.

Tyrone pointed to the Maestro. "Of course, of course, I will get them from him. Thank you for your time."

"You don't understand. We are one."

"You already told me."

"The motorcycle expert it is me." Henryk pointed at himself. "And he gives Spanish lessons."

"Impossible!" Tyrone said.

"I am best damn motorcycle expert in Canada — no, in whole America. You are wasting my time." Henryk glared and got up so fast he knocked his chair over, leaving it on the floor. He was wearing beat-up leather boots and a black leather jacket over a grey T-shirt that may at one time have been black. A wide man made bigger by arrogance.

"Crazy Pole, he will leave me here," the Maestro said, taking off after him.

Through the diner window, Tyrone watched Henryk jumping with dramatic flair onto an ancient motorcycle parked across the lot and the Maestro running to catch up. In the next split second, he decided he did not want to feel guilty about another missed opportunity in his life.

"Wait!" he roared in his best lecture-hall voice, running in turn after them.

The biker stopped, motor still running.

Tyrone leaned over, fearing a heart attack. Eventually his breathing calmed and he managed to gasp, "All right. Both of you. When do we start?"

They agreed the first Spanish lesson would start the following morning and motorcycle lessons the day after that. Henryk pointed at his watch, a complicated-looking Omega with dials within dials. "I will come to you at ten o'clock exactly," he said.

Just before they parted, while the Maestro strode into the men's room, Henryk pulled Tyrone aside, glancing in all directions.

"Listen, my friend," he said, smelling of minty chewing gum. "You must listen to me. You must pay only me. One day

47

he will ask for money. No, he will beg. He will swear anything and everything. You must absolutely not give it. You must give him nothing. You understand me?"

Tyrone glared, anxious to get rid of this volatile poseur. His back was up. How dare this man give him orders?

"You must promise," Henryk whispered, holding Tyrone's arm as the Maestro came towards them with a faint smile and a glint in his eye.

"I will do what I judge is best," Tyrone snapped as he disengaged himself and headed back to his car.

Two days later, Lawrence Tyrone was by the red mailbox at the entrance to his farm. It was ten in the morning. His motorcycle was beside him. With great difficulty, he managed to walk it over the dirt road with the clutch disengaged even though he suspected it was a mistake to do so. He looked at his watch, paced, and sat back down.

The fields were lit by sunshine. The lazy smell of warm grass and clover filled the air. The road was lonely in both directions, with only the occasional bee flying by with purpose.

At twenty after ten he was shaking his watch when he saw something smaller than a car appearing over the crest of the farthest hill. The more he squinted in the bright light the more his eyes watered until all he could see was a moving target of shimmering dots.

Standing up, he waited.

At last the biker came to an abrupt stop before him, engaging the kickstand and removing his helmet. His thin flax hair was in a ponytail. There was a small pressure mark on his forehead from the helmet padding.

"There you are," Tyrone said, trying not to show his relief.

"Aha! An accident." Henryk examined the fender and the left fairing on Tyrone's bike.

Tyrone shrugged. "The Maestro came yesterday as agreed."

Henryk was perfectly still.

"I picked him up at the bus station in Milton."

"Hmph," Henryk managed to say, his eyes narrowed.

"He asked me for money," said Tyrone.

"You didn't …"

"He said his mother was ill and he had to get to her."

"Hot shit damn, I told you —"

"He said his father was in hospital dying. What else could I do?"

"He is crazy demented gambler. You will never see this money again!" Henryk exploded, his large forehead damp. "How much you give him?"

"Spanish lessons!" Tyrone snorted, enjoying himself.

He had been planning his strategy all morning.

"How much?" Henryk persisted.

"Well," Tyrone drawled. "I lent him the car."

"What!!"

"No money, just the car to get to his sick mother."

"Are you idiot, mister very great professor of law? Did they teach you to be idiot?"

"Oh, very well, he asked for the car and I agreed to lend it to him. Relax. The transmission was shot. By the way, did he make up his Spanish name in the letter you sent?"

"He has sense of humor," Henryk said.

Out of curiosity, just before his first Spanish lesson, Tyrone looked up the Maestro's supposed last name, *Barajador*, in an old Spanish dictionary that had been wedged in a carton of law books and case studies he hadn't had the courage to let go of. There was no such word. But *barajar* meant to shuffle, as in cards.

Henryk sighed and looked away. "I know this man. I would never work with him in a normal way except you did say double pay for Spanish lessons."

"He wasn't much of a Spanish teacher," Tyrone said.

Henryk kicked the ground and then pulled up a stalk of stray alfalfa and chewed the end. "I did warn you," he finally spoke.

"Well now, I'll just have to learn to ride," Tyrone said.

He glanced over at Henryk and for a moment wondered how his initial instincts could have been so wrong about the man. He realized, in spite of everything, he just might be looking forward to what came next.

[6] The Insomniac of Rattlesnake Point

During his first riding lessons Lawrence Tyrone began to notice many things he had previously been oblivious to. He was aware of the slim birches and straight maples, tall cedars, spruces and pines as he rode over tarmac on the paved shale of the Niagara Escarpment while Henryk, his maniacal riding instructor, shouted instructions to lean this way and that, throttle this way and that, pull the handles this way and that, over the roar of their two engines. Half the time he could barely hear him and had to guess what was meant by the way Henryk was leaning into the curves and waving one arm.

Tyrone was never a clumsy man, yet he managed to examine the ground from an intimate position a number of times while rounding curves. Once he even bit the dust on a straight stretch while attempting to avoid debris diabolically appearing from nowhere.

"You stopped watching," Henryk stood over him with what appeared to be a smirk.

"Your directions are lousy," Tyrone managed to say while struggling up on his bruised knee.

At first, he swore at Henryk for making him spend what he felt were unreasonable amounts of money on such things as leather boots, a leather jacket and gloves. He argued about the gloves until he realized how damaging even little stones kicked backwards from wheels could be to hands and fingers. Then he started swearing at the road. Riding took more concentration than he remembered or had been prepared to allow for.

His fingernails used to be clean before he took up mucking around the farm and then the dangerous abrasions of riding a motorcycle. And yet he was determined to master it, just as he had mastered most things he set out to do in his life, even if they were self-destructive. Especially if they were self-destructive, remarked the insidious voice in his head.

One evening, after Henryk complimented him on his surprising lack of wobbles or falls, Tyrone stared at the shiny roadmaps of Mexico which were spread over his kitchen table without useful purpose. Gathering the maps together, he threw them into the top drawer of the buffet among the old candle stubs, elastic bands, pieces of string and crumpled napkins he stored there.

He opened his freezer. The Deluxe Four Cheese Pizza, in his opinion, was the only pizza worth buying. There was a stack of them lining the wire shelves together with one bag of broccoli solidly frozen to the side wall.

As the pizza was baking, he pulled out the wrinkled maps of Ontario, Guelph Line and Milton from the buffet cupboard where he used to keep his liquor. It sometimes disoriented him to see no bottles there.

Flattening the map of Milton and surrounding area, he peered at a secondhand book on the riding trails and country roads of Ontario he picked up at a yard sale. Taking too much time for even the smallest decision was an annoying habit that appeared as soon as the Scotch had disappeared. He was determined to do something about it.

The next afternoon, after pulling on leather boots, zipping up his leather jacket and strapping on his helmet, he got out the bike, turned the ignition and slipped into first gear with his left boot just as if Henryk were still shouting instructions.

Taking a deep breath, he cautiously eased himself out in search of the country roads of Rattlesnake Point south of Highway 401 which the yard sale book assured him were wondrous.

In particular he wanted to try a few of the side roads. There was a paved road supposed to take him through a deep canopy of trees. He was working up his courage to give the bike full throttle, reasoning he could do what he wanted without Henryk's wild directions.

The wind was mild, the curves he encountered made his heart pound and suddenly gave him a desire for greater speed. He roared past densely packed trees heading for the foothills. As he leaned around a curve and into a straight stretch on Appleby Line, he saw a small figure leveraging itself out of a parked car far ahead. An instant later there was a flashing cherry on the distant car roof, and, in the middle of nowhere, on a quiet nobody's business afternoon, he was being pulled over by an irritated plainclothes cop.

Put off at being caught like a teeth-clenched joy-rider, Tyrone almost lost his balance as he steered his bike from

53

pavement to gravel at an unsafe speed. He knew exactly what Henryk would have yelled at him. But Henryk wasn't there and the cop was demanding identification.

The former professor took off his helmet. "I'm afraid I've left my wallet at home, officer. What seems to be the problem?"

"Do you know how fast you were going, sir?"

"I'm afraid not," Tyrone said, in a deep melancholy voice.

"Let me suggest you should know."

Staring at the man from up close, Tyrone was no longer paying attention to what he was saying. He reached into his memory and was surprised how quickly it came back to him. "Brampton Court," he said. "You were testifying at that murder trial."

The cop narrowed his eyes for a moment and waited.

"Detective Brian Resnick." Tyrone pointed his finger at the man and raised one eyebrow.

Detective Resnick, broad-faced, red-eyed, clean-shaven, was wearing a dark jacket and pressed slacks. His new growth of beard was already apparent even though he had a few nicks on his left cheek where the razor must have slipped. What was he doing dressed so neatly on this lonely road, stopping joy riders?

Tyrone held out his hand. "You may not remember me exactly. I'm Professor Lawrence Tyrone. I brought four children to court the day we saw you on the stand. When was that? Four years ago?"

"Almost six," Resnick said.

Resnick had been in the process of giving testimony during that hellish time.

"Sorry about the commotion when the kid threw up," Tyrone said.

He didn't elaborate that he'd been playing uncle to Spenser's only daughter when he and Spenser were still on speaking terms. In a fit of altruism, he suggested taking the children, all from his niece's class, to a real live courtroom trial so they could see for themselves how the law worked. It was at the lunch beforehand that Billy or Marky or whatever the hell his name was finished off Tyrone's vodka on a dare when Tyrone was in the men's room.

The judge had to postpone the trial for half an hour while the mess was being cleaned up. Tyrone didn't remember much else from that afternoon; he did remember the patience of Detective Resnick as he sat waiting for the cleaning staff to finish. It impressed him. He was surprised he remembered so much about the man including his name.

"You have a good memory," Resnick said, folding his big arms across his chest with deliberation. "You need to slow down on these curves. Especially on a bike."

"Yes, officer," Tyrone said with as much humility as he could muster.

He rode off wondering how a man, a top-ranked detective who took meticulous notes, went from testifying at a high-profile trial to a posting on a lonely stretch of highway in the outback on Rattlesnake Point. Despite his curiosity, the only thing Tyrone left with when they parted was a warning to watch his future speed.

Back home, Tyrone paced for a while between table and buffet. Having had a taste of riding on his own in the freedom of the open air, he saw himself as a man on a mission to find other roads to explore, hills to fly over.

He went outside to inspect his derelict orchard and to give himself time to think. When he first took over the farm the apples were large, shiny and bursting with juice. The previous owner was a farmer with a bad heart and an intense love of the land, but with a dead wife, no sons and a daughter who wanted out, he mistakenly chose Tyrone to fill his shoes.

At first Tyrone thought the man must have been somewhat off kilter. Selling out to a law professor with two brown thumbs was surely both careless and showed a lack of good judgment. In fact, the very first year Tyrone let the apples fall on the ground and misplaced the careful instructions the farmer left him about spraying, pruning, tending and making sure there was a place for wild bees. A directive he hadn't paid attention to at the time. Besides, it was before his disgrace when he spent most of his days in the city with no time for such things. Although the fallen apples were allowed to rot in heaps for a couple of years already, while the trees remained unpruned and were buzzed by drunken wasps, Tyrone had time to reflect how shrewdly the farmer read him after all. If the old man's intentions were to preserve the land no matter how wild it grew, then Tyrone was the perfect landlord, given his disdain for real-estate developers who took pristine land and turned it over to bulldozers and destruction.

As he walked among the bent and gnarled trees in the orchard with their promise of wormy fruit, Tyrone discovered the latest hive of wild bees tucked away in a mound by a mess of wildflowers, clover and bushes and kept his distance. On this late afternoon, the bees were buzzing around the clover and the riot of flowering plants as if they were part of a living, mobile display. He stopped and watched them as his mind calmed and grew clearer.

He'd become intrigued by them as he walked around his acreage. Once he even sat for hours and watched them going about their business. His fascination led him to visit the local library where he combed the stacks and checked out *The Bee Keepers Bible*, reading it cover to cover on some of the long nights he couldn't sleep, like a secret vice.

He still considered the biography of Franklin D. Roosevelt to be a more impressive book. He just didn't have the heart to read it.

What he found interesting about bee keeping, or apiculture, was that it went back to ancient times — as far back as when Alexander the Great crossed the Hindu Kush mountains in 327 BC. The hives discovered by archaeologists in ancient Greece were remarkably similar to more modern ones. More interesting still was the fact that ancient tablets discovered in north-central Turkey set out penalties for stealing bees or hives. The bee economy generated by honey, and therefore the bees, were both important enough to be incorporated into the law. Now there was something he could have included in one of his seminars on how laws changed or were modified as times changed. The thought gave him some pleasure until he realized what he was doing and got angry with himself for having such a bloody useless thought.

He made note of a site on the internet that promised to supply him with a bee colony and teach him how to tend it, but he kept putting off the actual follow-through, knowing himself well enough to realize he was never going to do it.

At his wobbly kitchen table, curious about Detective Brian Resnick, and having nothing better to do, he got out his address book and planned three calls: a judge, a court administrator, a police inspector — people he hoped were unaware of his reputation at his drunken worst. He searched his pockets for quarters before leaving the farmhouse. Finding none, he kept going anyway while arguing with himself about calling in favors.

"Back at your office, I see," the quietly humorous variety store owner jerked his head towards the phone booth while giving him change.

Affecting a suitably agrieved manner, Tyrone listed mysterious home telephone problems no expert seemed able to fix. The owner smiled in the manner of country folk too polite to contradict an occasional paying customer.

In the end, after speaking to two of the three targets on his list, Tyrone cradled the receiver thoughtfully, thinking over the information he'd been given about how the big detective was so driven towards justice he couldn't let go.

That night, by the light of the moon, after eating the other half of the previous night's pizza, Tyrone eased the motorbike over the winding dirt path from his farm. The pavement was black and so were the trees at the highway exit leading to Appleby Line. It was a night for a stealth rider. If he couldn't ride the way he wanted in daylight, he was determined to do so at night.

His headlight cut a dim swath over the tarmac. There was just enough moonlight to increase his vigilance, jolt him awake. Recklessly he pointed the bike straight ahead, opening up the throttle on the wonderful flat stretch of the two-lane road under his wheels.

And then he couldn't believe his eyes. He blinked twice and continued to see a pulsing cherry on top of a shadowy car positioned in the exact spot it occupied that afternoon. "Shit, no," he swore.

A dark figure was waving the beam of a strong flashlight in an arc, reeling him in.

"Second time, sir." Detective Brian Resnick's voice sounded morose.

"Just who were you expecting?" Tyrone snapped.

"It's for me to ask the questions."

"You're going to tell me they posted you at night in the middle of nowhere on this godforsaken road so you could stop occasional joy riders?"

"I posted myself," Resnick said.

"Well then, what *exactly* are you after?"

"Sleep," Resnick said.

There was a moment of silence as Tyrone placed his helmet on the seat behind him and peered over.

"Ah," he said, the way a lawyer says it when he already knows the answer. Or the way a person says it when recognizing a familiar thing.

They stood together as the red light flashed nonstop. By the intermittent bursts of light, Tyrone noticed a cribbage board on Resnick's dash.

"Do you play?" he asked.

The detective nodded. Tyrone saw Resnick's hands were clenched. He felt immense pity given what he learned from the phone calls he had placed in the afternoon.

Neither man said anything until Resnick pointed towards the car door.

They sat together in the front seat of the dark vehicle while Resnick dealt six cards, their game crazily lit by the flashing cherry. Every once in a while, Resnick reached over for a bottle of Tums and chewed on a tablet.

Tyrone didn't question why he was sitting in an unmarked car playing cribbage with a sleepless cop. If it was a rescue mission he was unwilling to find out who was the rescuer and who needed rescuing.

[7] Rescue Mission

After the first evening playing cribbage in the front seat of Resnick's car, Tyrone would get on his motorbike at dusk every second or third day and head out for Appleby Line. Resnick's house was just up the road from where they first met.

They watched sports events or even reruns of sports events on Resnick's big-screen television. It didn't appear to matter to the detective what sport he watched, he seemed to love them all while Tyrone never had enough interest in sports to care. At first, he sat there just for the company. Eventually he became curious enough to ask questions. Resnick would go over the intricacies of each play with great patience. In the end, Tyrone decided there was a certain excitement and tension in trying to determine the best team or the best play. He even found himself clapping enthusiastically but could never bring himself to stand up yelling when his chosen team scored.

"How about a beer?" Resnick asked the first time Tyrone stood in the kitchen.

Tyrone looked into the otherwise empty fridge and shook his head. He walked over to the sink and poured himself a glass of water, taking a long sip so he wouldn't have to meet the detective's eyes. Resnick didn't comment. After that first visit, there was always a water jug and glass waiting on the counter. Tyrone felt uncomfortable with such accurate scrutiny. He preferred knowing to being known.

Besides water and beer, Resnick would rip open a bag of chips and shake them out into a glass bowl as his concession to being a good host. Mostly, the remarks Resnick made when watching sports events were the usual: "Those Argonauts, what a bunch of fuckin' losers. Can't win their way out of a paper bag." Or more often, "Did you see that? Snatching defeat out of the jaws of victory. How oh how do they manage it every time?"

Even though sorely tempted to make some comment, Tyrone held his tongue, figuring Resnick was deliberately dumbing himself down so he wouldn't have to talk about anything painful or important.

But one evening, Resnick turned to him and said, "You have a lot of time on your hands, what's up?"

Tyrone's instinct was to shrug stoically and remain silent. He had been thinking along the same lines. But why should he want his old life back, his old job? It was nothing but trouble. People dictating his life. Telling him when he could and couldn't drink or teach. Why should they care as long as he did his job? And he had been — was — good at his job. But teaching law was so simple compared to everything else.

One evening the detective went into the bedroom and came out carrying a photograph in a clear plastic frame. A little blond boy and an equally blonde woman who was smiling joyfully with her arm around the boy.

"My wife and kid," Resnick said with such longing that Tyrone sat up and took notice.

"You have a son?" Tyrone said, feeling envious and at the same time tempted to pry, to get at reasons. But then Resnick took the picture away. Side by side they continued to stare at a game of golf being played in California on green manicured lawns and the moment passed.

The last time they were together they took a short walk in the night air. There was a sliver of a moon above them, a silver gold sheen on the ground. Tyrone, to his surprise, found he was walking easily in his black jeans and leather jacket without having noticed the point at which he started to get used to them.

"You were really at that second trial?" Resnick asked in the dark.

"Sure was," Tyrone said.

They walked on in silence, their footsteps crunching dirt.

"You stood up very well to cross-examination," Tyrone finally spoke.

"If they listened to me the first time there wouldn't have been another trial." Resnick stopped walking and punched his fist into the palm of his other hand. The sound was loud enough for the punch to have hurt.

"It wasn't your fault."

"I couldn't stop it."

"How could you stop anything?" Tyrone said in a neutral tone of voice. "You could only give the evidence you had. The rest was up to the courts."

"If I'd done better at the first trial the boy would be alive. They wouldn't have sent him back so that bastard could kill him."

"It was the rules of evidence and the court system, not you."

"They fucked up," Resnick said. "I've seen guys like him before. Everyone around them sons of bitches always has accidents. So no fucking way was I going to let him walk out of the murder charge. I knew he killed the kid. That's what you saw. A promise I made myself."

Resnick pried open the Tums and chewed on two of them as they walked back towards his car by the shadowy trees.

"It wasn't your fault," the former professor repeated again. "They ruled it wasn't murder; just another accident."

Resnick walked quickly and then he stopped, turning towards Tyrone. "Let me tell you something. That bastard knew and I knew it wasn't an accident but it wasn't enough. Don't you see? We spend our time bringing them in, thinking we're doing some good and it's all for nothing."

"Don't forget the rules of evidence. I seem to remember in this case it wasn't just a technicality. You were there. You heard what the defense had to say, like it or not," Tyrone said, a little too arrogantly. "That's what trials are for."

"The fuck they are," Resnick said, folding his arms across his chest.

They parted quickly, as if the big detective, in his pressed slacks and crisp white shirt, had more important things to do. Before Resnick turned away Tyrone saw a strange look on his face. Resnick appeared to be simultaneously thoughtful and angry, uncertain and resolved. It was just an isolated moment when the emotions crossed his face so quickly they could have been easy to miss but for the faint moonlight.

As he rode home in the night wind Tyrone couldn't put his finger on why he felt unsettled.

The next afternoon, a Friday, Tyrone rode over to their usual meeting spot. Resnick's last look was with him. The detective wasn't there.

Nor was he there on Saturday.

Resnick's house was in shadow. Lurking at the front windows and then peering in, Tyrone couldn't make out anything. Finally, not wanting to be caught trespassing, he left, trying not to rev the bike engine too loudly as he sped away.

His night was restless. At the dark hour of two in the morning, he gave up on sleep and went downstairs to stare out at the murky expanse of field from his kitchen window. The silence was intense.

In the old days, while he was married to Leah, he would read law journals when he couldn't sleep. On those nights, she would sometimes joke that her Russian Jewish parents obviously had no idea her name meant *weary* in Hebrew, and weary was what both of them would be if he didn't keep her warm by coming to bed. Then she would put her arms around him and lead him back under the covers. The memory did not bring him comfort, nor did the unbearable desire that accompanied it.

Back in bed he felt the urge to urinate so often he started to worry about prostate problems. This led to visions of himself in the hospital, alone and dying, being taken care of by a large-assed nurse and inattentive doctors all speaking a foreign language. At four o'clock in the morning, just as he managed to doze, the perverse wild rooster, jolted awake by the insane barking of the rogue dogs over on the next farm, began to crow.

He rode over to his phone booth the next morning at quarter to eight, too impatient to wait any longer.

"Do you have time for another lesson?" he said, the minute Henryk picked up.

"Of course, *for you*," Henryk said in the expansive European way of his that was often irritating. As if Tyrone were a long-lost friend who had strayed for inexplicable reasons.

An hour later Tyrone heard him ride up to the front of the farm with a defiant roar. Nursing a head full of barking dogs, crowing roosters and incomprehensible foreign medical staff, he considered going to the animal shelter and bringing home a big territorial dog, an Akita perhaps, who would attack noisy intruders on sight. He held his tongue along with all irrelevant chit-chat and got on his bike, leading the way to Appleby Line and then up the path to Resnick's house.

"Your new house?" Henryk said pleasantly, removing his helmet with wide hands and shaking out his long pale hair in an affected manner.

"A friend," Tyrone said, more anxious than irritated. "I want to look inside."

"You will buy it?"

"Not exactly. I wonder where he is."

"Well? Ring doorbell!"

"He doesn't answer."

"Maybe he's on big vacation?" Henryk looked as if he were enjoying himself.

"Just what the hell do you think is so funny?"

"I'm guessing your mood is not so good!"

Tyrone was turning the knob on the front door. "Let's just see if we can find anything."

"Door is locked," Henryk said smugly.

Tyrone scowled at him.

"You want help opening?" Henryk appeared to reconsider his misplaced jocularity.

"You have tools." Tyrone pointed to the metal box welded to the back of Henryk's bike.

"Of course." Henryk nodded and started to walk around the perimeter of the house.

"You can't let it show," Tyrone said when Henryk came back.

"Those are A-1 locks. This man knows locks."

"Then what do you suggest?"

"We will break window." Henryk picked up a rock.

"Not on your life!" Tyrone lunged to stop him.

"Listen, my friend," Henryk said, serious at last. "Unless this man you know is fixing plumbing, through back window there I see his feet and shoes lying by kitchen sink."

[8] The Finer Points of Death

After wrapping his jacket around a rock and breaking a rear window, Henryk cleaned up the jagged edges of the glass from the frame and climbed through. When he opened the front door for Tyrone, he was holding a hand over his nose and his eyes were watering.

"I hoped never to smell death again," he said.

They were days too late. Shocked and gagging, Tyrone followed Henryk into the bedroom. He called 911 from the bedroom phone, while Henryk shut the door and threw open the windows. Tyrone saw the family photo Resnick had shown him after he hung up. It was on the left nightstand by the bed, along with a paperback book on family secrets. He wanted to carry the photo out to the living room and place it on the ancient fireplace mantel so someone would notice Resnick had family, was not alone, but stopped himself both because of the terrible stench of the decomposing body and because he convinced himself it was a foolish gesture. And then, unable to stay put any longer, he went out into the cool, fresh air to wait for the police. Even there, he couldn't get far enough away.

He was never a patient man. In this surreal scenario everything that happened next conspired to try his patience further. The police asked unending questions which they kept repeating as if he might trip himself up if asked in five different ways. The coroner, an officious man with a ghostly complexion, finally arrived at the request of the paramedics. The ambulance looked sinister, impersonal and unforgiving. And after all that, the senior detective, seeing the picture of Resnick's wife and son, casually said he would contact the wife as if it didn't mean anything to him.

Once the coroner made his examination and the ambulance loaded Resnick's covered body and drove away, the senior detective glanced sharply at Tyrone. "This is still off-limits unless I say so. I want that window fixed. You goin' to take his keys to get the window fixed when I say so." He made it clear it wasn't a question but a way of taking care of one of their own.

A little too late for that, Tyrone thought. "Give me your card and I'll call in a couple of days," he said out loud. "My phone is out of order."

Hours later, by the time the last of the official and officious people drove away, the countryside was quiet again. Tyrone headed back to his farm with Henryk. He hadn't expected to feel so emotional about a man, an insomniac, he barely knew. Not wanting to sit by himself in his empty kitchen, he invited Henryk in for a cup of coffee or glass of mineral water and ignored the man's suddenly knowing smile.

After putting four teaspoons of sugar into his instant coffee and stirring non-stop for far longer than necessary, Henryk said, "You were good friend to him."

Tyrone, who had been watching the aggravating stirring motion as if mesmerized, was finally distracted. "I didn't really know him."

"Oh yes?" Henryk said.

"I saw him testifying at a trial once, that's all. He was so calm and self-assured. It's difficult to know anyone."

They sipped in silence. When Henryk moved his hand towards the spoon again, Tyrone grabbed it first and headed for the sink.

"Those pills. Those damn pills." Tyrone said, his back to Henryk.

He had been unable to look at Resnick's body. No matter how tough he wanted to be, what he noticed was how vulnerable and alone the big detective was. A man he watched television with and had spoken to, a living human being estranged from family, suddenly stiff and cold and putrid, beyond anybody's reach. He didn't want to know how much the two of them had in common. He had turned away.

"My friend," Henryk reached up to put a heavy hand on Tyrone's shoulder as he was getting ready to leave. "He was holding antacid pills. But coroner who came thinks he died from heart attack. You hear this? Heart attack. Your friend had stomach problems?"

"I don't know anything," Tyrone said, wondering if Resnick's death was an accident, a sneaky heart attack, or if the big detective knew something was wrong and had deliberately not sought help.

That night Tyrone was unable to sleep again. As he tossed he questioned whether he should have noticed or done something or perhaps not done or said something on the last night he saw the detective. He tried to remember the uncertainty in Resnick's eyes. Did the man know he was dying? The way Resnick dropped his head and shoulders — was that his heart signaling its distress or was it something else? All the answers were gone now, along with Resnick.

Two days later, Tyrone got up early. He sat at the kitchen table, staring at his cup of instant coffee. There was a swirl of iridescence across the top of the coffee from the instant powder as it disintegrated in the hot water. Practical things he could deal with, yet he couldn't bring himself to visit the dead detective's house just yet.

From his familiar phone booth, he called the precinct and asked to talk to the lead detective who had left him his card. "Go ahead," the detective said gruffly. "Autopsy's done."

Tyrone didn't have the heart to ask any more questions; instead he called a carpenter he knew in the area, a rough no-nonsense jack-of-all trades who replaced the rotting joists and beams in his barn right after he bought the place. He gave him directions to the house off Appleby Line. "You won't need keys," he told him. "Just do the window right away."

"How do I reach you?" the carpenter asked.

"Reach me?" Tyrone, startled, peered at the telephone keypad in an effort to give him the phone number in the booth.

"I mean reach you right away, not through a relay of smoke signals."

"I have a cell phone somewhere," Tyrone said. "I just don't have a charger."

"Charge it."

"How?"

72

"Who knows? Go to a Bell office and beg them or something. Or buy a charger. Now give me the number again. What? Okay get it to me when you remember it or maybe I have it somewhere."

Four days later, Tyrone was surprised to hear his pocket ringing.

He searched with clumsy fingers. "Yes?" he said, expecting the carpenter to give him a price for what he owed.

"There's a woman here," the carpenter said, sounding embarrassed. "She wants to know if you intend to return the keys."

"Woman? What woman?"

"I don't know."

"Is she blonde?"

"I would say so," the carpenter said carefully.

"Is there someone with her? A little boy?"

"You got it."

"Tell her I'll be right there," Tyrone said, putting the phone down on the living room sofa where it fell and buried itself behind the cushions as he was getting up.

The front door of Resnick's house was open. A woman with messy blonde hair was sitting outside on a tree stump. A little boy ran around the surrounding trees and thick grass making a racket. He circled one tree yelling, "Kapow!" circled the next holding on to the trunk, headed for a third and fourth shouting nonstop. "Kapow! Kapow! Kapow!" Tyrone was reminded of a windup toy gone berserk. The woman kept her arms around her knees, staring at the open door and seemingly unaware of the deafening little savage. Her blue sweater was buttoned wrong starting at the neck.

"Hello," Tyrone approached her, awkwardly wiping his hands down his jeans.

She looked up. Her eyes, a startling blue like the sweater, didn't quite meet his.

"Hello," he repeated, holding out his hand, not so much for shaking but in case she needed focus or some kind of help. "I'm Lawrence Tyrone."

"You knew my husband?" she asked in a low voice.

The kid twirled around the trees, a damned racket engine, Tyrone waited for her to say something but she was silent.

He looked into her startling blue eyes, unsure what she wanted to hear.

She waved her hand impatiently. "I didn't know a lot of Brian's friends. He was very private."

"I'm sorry for what happened," Tyrone said loudly. And then, because he didn't know what else to say, he said, "I saw him a few years ago testifying at that murder trial."

"Testifying at that murder trial," he repeated more loudly over the kid when she didn't appear to get it.

"Would you like to come inside?" She too raised her voice. "I didn't want to go in alone. I'm Karen, by the way."

What Tyrone wanted to do was leave. He was no good with emotional scenes or with comforting messy-haired widows in blue sweaters whether he knew them or not. He hadn't known Resnick either. What use could he be to this woman and her brat?

She was already entering the house without turning around to see if he would follow.

"I'm sorry, I have an urgent appointment," he said to her back as he ran up to the doorstep and laid down the keys to Resnick's house on the sill, wanting to get away as fast as possible.

On his bike, the sound of the engine was almost drowned out by a fresh wave of bloodcurdling yells from the kid. "BANG, BANG, KAPOW, I GOT YOU, TAKE A DIVE, NOT A MOVE, ON YOUR FREAKIN' KNEES, BANG, BANG. KAPOW! ZZZZZZZZTTTTT!"

Tyrone wondered how such a little boy could make so much noise. He turned his head and met the kid's eyes. The boy stopped yelling and was staring at him, looking frail and alone, causing Tyrone to feel something like shame. As if he himself had become a bully without quite understanding how it happened.

Halfway along the 401 he began to sweat. He wanted to recant everything he'd said and done back at Resnick's house, even though he couldn't face the disruptive chaos of a distraught little boy. More to the point, in his black jeans and on his macho bike, he wanted to reclaim something of the man he could have been before everything went so wrong.

He got off at the first exit and parked in front of a forlorn variety store. Inside, to the shriek of a heavy metal rock band blaring out of a boom box, he picked up an assortment of gummy bears, floppy worms in garish colors and candy-covered chocolate as well as two bottles of Sprite. He suspected it was not the best choice of edible items for a kid who was already bouncing off trees but he needed an excuse to justify his disappearance.

The spiky-haired teenager at the cash register stared at him when handing over his change, daring him to make a remark about the choice of cacophony passing for music. It reminded him of one of his classes where he instructed the students to debate whether rap music could lead to criminal behavior. They came up with impassioned arguments both for and against. In the end, the need to give voice to oppression and injustice won the day. He congratulated them for a strong debate in his usual conservative, half sarcastic manner. Even though he hadn't shown it, he had been secretly proud of them for working their way to the conclusion they came to in spite of the lurid headlines associated with the most contentious rappers.

As he rode up to Resnick's house, Tyrone noticed the door was still open. With his motor off the quietness was profound. He was relieved to note her SUV was there.

By habit, he ducked his head going through the door frame. She was sitting on the sofa opposite the large fireplace. The boy, sound asleep, was curled up beside her, his head on her lap. She was stroking his soft blond hair, so much thinner and neater than hers, and staring at the lonely picture on the fireplace mantel of the two of them in noticeably better times. There was a hole in the kid's dark sweater and his thin, bruised and muddy elbow was sticking out.

Tyrone fixated on the vulnerable elbow and noted how small and helpless the boy now looked. He cleared his throat.

"I figured you'd left," she said without looking up.

"I've brought something," he said.

She nodded down at the soft little head on her lap. "He'll sleep now. He just needs a little time."

Tyrone rummaged among the bags full of junk food and showed her the contents. "Can I pour you some Sprite?"

"Uh, no, thanks. Any of that stuff makes Briney really hyper so I stay away from it too. He left us, you know." She said the last sentence as if it was part of the same conversation. It took Tyrone a moment to figure out she had changed subject.

"I didn't know," he said. Deducing facts was not the same as knowing in his opinion.

"Right after the second trial. The one after the guy killed his kid. They said it was an accident. It just about killed Brian they let the guy go again. He kept saying it wasn't an accident and then he got very depressed. He said he wanted time and then he left us."

"I didn't know," Tyrone kept lying, thinking it was a big mistake to have come back. Neglected apple orchards and wild bees were so much more predictable and easier to socialize with than grief-stricken women.

"He said he sometimes really, really thought of hitting Briney. I didn't recognize him saying it, his face was so … so bloody different. That's when he told me it was better to leave us."

Tyrone snorted inadvertently and tried to cover it up. This was no time to agree with a dead man's instincts, no matter how accurate.

But it wasn't what the widow wanted to know.

"Do you really think that's why he left us?" she asked.

"Yes," he tried to say. It didn't come out loud enough. To give himself some time, he took out a plastic glass from the kitchen cupboard and half-filled it with Sprite. He longed for something stronger.

"Do you?" she said, looking over towards him.

He became alarmed at the tears in her eyes. "Yes," he said more loudly, gesturing with his plastic glass. He felt he wanted to complete a sentence, give an explanation to this distraught woman, but he wasn't sure what to say. All he knew was she wanted reassurance from him and he had none to give. His hands were shaking. He took a wild leap. "Look at that picture of you and the boy," he said. "It's the only one your husband kept in this place. That should tell you everything."

"I have to believe you, right?" she said at last.

Tyrone doubted any answers he could give her would be the right ones. Looking at his watch and feigning great consternation, he made his escape a second time. As he left he saw something both knowing and resigned in Karen Resnick's face.

Back in the kitchen of his farmhouse, Tyrone started to think of himself as the man who had been sleeping too much meeting up with a man who couldn't sleep. Something about the scene he'd just left, the emotions he never liked to acknowledge, reminded him of Leah, his dark-eyed first wife, rounder and softer than Resnick's widow, sharing the same sense of bitterness before she walked out. And it reminded him of what Leah hid from him, which he kept putting on the back burner each time he thought of it because he didn't have the strength to follow through no matter how outraged it made him feel.

Seeing Brian Resnick's boy once he was sleeping and calm touched Tyrone in an unexpected way. He was astonished at the sudden strength of his feelings. He too had a son, a secret son, didn't he? He felt ashamed at his apathy up to now. It was not his fault he let the son slip from him — yet he knew it was. Even though Leah never mentioned she was pregnant before she left him, he should have known or at least guessed from her odd behavior and even from that ill-fated time when she came to his office. It was time for action. Time to embark on a moral quest to regain a child who was rightfully his. But for that he would need Henryk and he was not about to tell Henryk his true purpose. It did mean the motorcycle was a liability, a mistake he should never have made.

Rummaging around for his newly found cell phone he discovered he'd forgotten to charge it so he called Henryk from the usual phone booth.

"I want to find the Maestro," Tyrone said. "I need my car back."

Henryk laughed.

"You understand? I'm not sure I want to keep the motorcycle," Tyrone said.

Henryk's voice was amused. "Another accident?"

"Of course not." Tyrone tried hard not to succumb to his usual irritation. "I'm not into motorcycles. I've learned I'm a car man. I made a mistake."

"My friend, my good friend," Henryk said loudly. "Car men. Motorcycle men. We are everything we want to be. What do you want?"

"I want —" Tyrone said and then stopped, reminding himself it was too early and too dangerous to share his thoughts about anything personal. He was determined to change things but didn't yet know how. "I want less sleep," he said instead.

"What?"

"That's it exactly," Tyrone said with more conviction, feeling his way to something painful and truthful at last. "I want less sleep."

[9] Raiders of the Far Casino

Tyrone was back in the phone booth the next morning arguing with Henryk. The biker, however, remained stubbornly unhelpful, not convinced about the wisdom of scouring the countryside for a '98 Audi with a bad transmission.

"I know this man. Your car is gambled away," Henryk spoke with great confidence. "It has disappeared on back of IOU note or into spare parts."

"It was a great car, the best," Tyrone retorted loudly. "It never gave me trouble. It's too good to be used as scrap because everything was in perfect working order." Enumerating the car's good points, he let himself grow fonder of it by the minute.

"I will not help look for this big waste of time!" Henryk shouted. "I will absolutely not."

But Tyrone was unwilling to give up his mission. It would start with the great car chase. Instead of buffalo or memories he was going to hunt down the remnants of his car, whatever may have happened to it and however far it may have gone.

On Thursday, a cloudy day with a cool wind which would translate to something much colder on a motorbike as it whistled for miles over his sweaty frame, he wore a scarf, a dark green cashmere sweater under his leather jacket, black leather gloves and black wool socks to warm his feet in his leather boots. Boots whose thick leather soles he hadn't appreciated nearly enough when he first complained about their cost to Henryk, silently wondering if the biker was demanding kickbacks after each shopping spree.

He fiddled with his scarf, trying to decide how best to tie it as he waited at the junction of Guelph Line and Highway 401 and ended up concluding that wearing it was a bad idea and squashed it into his saddle bag.

Henryk finally showed up, unapologetic, in a turtleneck sweater and an old leather bomber jacket. Tyrone stared at the red-and-white bandana under his helmet.

"Russian memories," Henryk said without further explanation as he removed his gloves. Tyrone assumed he meant the bandana and shifted his gaze to the cracked leather of the bomber jacket, which looked vaguely Russian and years out of style.

"Where are we going, mister famous professor of law?" Henryk asked.

"Orillia," Tyrone mumbled.

It was a town approximately two hours northwest of Toronto and he was already thinking it was too far north and not worth the trouble, even though it was home to the biggest casino in the area.

"You are serious?" Henryk contrived astonishment as if gazing at a fool.

"Of course, I'm serious. Stealing someone's car is serious business."

"He didn't steal," Henryk said. "You insisted he take it."

"I most certainly did not. I loaned it to him."

"Loaned! Hah! You gave it away. Forget this nonsense. I am telling you sincerely."

"Never!" Tyrone said, carried away by the confrontation. "Now I want it back."

They rode in tandem in the slow lane along Highway 401. An impatient Tyrone suspected Henryk was being moderate because he didn't trust Tyrone's riding skills. In retaliation, Tyrone insisted they pull off at the Brampton exit, pretending something was wrong with his motor. He knew there was a coffee shop at Derry Road, just west of Highway 10 heading towards Brampton.

Henryk leaned towards Tyrone's bike in the parking lot and listened for a moment, brusquely pronouncing the motor healthy. With a smirk, he pulled a Thermos from his saddle bag while Tyrone went in to get his cup of coffee and a needed rest.

It was the last thing he got away with.

A tough master, Henryk now pushed them forward over the miles towards Orillia, without allowing further prolonged stops. Tyrone, unaccustomed to such long rides was stiff by the time they got to the Casino Rama parking lot. He hobbled off the bike with an unforgiving ache tight as a tourniquet around his forehead, a numb ass and pains shooting up his legs.

In the dusk, rebounding through the air, he heard high-pitched screaming.

He saw rows of cars, dark windshields and tarmac black as soot while the screaming assaulted his ears nonstop. A young woman walked past him. Her black hair was piled on top of her head. The screaming continued; it was not coming from her very red shiny mouth. It was coming from somewhere behind her. She blinked nervously.

As he fought to ignore his aches it took him another second to locate the source of the noise. If he looked in a straight line from where she had just come there was a dark car with the windows cracked open an inch. He was feeling sensitized to sensory onslaughts given his various tender places and pains. The noise was unbearable and had to be stopped.

He hobbled after her. "Did you leave something behind?" he asked.

The young woman turned on high heels. Holding tightly to an over-stuffed little handbag, she smoothed down her very short skirt.

"Mind your own business," she said, giving him a sullen look.

He pointed his finger and lied. "This is my business. I'm with the courts."

"She's ruining my life," the young woman spat the words. She glared between Tyrone and a mocking, silent Henryk. "I can't even go out without her bawling her head off."

Tyrone was aware he was being sucked in by yet another confrontation. And yet… and yet, this felt wrong. All his training, all his teaching, had been an attempt to negotiate the ethics of the wider world even if in the long run it ended up in a crap shoot marred by his own personal leanings. He hesitated. Why should he bother? What business was it of his?

She had that right at least. And yet … and yet, she seemed so shockingly young.

She saw his uncertainty and came closer, giving him a practised smile. "I'm only going in for a sec. Honest. She's in her pajamas and everything. Like, I'd never leave her alone or anything. She's always been — oh —" she put a hand over her mouth as if realizing she had said too much.

And Tyrone became aware of two things staring him in the face, three if he counted the fact it was an expensive leather skirt she was wearing no matter how little material it contained. The BMW she was driving and her Valley Girl enunciation suggested privilege. In his estimation he needed to exert some authority.

"Listen, miss," he said. "If you leave that child in the car I will inform the casino management and they will ban you from the place forever. So what will it be?"

He was certain she was using fake ID, although she must surely be over sixteen to be driving.

"Fuck you," she turned unexpectedly. "Fuck it all!" she flung herself back at the car and jerked open the rear door.

"You stupid, stupid brat," she screamed at the screaming little girl. "Why couldn't you just shut the fuck up?"

Leaving the rear door open, she ran towards the casino, her ankles wobbling childishly in her heels. A snotty-nosed little girl peered out the car door and then ran after her mother on bunny-clad feet. Tyrone thought her mouth was open so wide you could probably see her lungs. Her pink fuzzy pajamas were clean and embroidered with a white bunny and her soft curls, in a miniature imitation of her mother's, were held up by a pink elastic band.

"I'll be watching you," he yelled, his voice brutal in the silent lot. "You can bet your life I'll be watching you. And I'll make sure your parents lock you in."

"What the hell do you know?" the young woman screamed back. "Leave me alone. My father will get you for this."

"I know everything," he said forcefully. "Go home, get back to your homework. You still have a chance."

"Pig," she sobbed. "Fucking asshole."

Tyrone's anger grew. To his surprise she came back to the car, barely waiting for her child to climb in and for him to slam the door shut before she took off, flooring the gas and leaving fumes behind.

"Bravo." Henryk laughed, clapping his hands. "Just what do you think was accomplished?"

Tyrone, who was thinking the same thing, shrugged. "One night when that baby will sleep in her own bed. Just one night," he said, making an effort to repossess his newfound zeal.

"And you believe it?"

"I suppose you think you should do nothing?"

"Not unless I am here when she comes back tomorrow," Henryk said as he started walking towards the casino entrance.

Tyrone was not prepared for the onslaught once they were inside. The intensity of people jerking at slot machines hurt his eyes. His head started to pound again. There appeared to be thousands of machines all whirring and clicking and spinning in eye-splitting colors, a strobe light of jumpy motions randomly lit by multi-eyed monsters. Amid the racket of clanging and clicking and buzzers going off, coins were shoveled into buckets or fed nonstop into slots.

It seemed to him the place was filled with robotic men and women turning grey from lack of sleep, while dealers and croupiers dressed in artificially shiny clothes waited behind tables covered in green felt cloths. The thought of the young girl dulling herself in this place made his eyes hurt. He looked around for Henryk and saw him grinning as if to say, *Now, mister fancy professor, see if you find who you came for.*

They walked through rows of slot machines over to the hotel lobby, a huge cathedral space filled with rocks, wooden beams and a waterfall. Everything in it, including the furniture, was oversize. There was a giant circular carpet on the stone floor.

At the desk, Henryk asked if the Maestro was registered. He gave a name Tyrone didn't recognize, and then another. Each name drew a head shake from the manager on duty. Artificial air blew over them, simulating a breeze. The Maestro, Henryk said to Tyrone, was always trying to stay one step ahead of somebody so it was possible he registered as an entirely different self. Information that was not comforting to the sharp-eyed manager, who felt he had to show incredulity mixed with displeasure when it came to people registering under false names.

Tyrone eyed the manager's pursed lips with amusement, certain he was overdoing the act for their benefit.

He glanced over the manager's head at the clocks positioned in a row on the wall behind the front desk. New York, London, Tokyo and Orillia. As if Orillia was in the big leagues. The hands of the Orillia clock had just moved to nine thirty. He was used to going to bed before ten at night and sometimes even nine and was seized by an enormous weariness. He could barely keep his eyes open. At the same time, he was very much aware that somewhere on the other side of the floor was a bar serving cheap booze. And to think he recklessly told Henryk he wanted less sleep.

"We will need a room for the night. Too late to go back now," he said to the manager on impulse. The manager took one step back, looking wary. Tyrone wondered whether the man was assessing his bloodshot eyes, helmet hair and five o'clock shadow and categorizing him as untrustworthy.

Henryk, stepping forward at the same time the manager was stepping back, came to the rescue. "You heard this man," Henryk said, resplendent in his biker's bandana, folding his big arms across his chest. "We thought we could use less sleep, now we are not so sure."

"A room with two beds." Tyrone shook out his credit card, not caring anymore what the manager thought.

"Excuse me, sir," the manager said, "we are fully booked."

"Business must be good." Tyrone smiled, a wolfish smile that never quite reached his eyes. "And I suppose you let underage girls in here who leave their babies in the car?"

"I beg your pardon?"

"I'm with the courts. We are investigating the case for her parents. We just saved you a great deal of trouble tonight. Are you sure you don't have a room?"

The manager looked nervous. "Do you have ID?"

Tyrone fumbled in his wallet. With great luck, he still had his Osgoode Law School ID which the administration had not thought of reclaiming. It identified him as a senior faculty member. The fact that all it was good for was unlimited library privileges was not specified.

"I see," the manager said, a little more relaxed once he realized they weren't plainclothes cops. "I can offer you the Vegas Suite."

"Excellent," Tyrone said. "The Vegas Suite better have two beds. We will continue our investigation in the morning."

He got up once in the night to relieve himself and noticed Henryk was not in the other queen-size bed. Unable to sleep, he read hotel brochures, tourist materials and catering menus until four in the morning, wondering where Henryk was. When he finally closed his eyes, he slept way past his usual time.

On waking he heard a soft snore. It was nine in the morning. The stocky biker, fully clothed, was lying kitty-corner on top of the other bed, his head thrown back and his mouth open. His boots were neatly lined up on the floor.

Tyrone got up to use the washroom and have a shower. There was a plastic package with a razor, shaving cream, toothbrush and toothpaste laid out in a rattan basket at the sink. The razor was cheap but he managed to only nick himself once.

When he came out of the bathroom, Henryk was still snoring. Tyrone cleared his throat. The biking instructor's left leg twitched twice spasmodically on the garish red bedspread and then once more, still switching gears in his dreams.

Ravenously hungry, Tyrone set out in search of the promised breakfast buffet included in the room price. Loading up his plate, he devoured eggs, bacon, sausage, potatoes, toast and jam in keeping with a man starving for variety, whose usual diet was frozen Deluxe Four Cheese Pizzas heated and reheated in a faulty oven.

Henryk joined him at the table carrying a full plate while Tyrone was on his third cup of coffee. The biker sat down and started eating enthusiastically without saying a word. Tyrone found this irritating. Even his own free-spirited mother taught him a few manners before she died, and he remembered them when it suited him.

"Good morning. You had a good night?" he said.

"The best," Henryk looked up at him clear-eyed, clean-shaven, his red-and-white bandana wrapped around his head at a rakish angle. He must have used the razor and shaving cream which Tyrone had carefully dried and laid out on a hand towel.

"Glad to hear it." Tyrone fought the urge to question Henryk about his whereabouts in the pre-dawn hours.

"The best night." Henryk grinned and pulled out a wad of cash. "Blackjack is my game."

As Henryk munched contentedly, Tyrone felt guilty for sleeping too much yet again. Blackjack was one of the games he played with the other students when he was studying for his law degree, egged on by cheering onlookers. He trained himself to count cards — up to three decks — so he often won. It seemed so long ago now. And then casinos had started to stack eight decks in automatic shufflers and the odds went against him. That wasn't why he stopped gambling. After Leah, he gradually lost his taste for it.

"The Maestro was not here last night. I looked for him," Henryk said sounding as fresh as if he had put in eight hours sleeping. "I asked dealers too. He was not here all week. We must look somewhere else."

Without replying, Tyrone got up to give the buffet another scan. He came back with a plate of sweet buns, slices of yellow and orange cheese, crackers and a piece of carrot cake.

"She did come back again," Henryk said casually, chewing a piece of sausage. "Your young lady."

"She's not my young lady," Tyrone snapped.

Henryk shrugged, his mouth full. "She did, anyway, return."

Tyrone folded a slice of cheddar on a cracker and popped it into his mouth. He had no intention of pursuing the matter, reasoning that what he didn't know would allow him to sleep at night, the sleep of someone with, laughably, a clear conscience.

"She gambled," Henryk said. "And then she left."

Unable to maintain his equanimity, Tyrone threw up his hands. "And the kid? Did she bring the little girl back in the car?"

Henryk shook his head, enjoying himself.

"Well, then what happened?" The words left Tyrone's mouth against his will, which was why he was always a better teacher than a lawyer. Never having experienced his own child, he suddenly found himself — at this late stage — meddling with other people's children.

"Relax, relax," the biking instructor said. "When she left, I followed. She will not gamble no more."

"What have you *done*?" Tyrone asked, alarmed.

"I meet her father this morning," Henryk said, wiping his mouth with a cloth napkin and leaving a greasy smear. "She lives with him. They live together in his house. Just imagine — ha — he is bigshot lawyer, maybe works all night. Doesn't want to see what is inconvenient. He was coming home. Of course, she was sleeping. I told him few things."

"What *things*?"

"Gambling, drinking, bringing child in car at night to casino, using fake *papieri*, shit like that. He said, leave it to me, I know what to do. He told me this girl she left her mother — his ex-wife — to be with him, the bigshot lawyer, and did I see how important it was? She trusted him. He would have to move softly not to lose trust. Did I understand the importance? Blah-blah-blah-blah." Henryk waved his hands around with animation. "I understood this: he was thinking I was some crazy man and he was important lawyer. He was absolutely not happy when I told him thank you very much on behalf of Professor Tyrone of the court system who started this case and would like to see it finished with proper ending. Right and serious ending. Think of the little girl, your granddaughter, I said. He changed tunes immediately. He knows you, did I tell you?" Henryk spooned a forkful of scrambled egg into his mouth and chewed with enthusiasm so his next words came out muffled.

"What's that?" Tyrone asked suspiciously.

Henryk swallowed a mouthful of egg. "One of your old students."

"You had no right to do that! How could you? What student?"

Henryk shook his finger. "That is unimportant. It is not our next lesson."

"You went too far! What gave you the right to talk to one of my students?"

"Because, my dear Professor who wants to ride motorcycles and poke stick into hornet nest, you started something and we must always finish what we start or hornets will swarm and sting. Were you not aware of it?"

In truth, Tyrone was only too aware of it from a painful encounter with a wasp's nest as he rambled around his land, but he was not about to let Henryk have the satisfaction of being proved right.

"You could have been arrested for stalking," Tyrone said to Henryk when he was calm enough to speak to him again. They were at a gas station to fill up and to relieve themselves. Henryk was zipping up in the next urinal.

The biker raised his voice as he noisily dispensed pink soap to wash his hands, "Result, my good friend. There is most important thing."

Tyrone bristled for a minute at being told something so obvious in such a patronizing manner.

"You just made that up?" He said while looking around for paper towels. Finding none, he dried his hands on his jeans, something he would never have dreamed of doing when he was wearing made-to-measure suits and shirts.

"Made it up?" Henryk said, astonished. "Of course not. I am repeating only."

"Repeating? How refreshing."

"You are serious?" Henryk's attempt at looking puzzled was comical.

"What? *What?*" Tyrone's headache was returning. This was his punishment for trying and failing to rescue a high school gambling addict and feeling sorry for her child? A biker who hadn't seemed to care had gone and done something meaningful about it while he, himself, slept.

"Is the first thing you said to me. Our first riding lesson. You said it doesn't matter how I do it, result is most important thing." Henryk said.

"Oh, that." Tyrone waved a free hand. "A lot of good the results would have been from a jail cell."

Henryk regarded him, weighing the truth of the matter, looking vaguely uneasy. He took the time to think, while examining himself in the smudged bathroom mirror, adjusting his red bandana. His stint in the Russian army and all the uncertainties engendered by that regime must be reminding him of how quickly things could get dangerous. It was enough to make Tyrone feel better, even if only a little.

Outside once more, ready to mount their bikes, Tyrone felt it was up to him to take the initiative. Resume control.

"No more casinos until we are certain of where he is, the Maestro, that is," he pronounced, making it sound as if the bad idea was Henryk's alone.

Henryk raised his eyebrows and folded his arms, waiting. It was as far as Tyrone had reached in his thinking. "Shall we get going?" Tyrone said with a scowl.

They didn't communicate until they parted at the junction of the Milton cutoff and, even then, Henryk only revved his engine and waved mockingly as he leaned into the curve and sped away.

Tyrone stopped his bike on the soft shoulder. It was full country here with stands of trees and long roads disappearing behind hills. The sun streamed briefly through the late afternoon bleakness. As he looked up the road where Henryk had disappeared he crossed his arms and swore he wouldn't keep putting it off, nothing more would distract him from his purpose. But he needed a better plan.

Back at the farm, Tyrone walked through his apple orchards, pored over road maps, tried to watch TV, dipped into the Bee Keepers Bible and went on solitary motorbike rides while formulating all sorts of plans that ended with his triumphant appearance at Spenser and Leah's doorstep waving legal papers, ready to reclaim his son. Unfortunately, on further examination, although he was gaining an encyclopedic knowledge of bees, none of his plans led to reclaiming his car. And there he was stuck. He was not prepared to move past this stumbling block. No other car would do but his, he convinced himself, unwilling to admit it was just an excuse not to act.

At night, he came awake, hoping to hear frenetic barking and demented crowing in the vast landscape around him just for the company it suggested. Under dark clouds, the countryside was perversely silent and uncooperative. Even the moon was hidden.

He had not seen Leah until after their divorce became final. In spite of his resolutions never to contact her, he tried a number of times after she left him. She refused to answer his calls, preferring to let him deal with her lawyer. She unlisted her number. And then, three years later, he heard through a lawyer he bumped into on the street that she was planning to tie the knot again and he was shocked. He asked the lawyer, someone he didn't much care for, whose specialty was family law, to have a drink with him so he could hear all the details. The hapless lawyer didn't know much, or pretended not to, even though Tyrone plied him with hard liquor.

At first, he managed to find out she was marrying a lawyer or perhaps another professor of law or a professional businessman, rich and successful. In his obsession, he convinced himself he knew who it was. Of course, given later developments, he didn't have a clue. He called in all sorts of favors — legal and illegal — to find her.

"Leah? Leah? Why?" he said, fortified with a few glasses of whiskey, when she came out of her house in Rosedale, a renovated artist's studio with stained glass whose address he managed to unearth through one of his contacts. For the first time, the question was torn from his heart. He was not too unaware to notice the house and the little boy — perhaps two or three years old — who peered, frightened, from behind her skirt.

"You're drunk. Leave us alone," she said firmly, keeping her head down.

"I'm not drunk," he said, looking at the boy. "Really. It's just a few—"

And suddenly a thunderbolt hit him, an impossible revelation. He couldn't believe how duplicitous she'd been. This had to be his son, who else could be the father? She must have hidden the fact from him, snuck away during the pregnancy and deprived him of his lawful paternal rights. He worked himself into a state of righteous anger, conveniently forgetting how clear he'd made it that he wasn't ready to have children: the conversations he initiated in order to convince her of the rightness of his position, the abortion clinic he suggested just in case. Damn it, he had a right to know. She failed in her obligation to tell him and he would drag her to court and reclaim his rights and so much the better if it caused her trouble. If this was his son ... she thought she was going to marry someone else with impunity, without the smallest hint of trouble? As far as he was concerned what was his was his, and he wasn't going to make it easy for her.

She prepared to walk past as if he weren't there. To his everlasting regret, he reached out, trying to hold her back, trying to get her to look at him, but it came out as a push or something close to it. The next day she took out a restraining order against him and he went back into his black hole, until the day he found out who she was going to marry.

He told himself a son would have been a hindrance, so what did he care? The boy probably wasn't his anyway. She'd no doubt had affairs. An insidious voice in his head said quietly, *she wasn't married yet, was she, when you last saw her? Whose son was it if not yours? What kind of a man were you to let them go?*

In the end, it was too much. The continued comfort in a bottle was much safer. She left him and rejected all contact and he refused to examine why. She was firm-fleshed, dark, comforting, exciting and histrionic. She had been his and then everything changed.

Not even Irene, his second wife, especially not his blonde, Canadian, very brief second wife, possessed the same power. He came into the bathroom once when she was showering, soaping her small breasts and golden pubis, the lather snaking down into hidden places and his first thought was of Leah. To his fury, after so much time, his first thought was of his first wife in her round-limbed sexiness and unfathomable moods. The thought took hold of him so violently he left the bathroom at once with a painful erection. Even Leah's nose, aristocratic, hooked like Cleopatra's, was an asset, drawing attention to her turned-down sexy mouth, an erotic mouth forever discontented for hidden reasons or bitten softly by her sharp teeth.

In the morning, he rode over to the variety store and called Henryk. The phone rang and rang. Henryk didn't have an answering machine.

He gunned the bike for a mile around the side concession roads and returned once again to the phone booth, impatient to find the biker. Just as he was about to hang up, he heard Henryk's curiously accented hello.

"Ah," Tyrone said. "There you are."

"Yes?"

"Where would you suggest we look next?"

"You are determined about this?"

"Of course, you said it yourself."

"I said it?"

"You know. The spiel about finishing what we start."

"You are not by any chance willing to forget?"

"What you said?"

"What you wish to pursue."

"Not on your life," Tyrone said firmly. "I keep thinking about those angry wasps coming after me. I am certain I will get away faster using my car if I can find it."

Henryk laughed at Tyrone's attempt at humor with a touch of bitterness. "It will not be so easy."

"You have an idea?"

There was a long silence.

"Unfortunately, yes," Henryk said.

[10] Beware and Fall in Love

"And just where are we going?" Tyrone asked two days later as Henryk pulled up to the junction of Guelph Line.

"Home of Alexander Graham Bell," Henryk said.

Tyrone felt he had been supporting himself against his bike on the grass verge off the highway for at least half an hour while the wind whistled past his face. His watch informed him it was only ten minutes. He tapped the watch face to make sure the battery was working.

The man before him was one he had never seen before: a subdued Henryk wearing a clean shirt and sweater stretched over his broad chest, pleated slacks that looked to be thirty years old, a paisley ascot and a hip-length leather jacket probably the same vintage as the slacks. The bandana was gone and his thin, colorless hair was brushed back neatly in a ponytail. Smelling aftershave, Tyrone stared at him, astonished. For a moment, he remembered his own clumsy attempts to impress Roxanne, the motorcycle lady, with new black jeans and T-shirt and copious aftershave. It was painful to see Henryk in this state and be reminded of his own follies. While assessing the outdated sartorial attire of the biker, Tyrone hesitated. To ask Henryk what was going on was too much prying.

"What's up? Is everything all right?" he said.

"Of course, everything is fine," Henryk said, looking angry. "Why should it not be all right?"

It was only when the fashion plate swallowed that Tyrone realized it wasn't anger Henryk was feeling but nerves. He reassured himself he wasn't curious in the least. Of course, he couldn't ask any more questions. It was enough the biker was coming with him, so better to allow him some privacy.

"You're all dressed up," Tyrone said. "I wish you told me this was something special."

"It is nothing special," Henryk said with irritation. "Only a change of clothes."

"Well then, why are you nervous?"

"Nervous? What are you talking about? You think I am nervous?"

"Are we in danger from something to do with the Maestro? You can tell me the truth."

"The truth is we are going to Brantford, mister clever professor. We are doing exactly what you wanted. What difference is anything else to you?"

Walking towards his bike, Henryk trailed aftershave as if he had bathed in it.

"Just asking," Tyrone drawled.

"Better concentrate on ride," Henryk said with a narrow-eyed scowl. He buttoned up his jacket before putting his helmet on. During the journey, he never once looked back at Tyrone as they rode in tandem all the way.

The house they reached was neat, painted a pastel ochre with white shutters. There was even a white picket fence around it.

Before knocking, Henryk placed his leather gloves in his pocket, swallowed and rubbed his hands as if to warm them. It reminded Tyrone of the day he came home from the hospital and paused at his front door, afraid to open it, wanting and not wanting to know whether Leah would still be there.

The door was opened by a young woman in her early thirties. Her black curly hair was very short and her wide eyes were very dark. Tyrone had never seen such dark eyes before, so dark they appeared to have no pupils or perhaps were all pupil.

"Henryk," the young woman said happily and threw her arms around him. They kissed on both cheeks, the biker holding her tenderly.

"I have brought a friend," Henryk said, taking her hand and turning around.

Tyrone waited, fascinated by those eyes.

"Teresa Mendes de Arroyo," Henryk said formally, with surprisingly impeccable pronunciation, "I present Professor Lawrence Tyrone."

"Pleased to meet you, Miss Mendes," Tyrone said, putting out his hand.

"You are to call me Tess, Professor, okay?" The young woman said, not taking his hand but moving her head towards him with a charming smile.

101

"And you may call me Lawrence," Tyrone said graciously, taking his hand back and giving her a slight bow.

She led the way along a broad hallway, past the living room and into the kitchen at the back of the house which smelled of baking and furniture polish.

"You will excuse me if we sit here," she said to Tyrone, placing her hand on the kitchen table. "Beatrix went to her mother today and I am alone so it will be easier."

"Of course, of course," Tyrone said, watching as she made her way to the counter to turn on the kettle and pick up a cake sitting there. Her movements were smooth, practiced. Her cheeks bloomed pink. She was wearing slim pants and a red pullover, her shoulders straight and strong. She brought a knife to the table and laid it next to the cake, went back to get napkins, hesitated for a moment before reaching for them. Everything was laid out on the counter, even the tea bags and teapot. She was very sure of herself.

Tyrone suddenly realized she was blind.

He turned to Henryk and caught the biker watching him intently. Tyrone opened his mouth and Henryk shook his head infinitesimally in warning. What was that about? Was he not supposed to say anything? He certainly was not going to be so rude.

"May I be of help?" Tyrone asked.

"Why?" she said. "Am I doing something wrong?"

"I —"

"Substituting the salt for the sugar, perhaps?"

"No, of course not. It's just...." Tyrone let the sentence die.

There was a smirk on Henryk's wide face.

"There, all done," Tess said in the silence. "I hope you like the cake, it's a *Tres Leches* — a special cake made with three kinds of milk — Bea prepared it all just before she went, so you see I am quite capable of doing the little she left me."

After the cake was cut, the forks and spoons laid out, the tea poured and the whole spread laid out on the table in front of them, she sat in the chair closest to Henryk and lightly placed her hand on his arm.

"You don't come anymore, Henryk," she said.

Henryk's expression, once the smirk was gone, was impassive, although his neck reddened and his eyes glittered.

"You're being mean." She smiled. "Say something to me. At least explain yourself."

"Excuse me, my dear Tess, I am very busy man."

"Busy? With what?"

Henryk was silent.

"Riding lessons," Tyrone said. "I am to blame."

"And why is that, Lawrence?" she asked pleasantly, biting into her cake with zest. She was obviously a woman of extremes, annoyed one minute and enthusiastic the next. Tyrone warned himself to be careful.

"I am a very bad pupil. He has been trying his best," he said.

"Big job," Henryk added. "Day and night."

Tess laughed. "Isn't he full of bullshit?"

Tyrone nodded and then caught himself. "Yes," he said.

Henryk was gazing out the window. He hadn't touched his cake.

"Now for the reason we are here," Henryk said.

"Yes?" Tess bent her head towards him.

"We need to find Juan Carlos. And do not worry. The professor is harmless. We only wish to talk with him."

"But why?" she asked.

"A private matter," Henryk said. "You understand?"

She waited, her dark sightless eyes turned towards his voice.

"Juan Carlos is the Maestro?" Tyrone asked Henryk. "That's his name?"

The biker nodded without speaking.

"It's about my car," Tyrone said to Tess. "I loaned it to him and now —"

"Ah," she said. "I understand. He called me last night."

"Where from?" Henryk said quickly. "The professor saw him weeks ago. He was giving Spanish lessons — did he tell you?"

"Spanish lessons?" she looked startled and pleased. "*There's a change.*"

"Where is he now?" Henryk said.

She hesitated. "Henryk," she said. "You know he is not a bad man."

"I know, my dear," Henryk said. "We need to find him. Better we find him than someone else."

"You will make sure he is safe?"

"Yes."

"Very well. You are the only one I trust. He's in the Thousand Islands. He swore he was not at the casino, but he is running out of casinos and we know better, don't we?" she sighed, reaching for Henryk's arm once more.

"You promise?" she asked.

"Always, my dear Tess," Henryk answered. "Always for you."

She smiled a small uncertain smile, listening for something not immediately obvious, her fingers touching Henryk's arm.

Some things continued to get to Tyrone, who liked to think he couldn't be gotten to anymore. He could understand the Maestro keeping in touch with home no matter how far he strayed. Was he her brother? Her lover? Her husband? Apart from this young woman being sightless and Juan Carlos being almost blinded in one eye as if he planned it deliberately, the coloring and features they had in common suggested a brother. Whatever the relationship, since he called here, he obviously considered this house, this young woman, home.

And despite the fact that Henryk wanted to hide his emotions, the way his body relaxed, the way he held her arm protectively, suggested Henryk felt it too. It was a familiar longing that gnawed at Tyrone. He had no home to keep in touch with. The apple orchards and wild bees wouldn't care if he was a day late or a year late. No one would notice or care. It was what made the house feel so empty after Leah left him.

"Must you go so soon?" Tess asked when they finished the cake and tea. "Stay. We'll go for a walk. We'll dress and put on scarves and walk like we used to, Henryk."

Tyrone pushed his chair out to help her clear the table. Moving lightly, no longer hesitant, between counter and table she suddenly fell over the chair.

Henryk was at her side immediately, examining her ankle. His other arm propped her up, encircled her so intimately it was both painful and erotic to watch. They stayed together in a way Tyrone interpreted as having nothing to do with ankles.

"I'm fine," she said.

"Can you get up? Put weight?" the biker murmured. He removed her shoe, a black ballet slipper, and massaged her ankle using thumb and fingers.

She was long and lithe with a deceptive frailty. Henryk's hand looked large over her ankle bone. Tyrone wondered if they were going to stay so intimately entwined for the rest of the afternoon. He tried to signal his presence with a dry cough. His opportunity to apologize had passed.

"Henryk," she said all of a sudden, holding the biker's arm. "I haven't seen you for so long. You don't come around anymore. I wanted to tell you I am getting married."

Henryk got up without a word, supporting her and making sure she was sitting.

"Did you hear me?" she said.

"Yes, my dear."

"Well, aren't you going to say *anything*?"

"Congratulations, I suppose. Best luck. Many happy years, best happiness and all that."

"You haven't asked me who."

"The schoolteacher, I am thinking. The one who teaches blind people."

Henryk's face was impassive, his voice calm.

Henryk and Tyrone left her house under a deceptively bright sky. The roads and sidewalks were coated with a thin film of rain. The green trees shone with smooth drops in the clear light.

Tyrone kept his eyes on the ground, rich with a million fractured specks. He needed to hold on to this image to keep from turning on Henryk after having witnessed something painful he wanted no part of. For a moment, he felt he was watching himself. Of course, that was nonsense. He was determined never to mention what he had seen or to ask why Henryk was taking leave of his senses. He didn't need to understand what crazy motives were going to destroy the biker.

"What the hell just happened back there?" Tyrone said before they got much further.

"Nothing," Henryk said.

"Nothing?"

"You pushed out chair, she fell on floor. Why are you asking?"

"That's not what I'm talking about."

"A very long boring story," Henryk said in a tired voice, brushing tiny water trails off his fancy outdated clothes.

"That's hardly an explanation."

"The only explanation, my friend. We have been successful as you saw. We know where to find car," Henryk said. "Nothing else is important."

"What I saw was important," Tyrone said. "You do love her, don't you?"

"It is not important!" the biker roared. "What do you expect me to do?"

Tyrone was agitated. "More than you did."

Henryk threw up his arms in a wide gesture embracing everything and nothing, got on his bike, put it into gear and took off without looking back or saying another word.

The obscure dusk swallowed him up until even the sound of his engine faded away.

Standing alone under the dripping trees, thinking of the young woman's tender, blind touch on the crazy biker's arm, Tyrone felt both envious and unsettled.

[11] "Chakalaka"

The sidewalks and roads were slick as the rain fell in a fine drizzle. Tyrone told himself it was too hazy, too uncertain to take off in such weather, especially as he would be riding alone on slippery highways. He told himself the fault was in the weather, and not in the fact that he was immensely curious and drawn to something he was uncertain about. Of course, it was the weather, not the puzzling scene he'd witnessed and couldn't shake.

As he rode slowly towards the highway exit he found himself wishing for something else. He passed a flower shop on the way and went in. He felt reckless. The damp, earthy smell of plants and flowers in the warm shop provided a high he could barely contain. He might have said he was happy if he knew the reason for it, this strange impulse towards the unthinkable, more precisely, towards the unknowable. Almost as if deep down he was allowing himself a second chance. He knew it was impossible. It didn't lessen what he felt.

When he walked up to her house he felt a moment of panic. He could feel his heart.

"Professor Lawrence Tyrone," she said when she opened the door.

"How did you know it was me?"

"You feel taller. There is more area of heat."

"Amazing," he said, handing her the armful of freesias which reminded him of spring. Roses would have been too serious and not at all what he thought he was there for.

"Thank you." She laughed. "And there is, of course, Henryk's aftershave."

"Ah." He smiled in turn. "I came to apologize for leaving my chair out like that. I hope your ankle is all right. I want to make sure. The weather has turned very wet."

"And Henryk?" she asked, puzzled.

"He rode off. I think another appointment. I hope you like flowers. He asked me to bring them." He convinced himself Henryk would forgive the lie, would of course approve everything because it was being done in a good cause.

"It's okay," she said. "You must not think I need excuses. Please come in."

They passed the living room where Tyrone noticed the baby grand, a small black affair with the top open. And behind it, a mantel of pictures. She was limping very slightly, favoring her left foot.

"You play the piano?" he asked.

"Well, I am not very good. It's for Bea. She loves to play and I sit and listen. It's very soothing, don't you think?"

"Depends who's playing," he said wryly.

They sat again in the kitchen. This time he noticed there were pictures carefully arranged on a small buffet behind the table. It seemed strange someone would arrange pictures for a blind woman. He walked over to take a look.

"My collection," she said, listening to his footsteps. "You think it's odd?"

He decided not to evade. "Yes, actually," he said.

"Bea tells me about them when I ask. When I am lonely, you understand?"

In the fading light, he saw older pictures of small groups and more recent ones of one or two people. Her brother, for instance, standing by himself in front of some building, the scar on his face not so noticeable as in life; a picture of Tess and Henryk out in the country, the sun on them as she squeezed his arm and smiled into the camera, blazingly happy, Henryk beside her in a relaxed pose suggesting hopefulness; a picture of a younger Tess with an elegant older woman in a black coat, their arms around each other. This woman, like Tess, had dark hair but it was long and clasped back. The similarity between them was striking enough it could have been her mother.

Tess went over to the sink and filled a vase with water, carefully arranging the flowers, her fingers playing the stems.

"May I turn on the lights?" he asked.

"Of course. Do you like Mexican food?"

"Mexican?"

"Yes. That is where we are from. Did Henryk not tell you?"

"He told me very little. I assumed Spain, I think, because you are so tall and so ... so—" he wanted to say dark-haired, elegant, beautiful, all those words, but he chopped them off as inappropriate. He didn't want to reveal himself as someone who was starting to yearn without meaning to. "So Spanish," he said.

"Do you like Pico de Gallo?" she asked. "It's just a little snack."

"I'm not sure."

"A Mexican salsa *cruda*. Fresh tomatoes, onion, cilantro, some chili peppers. I eat it when I'm upset. It reminds me of my mother. Also, I think there's guacamole here somewhere in the fridge and if you're very hungry I can make tortilla soup. Tonight, it's everything Mexican."

There was a large bowl of chopped tomatoes mixed with white and green bits on the kitchen table in front of her, tortilla chips in another bowl. As he sat watching her, not daring to offer a hand, she went to the fridge, felt around, removed a container after smelling it and poured the contents into a pot on the stove. Then she went over to the cupboard and brought him a plate. By the time she sat down, fifteen minutes later, there was guacamole, the Pico de Gallo salsa, grated cheese and steaming bowls of soup in front of them. The sink behind her was piled with discarded pots and serving dishes.

"I hope you like to eat as much as I do," she said before carefully trying her soup.

Then, picking up a serving spoon and putting the diced tomato mixture on a tortilla chip, she leaned over and bit into it, holding her other hand underneath. "How did you meet my brother?' she asked.

Between mouthfuls of tasty soup, he found himself telling her the story of the motorcycle and his wild idea about Mexico and Spanish lessons. Laughing, she went to the fridge and brought out a bottle of white wine and two glasses from the overhead cupboard. Tyrone was suddenly very aware of himself and his surroundings. The light sharpened. He didn't wish to break the spell. If he refused the wine he might even have to leave just as they ran out of conversation and he wanted to ask too many questions, some of which he didn't know how to phrase.

"Thank you," he said as she handed him a full glass.

Taking a long sip, she waited. Her short hair shone.

Tyrone held the wine up to his lips. Why not just this once? It certainly couldn't hurt. He could smell it, feel the desire for it, for the mellowness it engendered in him. He yearned for the man he used to be, the self-confident superior intellectual never at a loss for words. The professor whose status made students respect him. Words used to flow in such coherent sentences he sometimes amazed himself, especially when mellow. A proficient speaker who could hold his liquor while lecturing. Once in a while though, when Leah got through to him, he wondered what it would be like if he stopped cold turkey. He might have done it for her. He kept meaning to but time had run out on him, that's what he used to tell himself. Time had run out.

He took a sip of wine. Stopped. Took another sip.

Now in the blind woman's house, he realized what a delusional fool he'd been. But he wanted another sip. And why not? What harm could it do just this once? And besides, it was only wine.

No. Not this time. He forced himself to take a measure of the distance he'd come. He was done with all that. He'd always been a lucid drunk, remembered many things he was not supposed to remember. The psychiatrist he'd gone to once and only once after Leah was gone had rambled on about state dependent learning. People, he said, only remembered an incident or a fact in the state under which it had been learned. Tyrone was sure he was better than that. Except he wondered if he would be prepared to test himself and prove it.

With some difficulty, he put down the full glass of wine Tess had poured for him. He was through with courage that came in a bottle. He wanted a distraction yet couldn't very well ask her about Henryk even though it was weighing on his mind.

"Tell me about yourself and Henryk," he said.

She smiled at him with her fine, blind eyes. "You are a curious man."

"I'm sorry," he said.

"What are you curious about?"

Everything, he wanted to answer. Everything. The tenderness between you, that hopeless tenderness, how can you stand it? He was not a poet or even a man who was brave enough despite his pretend biker clothing and his wish to intrude; he was just a man who was once credited with having a good mind, a lucky marriage, and an enviable career.

"Tell me whatever you want to tell me," he said getting up and going to the sink. With the tap on he got rid of the wine in his glass and filled it with water.

"Some more wine?" she asked graciously, her head turned sideways.

"Just water for now," he said.

"We come from a small town in Sinaloa called El Fuerte, do you know it?"

"I don't know much about Mexico."

"It's at the rim of the Barrancas del Cobre Canyon. Way up in the northwest region of Mexico, close to California. Not many people know it."

"I hope someday to see it," he said.

"On motorcycle?"

"By car. I am a very green rider."

"But Henryk's teaching you." She laughed. "With Henryk, how far do you think you can go?"

"I don't know, what do you think?"

"May I touch your face? To know what you look like?"

He hesitated, startled and uneasy.

"When I was little, Henryk would let me touch his face. He doesn't want me to anymore," she said softly, taking his silence for assent and feeling her way lightly around the table.

"You have a short beard," she said, pleased. "Exactly how I imagined. And your skin is like the weather. Are these lines on your forehead?"

Unable to speak, he nodded.

"And look at your hair. Henryk's is long and thin, not as thick or short as yours. What color is it?"

"Salt and pepper."

"Salt and pepper?"

"Sorry. Do you know colors?"

"Don't feel sorry," she said abruptly, making him think it still mattered. "I'm used to it. Salt and pepper is black and white?"

"Yes," Tyrone said. "Why won't Henryk let you touch his face?"

"Selfish," she said. "My brother used to play pool. When my mother died, Henryk would come around to look after us. Just drop in, you know, to make sure we were okay. He liked …"

"He liked?" Tyrone prompted.

"He liked my mother, I think, but …" Tess said.

"But what? How did she meet him?" Tyrone asked.

"Oh, you know, just around. How do people usually meet? You must think I am a *chachalaca*," she said. She pronounced it *chakalaka*.

Her light touch was gone. In repose, her face took on a darker, brooding look and she pressed her lips together as if she had said too much.

"A what?" he said, to get her talking again.

"A *chachalaca*. It's a Mexican bird that talks too much. Makes all this noise and annoys everyone."

"Would never have thought of it," Tyrone said, dead pan.

"Well, that's exactly what I am. It's what Henryk used to call me when we went for our walks. It was the air or the motorbike or getting there that was so wonderful. It made me want to talk and talk and embrace something. I used to be so happy. I would touch the trees and the grass and the cold stones on the ground and hear the wind in the hills and all those noises in the fields and country roads. I was so happy. And Henryk was so good." She sounded wistful.

Her sunny expression was back as if nothing had happened. It made Tyrone wonder what it cost her to constantly hide her darker side, the one she had to confront on sleepless nights.

He got up and poured himself another glass of water.

"Hmmm," she said, her head bent in her curious listening attitude. "I am getting high all by myself. This is not very gallant of you. I used to make him promise he wouldn't leave us. How stupid can that be? I thought we could keep him forever." Her smile was careful.

"And then what happened?" Tyrone said.

"Nothing," she said.

"It's the same thing he told me." Tyrone was impatient.

"Don't you think he is the most stubborn man?" she asked.

"I don't know him as well as you do," Tyrone said. "I don't believe nothing happened. Something must have happened between you, it's so clear."

He couldn't believe he was having this conversation with a young woman he barely knew. For a moment, he was ashamed by the depth of his curiosity and of his impulse to buy flowers.

She shook her head. "You're being too logical. Nothing happened. Really. One day we were the same like everything would stay forever and the next he suddenly wouldn't let me touch his face anymore. And then he went away. See. *Chachalaca*," she said. "That's what I told you. I talk too much."

She turned towards him innocently even though he was sure she was hiding something from him because it either shamed her or was too painful to share. Her eyebrows were like beautiful dark wings. He imagined her body floating in the air over the fields intertwined with Henryk's like some lovers in a painting he'd seen once in one of his mother's beloved art books.

As he reflected about it, it seemed very strange to be sitting in an unfamiliar kitchen talking to a young woman in such a familiar way. Years ago, she could have been one of his

117

students. It was a paradox. He didn't know her yet he knew her. She was Leah in the full splendor and daring before the fall. Leah, who used to be one of his students before she gave it all up for art and being someone else. Someone mysterious whom he guessed was pulling away from him. It was something about Leah he was never able to own. Not knowing her fully, not able to possess her made him try all the more until she couldn't wait to get away from him. She even rented a studio across town so she could paint uncontaminated by his presence.

It wasn't until she said he was trying to invade her that he began to suspect something was very wrong. He even suggested a psychiatrist. It was after he came home late one night and his cold supper was piled dramatically in the garbage can right in his path by the front door. "You're acting crazy," he said. "You probably should look into it. Here, I found someone in the court who will see you. He has a private practice. I've got his card somewhere."

He started rummaging through his briefcase, scattering papers and journals and would have pursued the argument further but she cursed him at full volume and left the room.

"It's getting late. I'd better head home," Tyrone said reluctantly, spooning some more guacamole and Pico de Gallo on a tortilla chip. The green chilies burned and he was glad Tess couldn't see how some of it missed his mouth and fell on his plate. He hadn't learned anything to ease his curiosity and it was nagging at him.

"Thank you for coming," Tess said. "I liked talking to you. You made it easy."

He chuckled without humor. Ever since he felt he'd become less articulate, or more silent, he appeared to be easy to talk to.

"You don't believe me?" she asked.

"No. Yes. I was just thinking of life's ironies."

"How so?"

"You find me easy to talk to. Others used to have different opinions."

"Like who?" she said. "You will have to excuse me, we are much more open in our culture. You Canadians are so unsharing. Henryk too. I think he has practiced very hard being Canadian."

You too, he thought, especially when it comes to Henryk. "Well, Henryk is a strange element in the mix," he said, very aware he was changing the subject, not wanting to discuss Leah.

"What do you mean?" She sounded defensive for the first time.

'You know," he said. "The mix." He waved his hand around, then stopped, aware she couldn't see his inarticulate attempt to substitute gestures for words.

She put her hands on her hips, facing him, waiting for him to say more.

"I don't know," he finally said. "I am sometimes at a loss for words. To tell you the truth I don't always know how to say things, express what I feel and want to say. I want to, but I can't. It's never been easy."

What he didn't say was she was the first person he had ever said this to. In his whole life, she, a stranger, was the very first.

After seeing the ease between Tess and Henryk, the outward tenderness, what hit him was how fearful of tenderness he had been his whole life. With Leah there had been passionate sex, there had even been a kind of intimacy in their deeper moments together, but he had never been able to give her the tenderness he might have allowed himself to have. It would have made him feel too exposed. After what happened in Tess's kitchen it was so clear to him this night. He always held back.

[12] The Wild Art of Bees

He rode away from Tess's house down the dusky street, passing a slim woman walking with long, steady strides in the opposite direction, a dark hood pulled over her head. She was tall and there was dark hair under her hood. He didn't see much of her face. He felt her gaze as he got closer, felt her eyes examining him carefully, perhaps critically, judging him. Something about her was familiar. For a brief moment he thought of Roxanne, the motorbike woman, deliberately plotting to sell him her rogue bike. The encounter jolted him into a super awareness of the road, the glistening trees and the mysterious woman walking past him, making his heart race. When the woman passed beyond his vision, he didn't dare turn his head to watch her. It was better for his safety to keep looking straight ahead.

He kept going. The last faint rays of sun were trying to break through and dry away the slick of rain. It was the hour when roads darkened and light faded, the hour to hurry home.

As he covered the miles heading back to his farm, he thought about the parting conversation with Tess because it had surprised him, and also because he'd had an unorthodox idea he wanted to think about.

Tess had said, "The mix? I hear you, Lawrence."

And then, when he hadn't replied, she said, "Okay, the mix? You mean I'm blind, my brother's a gambler and then there's the element of surprise, a biker with no familial obligations to us, who has possibly taken on responsibilities? Something like that?"

Startled, he examined her face. "Something like that," he said carefully.

"Ah," she said, "I have surprised you."

"Yes, you have. It was something I wondered about, but you read my mind."

A few years ago, he used to think he was the one who could notice and know everything about anyone. Even Leah. And with her he had been so oblivious.

"We all have our stories," she said. "Thanks to Henryk we have been perfectly legal immigrants for years now. What I haven't told him is I'm going to university."

"Good for you," Tyrone said with false heartiness. "What are you studying?"

"Law."

"Why?" he asked bluntly before he could stop himself.

"I want to help immigrants, like we were. It's frightening when you don't know where to turn."

"Oh?"

"I have surprised you again!" she smiled, pointing her finger playfully in the direction of his voice. "Of course, I have someone to drive me four times a week."

"That's not the reason I was surprised."

"Of course! Professor!" she exclaimed. "Henryk never said, but of course. Wow. Can you believe this? Where do you teach?"

"Taught," Tyrone said. "Osgoode Hall."

"You're retired?"

"More or less retired," he said reluctantly.

"Well, which is it, mister reluctant professor? Is it more or is it less?"

"More. Totally retired."

"Oh," she said. "Do you miss it?"

"Every day."

"I see." She was silent for a moment. "You wouldn't think a blind person should be saying, I see, would you? I sense you have a reason why you don't wish to talk about it. I think you are sad. It's in people's voices, how they speak. There is a difference, did you know? Even when people are lying, there is a change in voice. They say things differently or they breathe differently or the pitch of their voice changes. Whatever it is, I can sometimes tell. One of my profs has joked I could be a walking lie detector test. Not strictly admissible, but funny. Not that I'm saying you're lying, it's just an example. With you I feel it's something else. Something you're trying to keep to yourself. Just like Henryk."

"And what is Henryk trying to keep to himself?"

"He has a wife; did he tell you? A sixty-year-old wife back in Poland he hasn't seen for years."

Tyrone took a deep breath, wondering what he could say. Nothing came to him.

"Henryk has two daughters about my age who won't speak to him even though he has written to them, or says he has. To be honest, I can't tell if he has really tried to get in touch with them or not or if it's the other way around. Henryk is very hard to read sometimes. One of the hardest people I know."

Tyrone's laugh was genuine for the first time in a long time.

"If you need anything," he surprised himself at how freely he spoke, "anything at all, let me know if I can be of help in your studies. I have some connections that might prove useful, though they might not be as good as they once were."

She taped his phone number on a small recording device she kept in the pocket of her pants. Her day-to-day miscellaneous recorder, she explained. And then, taking his hand in both of hers, she said goodbye.

He looked back to see her standing at the door in her dark pants and red sweater. On hearing his motor start she gave a little wave.

And it was at this point that he rode back towards her. "May I have something of your brother's — a scarf, a piece of clothing?" he asked.

A vague, crazy plan was forming at the back of his mind.

[13] Second Chance

Tyrone let a few days go by and then rode over to the phone booth early one morning to call Henryk. No answer. No answer half an hour later, either. As he sat at his secondhand kitchen table he thought about what to do while tracing the scarred surface with a coffee spoon. Owners of the table before him had made different patterns and whorls but he was becoming partial to the one he was carving out at his end.

The frenetic dogs in the next farmhouse were barking again, working their way up to a crescendo that sounded like they were just outside his kitchen. His coffee spoon dug deeper into the table. Of all the farmhouses he could have chosen, of all the counties and districts, it had to be the one next to these banshees. He pushed his chair away and walked over to the bay window remembering his vague idea just before he left Tess.

If he wanted to get his car back, maybe the dogs could serve a purpose after all. It just required the capacity for boldness, the chutzpah that had seemed so natural in his drinking days.

He discarded the idea of a noisy, aggressive ride up to the next farm on his motorcycle in favor of a long, quiet stroll signaling peaceful intentions. Gravel scrunched under his boots as he walked and planned what to say. The sky was a vast grey slate. The closer he got, the more he tried to convince himself the mad barking sounded friendly and benign.

The neighboring farmhouse was a red brick two-story, just like his. Unlike his, there was a wide porch wrapped around the entrance and a small table between two Adirondack chairs with flowered cushions. White shutters surrounded the front windows.

The door was opened by an ample woman in a large purple top covered in dog hair. She had a porcelain smile. Straight, even teeth gleamed at him out of a weathered face that could have used more obvious skin improvements. The smell of dog wafted out from beyond the door. It hit him so hard his eyes began to water.

"Hi there," the woman said brightly. "Have you come with the trailer?"

A nervous cough escaped his throat. "My name is Lawrence Tyrone, I'm your —"

Just as he feared, the dogs started an immediate racket, drowning him out.

"Excuse me a moment. I don't know what gets into them sometimes," she shouted and disappeared into the back of the house, leaving him to think she knew exactly what got into them but was keeping it to herself.

He heard a raised voice and then a soothing tone as the dogs grew quiet. She came back wiping her hands down the sides of her purple top as if it were a towel. There was a spot of wet slobber under her right breast.

"My name's Audrey," she said, peering down the driveway behind him. "I guess you didn't come with the trailer."

Anxious not to lose his opportunity, he spoke quickly, explaining what he had in mind.

"You want to rent a dog?" she asked, puzzled.

"A special dog, you understand. A dog I can trust, with an exceptional sense of smell. For a week. I'm willing to pay a reasonable sum."

"You can trust all my dogs. Let me think. A special dog with a sense of smell? You do realize they all have a special sense of smell so why do you want a dog with a sense of smell?"

"Uh. I need to find something. Just want to see."

"You don't have anything to do with drugs, do you?" she asked.

"Of course not!" Drugs? Him? What kind of people lived on this dog farm?

She stared at him, her hand up to her face, scratching her cheek. He stared back, not hiding his indignation.

"Okay, okay," she said. "Let me think. Let me think. Not Caesar, he's about to be picked up. Not Sammy. Hmmm. You're willing to pay a reasonable sum? Okay, I've got it. Sheba." She snapped her fingers. "She's just what you need."

"Is this *your* dog?" he asked suspiciously.

"Of course she's my dog. What do you take me for?"

"All right then, do you think she'll come with me? Work for me so to speak?"

"If she decides she likes you, I'm sure she will. You'll have to meet her and then we can decide."

"Excellent."

"There's just one thing — not a big problem, really — it might take a little time. It's just..." she hesitated, looking around him and beyond him and then to left and right.

She looked furtive when she wasn't smiling, he decided.

He waited.

"She's a good dog, really. Very reliable. But it seems..."

He waited some more.

"Well, I might as well tell you. I'm gonna have to find her."

"She's lost?" he said with as much incredulity as he could muster. Bad enough this woman gave him the impression she might have been willing to rent out other people's dogs, now she was also admitting to losing them.

"No, she's not lost," Audrey said impatiently. "She knows exactly where she is. It's me who doesn't know where she is."

She gave him a defiant glare.

The dogs in the back of the house started to bark again.

"Madame," he said dismayed, wanting to be humble rather than angered.

"Sir!" she said, perhaps guessing at his growing prickliness or just reading the look on his face.

He meant to be pleasant, he would have sworn to it, but he was already on edge and the dogs, perhaps sensing something brewing began yapping and then yowling and frantically barking in a rising crescendo. These were the most ill-behaved, bad-tempered dogs he had ever encountered. Kennels like this ought to be outlawed. The tone of her voice, the large red arms bunched around her purple top and the persistently barking and growling and yapping fiends set his already frayed nerves on edge. He was reminded what a hostage he was to their erratic uproar at all times of the day and night. He forgot his desire for a dog.

"Madame!" he shouted over the cacophony. "Control your damn dogs. Barking. Always barking. A public nuisance. Dangerous too. Next time I'm calling the police."

"I work hard with my dogs!" she said loudly, crossing her arms over her chest. "If my husband was here he'd tell you."

"The dogs should be shot!" he yelled.

"Say that one more time and I'll fix you myself. Get off with you," she screamed back at him, the dogs continuing their uproar behind her. "Son of a bitch bastard. How dare you harm helpless animals? Don't ever set foot here again, you hear?"

"I could personally shoot them myself with great pleasure," he shouted back.

This from a man, a professor of law, who never owned a gun and had taught a semester on the consequences of criminal violence.

Her answer was fortunately drowned out by the frantic hellions. There appeared to be hundreds of the murderous creatures ready to spring loose and tear him apart.

He turned with great calm, given the circumstances, his calves and ankles tingling at the thought of being torn apart, and tried to slowly retrace his steps. Not because of her, but because he read somewhere that fleeing from a pack of angry dogs was asking to be mauled and he didn't trust her not to set them loose.

The minute he rounded the curve, out of her sight, he sprinted towards the road until he was out of breath. He could still hear the barking when he got to his front door.

Locking himself inside his farmhouse, he peered out the kitchen bay window. He knew it was an unreasonable thing to do but he wasn't willing to be reasonable. Her reaction unnerved him. After all, he had done nothing wrong. He only asked about a dog and she reacted like a madwoman, turning on a dime without the slightest provocation. It was people like her who made the world the difficult place it was. If he ever needed proof that withdrawing as far from it as possible was justified, this was it.

His career, his first marriage, his life, dependent on the whims of incomprehensible and crazy people. Nothing ever seemed under his control. Attempting to calm his temper, he searched every inch of the house trying to find a bottle he might have hidden and forgotten. His anger vanished as suddenly as it came. On thinking it over, he was astonished at how fast it had overtaken him.

For the first time in a long time, he went to bed fully clothed, shutting off the lights and lying across the bedspread, staring at the darkness of the ceiling.

He wanted to keep his mind a blank. It didn't work. Here was Leah before him, so long ago, as a student. Smiling at him from the front row in a soft green sweater, she asked a question, deliberately crossing her legs one over the other and then switching back a few minutes later. Her black silk stockings made a seductive rubbing sound. It was beginnings he loved, the freshness of the unknown when it was still unknowable. She had smiled her full-lipped smile and then left the room, whispering to one of the other male students who put his arm around her. She glanced back at Tyrone as if challenging him. It was a watershed moment, seeing her with that young, arrogant male, a moment when the professor made a reckless decision to take a step into the unknowable. She told him soon enough, when they were together and there was hope, that he was too smart to insist things were unknowable. She insisted he stepped into the unknowable and made it known. It was when he was both clever and cautious, could make plans, stick to them and bide his time.

Once upon a time, he acknowledged he'd been a more patient man. He couldn't articulate the precise moment his suspicion, and therefore his disintegration, began. Was it the moment, the terrible moment, when he came into his colleague's private office?

Leah and his colleague were sitting there on a couch, too close together. They heard him stumble against the half open door and turned to stare.

Although afterwards Tyrone stuck to his arguments, he couldn't have said for certain if there was anything erotic in what he saw. What was certain, because he knew her expressions so well, all the lines and frowns and passions of her face, was that her quick red flush and sullen dark look signified guilt of some sort.

Outside the farmhouse the night was very dark and quiet. Not a peep out of the dogs and good riddance. Perhaps Audrey had taken him seriously and sedated them all.

To make up for the dogs, the unnamed feral cat who came with the farm and who usually prowled all night and slept all day in the bottom desk drawer, started to vocalize loudly and persistently beneath the bedroom window until he was let in. Tyrone was relieved by the distraction. The cat settled comfortably on top of his chest purring loudly. Just as Tyrone was drifting off to sleep, the cat decided it wanted out again, head-butted him to make the point and leapt to the floor, mewling aggressively. Tyrone threw his pillow at it and slammed the bedroom door, figuring the creature would shut up if he just outwaited it. After half an hour, he got up, defeated, and let it out the kitchen door. It stalked off with a swagger, tail high.

At five o'clock in the morning, when the light outside was blind and murky, Tyrone got up in the clothes he'd slept in and sat at the kitchen table with a glass of water. While he was wondering how many more endless nights he could tolerate, there was a brushing, or perhaps the sound of a twig rubbing against the back door. He lifted his head, wondering if it was the cat trying to fool him. There it was again. Something persistent and faint as if it was coming from far away.

If not the cat, it was a welcome danger, given how unbearable the night had been.

He got up and threw the door open.

An alert, cream-colored dog with a brown muzzle, brown ears and dark circles surrounding each dark eye was lying there. Its coat was short and gleamed by the kitchen light. The dog looked at him, head to one side, in a most confident and knowing manner. Her name could have been anything at all, but Tyrone knew with certainty who it was. He heard a short growl from the shadows and assumed the cat was keeping a carefully jealous watch. This bright-eyed dog could be none other than Sheba come to his rescue.

Looking in both directions, wary but also pleased, he opened the door wide and invited her in.

[14] Sheba's Will

A few hours later, there was a soft knock on the French doors leading to the kitchen. Tyrone was sitting in front of his computer in the kitchen nook, catching up with the morning news over the satellite internet. The nook consisted of a mid-floor-to-ceiling bay window with three large panes, two of which could be opened at the top if necessary. Like the kitchen, which overlooked the barn and the fields, the nook faced out towards the northern part of the farm, filled with the clear northern light Leah had so loved in her own artist's studio.

Sheba, after making a brief tour of the entire downstairs and then the upstairs, settled herself under the kitchen table. On hearing the knock, she opened one eye without moving, which was perfectly acceptable. Tyrone was not accustomed to sharing his space with a large dog.

He tried to peer carefully through the rightmost bay window without being seen by the invisible knocker, but the metal trellis, which was positioned on the outside between the bay window and the French kitchen doors, was covered in large floppy vines and prevented him from seeing who it was. He would have to approach the door and show himself.

The knock came again a little louder.

It didn't sound angry or vengeful, certainly not what he expected after his ill-fated encounter with Audrey.

Deliberately, Tyrone laid down his reading glasses and clicked off the news site before slowly getting up. He stared at his visitor through the glass pane on the upper part of the kitchen door before he turned the knob to let him in.

The man was in work boots and grey coveralls. He removed a cap from his head and stared back at Tyrone. His pale eyes were bright. No comb had recently touched his sparse hair.

"I see she made it," the man said, looking behind Tyrone at Sheba, who thumped her muscular tail once under the table.

"Er-hmm." Tyrone cleared his throat, feeling caught out.

"Not to worry," the man said. "The name's Wills. I'm over from next door. We haven't met."

"Lawrence Tyrone," Tyrone said as he shook Wills's calloused hand. "This your dog?"

"She is," the man said. "Biggest food lover I know next to the missus, don't tell her I said that." His smile was large.

"You've come for her, of course," Tyrone said.

"Nah, I sent her to you last night. Just checking up she decided to stay."

"I don't understand."

"I heard what happened. The missus told me. I laughed so hard she nearly shot me. She's sensitive, you know, but what can you do, eh? I said to her this morning, I said, I'm going to get over there and check her up."

"You mean you both — that is, you and she — decided to lend me this dog right here?"

Wills looked over at Tyrone in the friendliest manner. "You got it."

"Why?" Tyrone asked.

"What?"

"You heard the story. Why does she still want to lend me the dog?"

Wills affected a look of profound hurt. "Well. Heh. Heh."

When Tyrone didn't speak, Wills looked embarrassed. He shuffled his feet.

"It's like this," Wills said.

Tyrone crossed his arms.

Wills's face turned red. He looked over towards the barn and moved his hand. When he spoke, he used the hand as if to give himself momentum to keep speaking. Tyrone watched, fascinated.

"You know that snow blower in your barn? Well, it's ours."

"What do you mean?"

"George bleeding Jessup borrowed it and never give it back. The next thing we know he sells the place and there you were."

"Why didn't you say something before this?'

"We didn't know you!"

"And now you do?"

"You asked for a dog."

"I see," Tyrone said. "Would you like to come in? Look around for other stuff?"

His sarcasm was lost on Wills, who now bore the virtuous look of a man who had accomplished his mission.

"I need to get back," Wills said. "Just so you know, Sheba is smart, more determined than most Labs. Does what she damn pleases when it suits her. It suited her to come see you, but here is some rope and chain in case you don't want her to take off on you."

"Is she yours?" Tyrone asked curiously. "I mean she's not someone else's dog?"

Wills was no longer smiling or looking relieved. "Why would we lend you someone else's dog, mister? Sheba's totally bona fidey. In fact, she failed that there test, the one for leading the blind, and that's how we got her."

Tyrone's first instinct was to remark pointedly about the uselessness of foisting a stupid dog on him. Just in time, afraid to take a wrong step yet again on this precarious road, he controlled himself with effort. "You don't say," he remarked in as mild a tone as he could manage.

Wills was not fooled. "She's not stupid," he said irritably. "Don't you get what I'm trying to tell you? Just has her own mind when she feels like it. She started taking the blind guy on garbage tours, if you're dying to know, which wasn't exactly what he wanted."

"What does she eat, besides garbage?"

This time the words left Tyrone's mouth before he could stop them.

Wills's eyes seemed to narrow for a second, then he smiled with satisfaction.

"If she don't like what you got, she'll go out and help herself," he said.

"Help herself to what?" Tyrone's voice rose. "Bloody rabbits or prize chickens from one of the farms?"

"Ha! The look on your face. Had you worried, didn't I? I brought a bag of dog chow. It's in the barn. She's very particular. Knows just how to get into it, so be careful. Just feed her twice a day and lay out some water. She'll let you know if you forget something, but don't let her fool you into thinking she hasn't been fed, eh? She's good at that."

Wills dropped to his knees by the table.

"You'll stay here?" he asked Sheba.

Sheba's strong, hard tail flicked twice and then she came out towards Wills, mouth open. They looked at each other deeply. Wills didn't even turn his head away as she opened her muzzle and yawned in his face. "You'll stay," Wills said.

"Well then, that's that," he said to Tyrone. "We got a deal."

"A deal with the *dog*?" Tyrone asked.

"Who else?" Wills said, winking at Sheba. "Don't forget the snow blower."

Tyrone could have sworn that wasn't the end of it. Maybe the wink was some sort of secret signal.

"We'll do just fine," Tyrone boomed with pretended heartiness, staring Wills down. "I can handle the dog even if she is capable of making deals."

Wills simply smiled his large, disingenuous smile. Anybody else might have been fooled, but Tyrone was quick to note Wills's left eyebrow twitched before he turned away.

[15] Open Season

After Wills left, Tyrone thought of calling Henryk, bemused at the thought he had transformed himself so easily into a country man with a hunting dog.

He felt his spirits lifting on this particular morning. Sheba seemed content enough under the kitchen table, so he told her he would be right back, suddenly aware that without his car he had no way of transporting a large dog.

He rode directly to his phone booth.

"I have a plan," Tyrone said, when Henryk answered on the first ring.

"Oh yes?" Henryk said in a disinterested tone of voice.

Tyrone suspected he wasn't the only one who'd had an exceptionally dark night.

"This time we will be better informed," Tyrone said. "And better prepared."

"Better prepared?" Henryk snorted rudely, coming to life. "My dear Professor, what is your description of better preparation? Another warm sweater? A compass?"

"A dog," Tyrone said.

There was deep silence from Henryk's end and then a strangled sound.

Tyrone kept his voice hearty. In his other life, he found it gave reassurance to his students no matter what he, himself, felt. He was unprepared for Henryk's reaction. It turned out Henryk was laughing and choking at the same time.

"Cof — coffee," Henryk managed to say.

"What's so funny?" Tyrone said.

"You are thinking maybe about joining Russian army?" Henryk asked.

"Of course not. What does it have to do with a dog?"

Henryk was still coughing. "You wish to hunt Juan Carlos down with your dog?"

"It's not my dog." Tyrone realized the conversation was getting away from him. "Yes," he added.

"Very well," Henryk capitulated briskly. "Juan Carlos is in Thousand Islands. How is this dog to come with us?"

Two days later, at seven in the morning, Henryk and Sheba were both seated on an old motorcycle with sidecar. The bike, in mint condition, was Kelly green with black flame designs. Sheba looked regal by Henryk's side in the large sidecar. The seat on the sidecar had been removed and there were makeshift rails on either side. Plus Henryk had laid down a thick blanket on the floor so she could lie down if she chose. She was standing upright, mouth open in anticipation, eyes bright, peering through the rails, with the appearance of a true hunting dog.

Thinking it was a good time to acquaint her with Juan Carlos's scent, Tyrone attempted to thread Juan Carlos's red scarf around her collar.

She moved her head, annoyed.

He persisted.

She outwitted him by first pretending she would keep still and then arching her neck away from him at the very last moment.

The dog was devious.

Mindful of Wills's description of her as stubborn and willful, Tyrone did not wish to have her take off on a whim and then be obliged to hunt for her while trying to explain himself to Wills's secretly knowing eyebrows and to the unpredictable Audrey. He spread his legs to give himself extra leverage and came at her again.

She waited, waited, and then moved away again the second she felt his hands on her collar.

"Will you hold still?" he said, completely out of patience, while Henryk watched with interest.

She looked up, bright-eyed, with no remorse, as if this was a game she had every intention of winning.

"Arghh!!" he grunted.

Taking pity on Tyrone's frustration, Henryk stepped forward. The minute he gave her a soft pat on her flank, she held still.

The trip was uneventful. The weather was milder, the sun shone warmly, the road was easy and surprisingly empty for mid-week.

If he rode more slowly than Henryk, Tyrone enjoyed the wind. For once he had properly layered his clothes so uncontrolled air didn't whip its way between his pants and jacket. His hands in leather gloves were more or less safe and comfortable.

He began to enjoy the ride and the feeling of freedom as the engine responded to him over the long road.

It was how he came to relax his guard.

They made a pit stop about ten minutes from their destination. Feeling sorry for the dog, who did not look in any way put out, Tyrone undid the loose rope from the sidecar rails in order to take her for a walk.

"I'll be right back," he said to Henryk, who regarded him with an unreadable expression.

Sheba walked beside Tyrone, wearing Juan Carlos's red scarf around her strong neck, her short coat sleek in the sun.

A calm and docile trophy dog.

It made Tyrone doubt what Wills had said about her stubborn independence and fondness for garbage. Obviously, the dog had no intention of going anywhere as long as she was with someone who knew how to handle her.

Congratulating himself on being a natural as a dog owner, Tyrone felt pleased.

Nothing to having a dog, he thought, as they walked calmly side by side. In fact, he might consider getting one. If not Sheba, maybe a similar cream-colored Labrador retriever, since they took so easily to him.

He placed her rope loosely on a bush while he turned to unzip his pants. He never heard a sound other than his own jet stream.

When he turned to reclaim her, she was gone.

Henryk's complete lack of surprise when Tyrone returned from beating the bushes as quietly as he could, grass stains and dirt on his knees from tripping over a hidden log, was immediately irritating.

"She would have run away from anybody," Tyrone snapped.

Henryk shrugged.

"You don't believe me? She's obviously a devious dog."

"Was obvious she was planning something," Henryk said.

"It was certainly not obvious. How would you know? What do you mean obvious?" Tyrone said.

"The way she was walking. She was considering exploration."

"She's never been here. Why would she do that?"

"My friend, because a dog like that gets bored and curious. A dog like that is always looking for food and company. Especially company who will give her food. So it is obvious she will take all opportunities to explore. Was she a wandering dog where she came from? Myself, personally, I would have been holding the rope very tight."

"Easy for you to say now," Tyrone said sullenly with no intention of answering Henryk's query about a wandering dog.

Henryk waved his hand in a careless and almost insolent manner and got on his bike with the now empty sidecar.

"We can't just leave her here," Tyrone said. "She's not my dog. We have to look for her." More than ever he couldn't bear the thought of facing Audrey's temper or Wills's maddeningly self-satisfied look.

"We better go," Henryk said.

"I just said we can't leave her here, wasn't it clear to you?"

"Don't worry," Henryk said. "She will find us."

"What if she doesn't?"

"She's a *hunting* dog. What more do you want?"

"But what if she doesn't?" Tyrone repeated stubbornly.

"Then we will get another dog," Henryk said calmly. He looked at Tyrone in the eyes and held his gaze as if willing Tyrone to get a grip.

Within ten minutes, as the garish silver and red casino came into view, Henryk gave the signal to pull over. Weary from losing the dog rather than from the long ride, Tyrone feared Henryk meant them to camp out in the parking lot. But Henryk had unassailable arguments. Sounding enormously reasonable, the biker pointed out Sheba might have a better chance of finding them in the open.

Tyrone hesitated. Confounded as he was by Sheba's loss, he almost bought the story until he realized that unless the dog could follow bike tracks, she didn't have a hope in hell of finding them anywhere, let alone in the casino parking lot.

While Tyrone waited outside, Henryk went into the casino and came out a half hour later looking troubled but saying nothing. They agreed Juan Carlos might show himself more readily at night and that led to a small victory for Tyrone: rather than camping out in the parking lot waiting for the errant dog, they checked into a small motel not too distant from the casino.

Henryk dropped his black bag on one of the cheap double beds and went to splash his face in the bathroom.

After taking his boots off, Tyrone threw himself with single-minded abandon on the other bed. Almost immediately he started to dream. Later, he was never sure if his dream was a figment of his tired mind or real. In his dream, he was wide-awake and wandering the countryside, concentrating on every sound, trying to spot the tell-tale signs of injury or blood, even listening for the faintest bark or movement. The dream was so vivid, so real, he was aware his senses were sharpened and found himself praying they would not be too late.

He woke up disoriented an hour later. Lying for a moment with eyes closed he tried to remember what was so upsetting about his dream. Whatever it was had already slipped away. The room's curtains were partially drawn and the late afternoon sun was creeping in large motes across the musty carpeted floor.

In the bathroom, he splashed cold water on his face and stared at himself in a mirror that was so disgustingly clear it spotlighted every wrinkle and blemish. His left eye had burst a blood vessel while he slept. He definitely looked the worse for wear. A few months ago, this would have made him anxious. Now he just toweled himself dry, zipped up his jeans and set out to search for Henryk.

He found the biker at a blackjack table in the casino, doubling down.

Henryk must have changed while Tyrone slept. He was wearing a tasteful dark long-sleeved polo shirt and his hair was neatly combed and tied back. He looked mildly disguised, respectable enough to be allowed to lose money at any table in the province.

Caught for a moment in the excitement of luck and flying high, the feeling that let you know the cards would fall right, Tyrone couldn't help watching the play and deciding what his own strategy could be. But they had business to take care of and he touched Henryk's arm. "Any news?" he asked.

"I am winning so far," Henryk said casually. "Up two Gs."

"Hmm." Tyrone was tempted to try his own luck.

Taking his eyes off Henryk, he reached for his wallet while Henryk was clearing the table of his winnings. "I have news," Henryk said, a fistful of chips in both hands.

Tyrone put his wallet away. They walked towards the cashier together. "Bad news," Henryk said.

Moving past white sails and decorative wooden ships hanging from a forty-foot ceiling, they avoided the formal and expensive-looking Marina Grill restaurant and found themselves in one of the casino bars. A large screen was showing a WrestleMania championship. The Gorilla was fighting Bonzo Man. The grunts were theatrical, the falls earth-shaking and the displays of power — including a lot of frenzied chest beating — were histrionic. The audience, on both sides of the screen, loved it.

To Tyrone's surprise, Henryk, looking faintly disgusted, led them as far away as possible from the show.

Once seated at their table, Henryk ordered a beer and a bowl of peanuts, while Tyrone settled for a tonic with lime. Henryk took a long pull from his glass, wiping his mouth on the back of his hand.

"You don't care for wrestling?" Tyrone asked.

"I have seen enough men behaving as animals from very close," Henryk said. "I don't choose to have more experience."

"It's an exercise in deception, can't you tell?"

"Everything is about what happens at the end," Henryk said. "Nothing else matters."

"You will have to be more specific," Tyrone said.

"The world is not such an innocent place. People get damaged."

"What does this have to do with my car?"

"Juan Carlos was here yesterday."

"That's good news, wouldn't you say? How do you know?"

"One of the dealers saw him outside."

"Where?"

"Out there in parking lot. The dealer was having cigarette. Juan Carlos played at his table until he was recognized and told he should leave."

"By the dealer?"

"No, the dealer would not give him away. Security."

"So, where is he?"

"That is big problem, my friend. Men were waiting for him in car just outside —please do not think of asking about your car —" Henryk fixed Tyrone with a hard stare.

"I have no intention of asking about my car. I get the picture," Tyrone said. "Now what do you suggest we do?"

Henryk sighed, a long, drawn-out sigh, and ordered another beer, all animation gone from his large, pale face.

"Did the casino call the police?" Tyrone asked.

"You are missing big picture," Henryk said, not bothering to raise his eyes.

"All right," Tyrone said. "I suppose nobody told them. None of their business. I'm not an idiot. What can we do?"

"I promised Tess," Henryk said.

"Ah, Tess." Tyrone decided to try a little jab despite the situation. "She thanks you for the flowers."

"What flowers?"

"The flowers you gave her the time we visited."

"What are you talking about?"

"All right, the flowers I went back and gave her from you after you left so rudely."

"Flowers? You thought to give her flowers from me and you say you are not an idiot?" Henryk asked.

The fire he might normally have displayed was missing. Not a good time to bait him when there was more somber news on his mind.

"All right, truce," Tyrone said. "What's your idea?"

Henryk looked exhausted. "I am out of opinions," he said.

They walked outside. Tyrone, itching to do something other than sleep, persuaded Henryk to go for a ride. Just around the area, Tyrone said, even if Henryk had already checked it out and found nothing. "What can it hurt to try again?"

They eased their way down the county road towards the lake. Dusk was a shroud, descending like a net over the blue air. Dark trees rose up on either side of the road. Behind them was the blaze of the casino; in front, the smell of open water with its potential for a stealthy boat ride across the border and a body weighed and thrown overboard to sink.

"What if —" Tyrone started to say at one point.

Henryk stopped him with a chopping off hand motion.

As they rode slowly, Tyrone found himself listening closely, straining beyond the drone of the bike engines. He couldn't have said what he was listening for. He listened with anticipation. He listened like someone who wanted to believe in miracles. But it was Henryk who heard it first: a measured barking and a fainter howling coming from somewhere deep in the woods. The howling made Henryk come to a full stop, turn off his engine and gesture for Tyrone to do the same. In the stillness Tyrone heard them too, one faint, the other slightly louder.

A wolf, and then, perhaps, an errant retriever, or maybe it was the other way around.

[16] The Tree of Prophecy

They guided their bikes off to the side of the road and entered the strip of grass and sedge bordering the wooded area. It was where the barking seemed to be coming from. Tyrone found himself thinking about snakes and vermin and was grateful for his leather boots and heavy jeans.

The former professor noticed how much cooler the air felt in the coming dusk. As he and Henryk stumbled through the unruly tall grass and undergrowth towards the shadows of the trees, the path was suddenly illuminated in a bright band falling along the ground and tree trunks. Henryk had pulled out a flashlight.

Just ahead of them, the barking came in bursts followed by silence. Answering howls, distant, less urgent, partially filled the stillness in between.

Henryk went first, peering for signs of a footpath, holding back branches so they wouldn't snap against Tyrone's face. Neither man spoke. Tyrone had no wish to speculate on what men could do to each other and how futile it was to stop them.

For one bright moment, an eerie trunk took shape up ahead, enormous with its branches. In contrast to the other trees, this one was dead and bare. Tyrone could have sworn the bare tree was familiar even though he'd never been here before.

It reminded him of one of his last visits to Leah's studio before he was barred. They were still talking, although their conversations seemed to go nowhere. Now he realized they hadn't really been conversations at all, except in the sense that they were both talking. Leah was trying to be heard. But Tyrone had been doing his best not to listen.

She stood beside him in front of her latest canvas so they could admire it together.

"Is the tree dead?" he asked, wondering why she'd paint a huge grey tree. He secretly attributed it to her growing strangeness, not for a moment imagining it had anything to do with him. Behind the tree, a dense forest was in full leaf.

"Not exactly," she replied, biting her lower lip, looking critically at the canvas with him, a brush in her hand.

The next time she showed him the canvas she put her arm around him and he could feel her solid warmth as they once again appraised her work.

The latest incarnation of the tree had leaves. But they were bird leaves, clusters of bright yellow breasts, striped black-and-white heads, tawny brown backs, a canopy of dense feathers. At the base of the tree there were snakes. Black snakes with red stripes, banded in yellow. The birds, huddled thick as buds on the branches, appeared unaware or unconcerned, even though one snake was already climbing the trunk, just starting its journey up the base.

"It's a tree full of Great Kiskadee birds," she said. "A Kiskadee tree."

"Why snakes?" he asked, on his way to a lecture, already feeling mellow and unaware she was trying to make a point.

"Coral snakes are their natural enemy, but they haven't seen them yet."

"But why?" he repeated.

"Coral snake venom is a strange thing," she said, looking at him obliquely. "It's such a slow poisoning of the nerves. You can walk around for eight hours, even longer, maybe even twenty-four, before you collapse from the bite. Until then you never know what hit you or bit you, you just walk around like a normal person with feelings and you don't know you're going to die."

"Interesting," he mumbled.

Later he thought how insidious, how diabolical, that tree was and only later still did it occur to him to wonder why she showed it to him at all. He now realized she started to paint the thing after they'd had another of their ugly fights about children.

What she showed him, how she communicated, was becoming increasingly bizarre and he found himself unable, or unwilling to analyze it at the time. He dismissed it with the thought she obviously was tied to her emotions, never understanding the unseen terror in paradise, the slow poisoning of innocence she was trying to portray. In this sense, he had also been inarticulate. What he kept wanting to say was any child would be a hindrance to his career and to his well-being. What he could never say was how bereft he had felt after his mother died and he was left alone with Spenser.

It was only now, when he was walking in the near dark towards barking, howling animals and perhaps something even more terrible, his career and his first wife both long gone, that what he had not wanted to see was finally making sense.

Tyrone heard the barking again, closer this time. Henryk put up a hand to halt their progress and then turned around, putting a finger to his lips, indicating they should walk with caution as they left the path and headed into the brush. The animal sounds were very close now. He could see a dark shape up against something on the ground, a brief red smear in the soft beam of the flashlight. If it was a wild dog or even a wolf, they had disturbed his bloody kill. It was too hard to see. Henryk tried to illuminate the area better. There was a feral shine. Tyrone thought of yellow eyes and lethal teeth. The next moment he saw Sheba, guarding something, Juan Carlos's red scarf still around her neck. He shivered. Behind him, he could feel the presence of the ghost tree.

[17] A Doubtful Law Does Not Bind

"Here, girl," Henryk said, not approaching the dog. Sheba raised her head, considered the situation, and then came towards him slowly. She pushed against his leg in greeting.

"Phew," Henryk said. "What have you been eating?" He took a deep breath and patted her head.

Tyrone could hear the volume of air drawn into Henryk's lungs and it made him anxious. Sheba took up a position to one side of whatever was on the ground. What Tyrone could see was a shape, and that was all. It could have been a muddy pile of rags.

When Henryk stepped towards the pile of rags, Tyrone followed. Sheba moved reflexively for a second and then let them get close.

Henryk squatted and turned the thing over, directing his flashlight on the face. It was hard to tell who it was or had been, there was so much dirt and slimy secretions. Henryk took a rag from his pocket and gently wiped the face, then shone the light on it once again. The lopsided scar was unmistakable now. Sheba whined softly as Henryk, taking deep gulps of air, tried to move Juan Carlos.

"Let me help," Tyrone said, not stopping to think about possible spinal injuries and attempting to pick up Juan Carlos's legs while Henryk was working his way under the arms.

The injured man let out a yelp before his head fell back once more.

"His leg is injured," Henryk said. "And we don't know what else is the matter. Please let him go."

"There must be a hospital close by," Tyrone said.

"No hospital," Henryk said. "We will take him to our room."

"But he may die!"

"He has the chance," Henryk said. "There is also the chance he may live. In hospital he will die for sure."

"What are you talking about?"

"The men who did this want him dead. If we go to hospital they will know for sure he is not."

"Come on, we're obliged to report this crime," Tyrone said.

"No," Henryk said coldly. "We are not."

Henryk shone the light around the area until he found some thick branches lying on the ground. He stripped off his jacket and took Tyrone's as well and created a makeshift stretcher as best he could, threading the arms of the leather jackets onto the branches. With effort, they managed to slide Juan Carlos onto the stretcher and started the journey back to the bikes. Juan Carlos groaned softly, as if by reflex, any time they jostled him or changed his position. Given the alternative, a deathly stillness, Tyrone found himself grateful for sounds of pain as they slowly dragged and sometimes carried him along the dark path.

Getting Juan Carlos into Henryk's sidecar past the makeshift rails wasn't easy. The injured leg, which looked puffy and bruised beneath his torn cargo pants was a tricky proposition. They finally succeeded in fitting his lower body into the floor of the side car in a semi-seated position and Henryk covered him with a sweater to shield him from the cool air.

After much uncertainty and angst, on the part of Tyrone at least, they staggered past the door of their first-floor motel room well past midnight.

Once they managed to settle Juan Carlos's battered body on Henryk's bed, Sheba positioned herself precisely between the two beds. Henryk brought a wet towel from the bathroom and handed it to Tyrone.

"Gentle," he said, watching the former professor's first awkward attempts at cleaning Juan Carlos's wounds.

"We have to undress him," Tyrone said. He could hear the testiness in his own voice. "Help me, will you?"

This process was also excruciating. Juan Carlos groaned in anguish, tried to fight them off, rolled into a ball and pushed their hands away as they attempted to undo his clothing. After a few minutes struggling with buttons and zippers and clothing that was plastered to the skin, Henryk got out his army knife and started slicing through pants, shirt and underwear. The sheets on the bed were now filthy, a russet red from the mixture of mud and blood. Once they were done, Tyrone pointed to the other bed, indicating he needed help to move the injured gambler.

Henryk said, "Better not move him. Clean him and then we will change sheets. I will be back."

"Wait a minute. Where are you going? At least let me call a doctor," Tyrone said, unwilling to face a naked man's dying body by himself.

"I am getting a doctor," Henryk said. "Wait here."

It was one o'clock in the morning.

"House calls? At this hour?" Tyrone said, trying to keep his voice down. "This man may die!"

"He will not die," Henryk said. "We are counting on you."

Left alone with Juan Carlos, Tyrone was repulsed by the damage his body had sustained. Then he filled the ice bucket with warm water. Using a hand towel, he worked around the bruises on the head, wiped the dark hair and gently sponged down the battered chest. The water turned a muddy red in seconds and needed to be changed frequently.

Juan Carlos moaned faintly each time Tyrone tried to get underneath a limb. When he stopped moaning, Tyrone became anxious. He put his ear to the man's chest to see if he could pick up anything, holding his breath in order to hear the faint thrum of the other's heart.

He continued to wash him. When he got to the genitalia, he hesitated. Taking a deep breath, he worked his way down around the battered penis and loose testicles, feeling pity and sorrow. Without warning, he found himself weeping, unable to stop. The more he tried to control himself, the harder it became. He put down the towel, grabbed Sheba and wept.

He cried for everything that was and might have been. He wept for the woman he'd loved, for the son he'd lost and might never see. Those were his deepest and most secret wounds, the ones he kept to himself because he didn't know how to share them or what to do. Whatever was his, whatever he was, it was gone. He wept for the mistakes, the people he failed, the life that could have been his. He wanted to howl from sorrow for every wasted opportunity. And yet somewhere deep down the irony was not lost on him at how a vulnerable penis and testicles were one of the few things in his life that made him shed tears.

Slowly, he pulled himself together, went into the bathroom to splash his face and refill the ice bucket once more before gently sponging Juan Carlos's bruised, swollen leg.

A little over an hour later, Henryk returned with a tired looking, clean cut young man smelling of antiseptic. An assured, compact young man who looked somewhat wary.

Tyrone, who had managed to compose himself, was sitting beside Juan Carlos on a chair that was numbing his ass. He'd stripped the top sheet from the clean bed and carefully rolled it under the injured man and then he'd covered Juan Carlos with a clean sheet and blanket he found in the hanging wardrobe when the man began to shiver. The soiled sheets and blankets were carefully rolled up under the bed. Tyrone hoped he and Henryk would be long gone before the chambermaid discovered the gory remnants and reported a murder. He did all this while Sheba continued to lie between the beds, head on paws, as if exhausted from overseeing the cleanup.

She raised her head and opened one eye while Henryk and the young man tried to maneuver their way to the bed.

Tyrone hunkered down beside her to try to get her to move out of the way to make room. Obligingly, she headed for the toilet and drank noisily out of the bowl. Tyrone turned away, reconsidering his opinion about owning a dog.

The young man washed his hands in the bathroom sink, unrolled a blue paper-like sheet he opened with gloved hands on the other bed and laid out instruments and packages on top of it. Then he tackled a blue roll wrapped in what looked like foil, which turned out to be a surgeon's mask and gown.

"Don't forget to bring in all the stuff out there," he spoke through the mask to Henryk's back as Henryk headed for the door.

"You a doctor, a resident or what?" Tyrone managed to ask while they waited.

"Resident," the young man said without elaborating further.

The packages of splints, bottles and bandages Henryk returned with made Tyrone guess they were a result of a raid on the hospital emergency stores. Wherever this young miracle worker might have come from, he never once mentioned getting the severely battered patient to a hospital. Henryk must have got his point across. Instead, he gave Juan Carlos a few injections, cleaned and stitched and bandaged, displaying a quiet competence and an excessively serious manner. He only looked up twice to let them know what he was doing and why.

At close to five in the morning, trussed and bandaged, Juan Carlos could easily have passed for an embalmed mummy.

"There is just one more thing," the resident said. He was swaying slightly with fatigue. "I can't tell if his spleen is damaged and I think his leg is fractured but I don't know how badly. You'll have to have him x-rayed very soon. Oh wait. Another thing."

"Yes?" Henryk paused on the way to the door.

"That sidecar isn't going to work."

"Pardon?" Henryk said.

"I figure you brought him here in it but you can't move him that way."

"How is he, you think?" Henryk asked.

"He's fairly young, which makes it easier, but you really should bring him round to the clinic for X-rays. I've taped his broken ribs and I think I took care of all the external bleeding. I don't think there's any lung damage, but he could die from something I couldn't pick up. Head trauma, for instance. Something internal. His leg. I have to see an X-ray. You could bring him round to the back of the clinic this morning. He's less likely to attract attention there."

"And how am I to do that, my brave young man, without using sidecar?" Henryk said.

"I'll bring the stretch limo round," the young man said.

"Ahhh," Henryk sighed loudly, rasping his hand across the grey stubble on his face. "What are we getting into?"

"I don't talk to anybody."

"I did say no one must know about this man. His life is in big danger."

"And besides, look at me," the resident replied. "I'm only doing my job. Do I look like I have connections?"

"Possibly not," Henryk said. "But I am suspicious."

"Well isn't that just great," the young man said.

[18] Black Maria

When the resident left, Tyrone let out a long sigh. It didn't look like their ordeal was close to being over and he didn't know how much longer he wanted to stick around.

How had something that started out as a simple adventure — Spanish lessons, motorcycle lessons — come to this?

Tyrone wanted to shake hands with Henryk and take off, leaving him to finish cleaning up the mess. He glanced over at Sheba, who was apparently deciding to end her nap. She got up, looked over at Tyrone and went to the door.

"She needs to go out," Henryk said.

"Damn," Tyrone said. "She needs food and water. Is she going to get sick drinking from the toilet?"

"What?" Henryk said. "When dogs stop drinking from toilets is when there are no more dogs. I will do it. Take her out, I mean."

"Disgusting habit," Tyrone muttered.

As Henryk was leaving with Sheba's rope wound tightly around his fist, Tyrone was going to mention dog food. Then he decided not to complicate things. The dog certainly didn't look starved and must have helped herself to something while she was running loose. He reasoned she would make Henryk aware of whatever she wanted so no need to worry. And if he mentioned dog food, Henryk might ask where it was and he'd have to admit he forgot it.

Tyrone watched the biker and the dog through the motel window. The day was getting brighter by infinitesimal degrees. The sun would be up soon. Henryk was whistling a familiar tune Tyrone should perhaps have paid attention to but didn't. The words of a song suggesting someone leaving on a freight train and not knowing when they'd be back did not bode well. He made a mental note of the things he'd need to gather up before he himself took off. It seemed cleaner that way, no explanations, no bad feelings, only the open road in front of him and the fickle freedom of the wind as he headed back to his orchards and his plans. He could always nap somewhere on the road if he felt sleepy.

He assured himself Henryk would do exactly the same in his position. The thought of Sheba made him hesitate. But he couldn't possibly take her with him. Henryk would have to bring her home in the sidecar. It was the logical thing.

Juan Carlos lay still, breathing shallowly, while Tyrone tiptoed around the motel room. Looking at the tall, wrecked figure on the bed in the growing light, Tyrone rubbed his face, trying to decide on a course of action. He couldn't very well leave the man alone in the condition he was in. He'd wait for Henryk and then leave.

But he had a strong sense that whatever he decided in the next few minutes would shape the rest of his life. In what ways, good or bad, he couldn't tell.

In the old days, once he decided on a course of action he never hesitated or questioned himself. Now things were not so clear cut. He took a deep breath, weary from the long night. By his third breath he was concluding his decision had always been obvious, he just hadn't grasped it because the terrible night was so disorienting. He had his own life to tend to after all. Personal commitments he'd kept putting off. It was time to stop procrastinating.

There was a soft knock on the door. Relieved that Henryk might have returned with a well-fed dog so they could wrestle things out between them, Tyrone was debating how to make his case.

It wasn't Henryk standing there.

"Raffaele Marino," said the resident, who hadn't changed his clothes or shaved. "Remember me?"

The young man pointed towards the parking lot where a sleek black limo was waiting.

Tyrone stared at him for a moment, feeling put out that his plans weren't falling neatly into place the way he'd expected and then focused on the limo. It was a stretch Rolls gleaming darkly as it sat in the small lot in front of them.

"You okay?" Raffaele Marino asked.

"Of course, I'm okay," Tyrone snapped. "Why shouldn't I be?"

Putting his bags down on the floor, Tyrone pointed to the man on the bed and then turned to face the young resident.

"He's still there. Still breathing," he said. "He's all yours."

Part Two

[19] Home from the Sea

For two days in a row, at six o'clock every morning, Lawrence Tyrone woke to the smell of coffee brewing downstairs in the kitchen and to the morning news on the radio coming from the bedroom next to his, delivered full blast by two male hosts. The subject matter of this news and the volume with which it was delivered was apparently geared to high-octane young males because the hosts themselves, long past their twenties yet aspiring to relive them anyway, kept bantering and laughing hugely at their own jokes.

The first morning, Tyrone stormed the room and turned the radio down, but that was when he mistakenly thought the purpose was to give him a headache. After Raffaele explained the program was meant to get through to Juan Carlos's comatose brain, he remained remarkably laissez-faire and let the program blare away as he showered and got dressed.

He made a daily habit of peering in on the patient just before going downstairs for his first cup of coffee. Juan Carlos lay stretched and bandaged on one of the double beds in the Rose Room, which was next door to his bedroom.

169

Covered in an abundance of pink roses, the room probably belonged to the previous owner's daughter. When he first moved in, Tyrone had stashed his business clothes in the cramped closet, the suits and ties he was never going to wear again.

Juan Carlos was hooked up to IV drips. A small machine on the wobbly antique stand next to his bed monitored his breathing or maybe it was his heart or even brain waves. Tyrone chose not to remember. And all the while Juan Carlos lay quietly without moving, a shallow-breathing mummy.

Raffaele Marino, known as Rafe, turned out to be a young man of persuasive words and impressive abilities. He was dark-haired, medium sized and compact. On closer inspection, he was deliberate in the extreme, as if he still had to keep reminding himself about the steps to a dance he alone was aware of.

After bringing Juan Carlos in the Black Maria limo to what turned out to be his father's clinic and tending to him in a location better equipped than a one-star motel room, he insisted he could accompany them both to wherever Tyrone wanted to go.

"Not up to me," Tyrone said. "We're waiting for the man who found you."

But the biker had vanished along with the dog. While he waited, Tyrone found himself unable to abandon Juan Carlos. More to the point, Rafe made him feel responsible, since, as he pointed out, the patient had to be someone's responsibility.

"I can travel, no question. Besides, I'm on vacation," Rafe said.

"Come on!" Tyrone eyed him skeptically.

Rafe sighed. "My father's a doctor. It feels like I've been at this since I was twelve."

"And where does that leave us?"

"This is different. Now he's my patient. I'm ready to take some time. I'm due for time off anyway."

Tyrone's suspicions kicked in. "But why?" Tyrone asked. "What's the deal here?"

"No deal," Rafe smiled and moved his hands out, palms up, looking clean-cut and sincere. "Just being a good Samaritan. That's what I trained for. He's my patient now. I want to make sure he's taken care of. What's wrong with that?"

Tyrone focused in on him with narrowed eyes, considering the pros and cons.

There was still no sign of Henryk. Juan Carlos had been lying bandaged up in the clinic for almost two days and needed to be moved. What next? Against his better judgment, he reached a fateful, though reluctant, decision. He agreed Rafe could wedge a comatose Juan Carlos into the stretch limo and drive it to Tyrone's farm while Tyrone would lead, or at least closely follow, on his motorcycle.

And thus, they set out early one morning in convoy.

It was a clear day with high clouds, a day made for adventure. As they traveled over the highway, the last few months were on Tyrone's mind. He wondered what he had gotten himself into yet again and how difficult it was becoming for him to extricate himself.

On arriving at the farm, Rafe rummaged around in the dusty hall cupboard under the stairs, unearthed the vacuum cleaner and made Tyrone get a mop and pail. To Tyrone's surprise, the resident proved to be clumsy the faster he tried to clean house and managed to trip on the cord twice, upend the vacuum once and disconnect the plug three times in his zeal to attack every speck of dust that existed, seen or unseen. As if his mind was on other matters, or more likely, he wasn't used to doing the housework by himself.

Ignoring Tyrone's barely suppressed smirks, the resident ordered him to mop the floor of the sick room before they moved Juan Carlos into it.

Once everything was cleaned and set up to his satisfaction, Rafe started to tend his patient earnestly and attentively, with none of his surprising housekeeping clumsiness in evidence.

And for two days now, Tyrone had been brooding over the whereabouts of Henryk, the missing biker with the borrowed dog, hoping man and dog would show up any moment so he wouldn't have to slink next door to admit his negligence to the unpredictable neighbors. From time to time he would go outside and stare at the gleaming black stretch limo parked right outside the front door under the sprawling oak as if all the answers resided within.

"Do you think he'll make it? Wake up at least?" Tyrone asked as he came into the kitchen on the third day. He accepted his morning cup of coffee from Rafe as if born to the habit.

"His heart is strong," Rafe said. "Would you like an omelet?"

The young resident had an appetite which was bottomless and went unpunished.

"No thanks," said Tyrone.

He watched Rafe beat three eggs, add a large pinch of herbs, grated cheese and a splash of cream, trying to decide if maybe he was hungry after all.

But then he reminded himself of his own plans and the actions he would need to take to follow through. He would need patience to succeed. Patience and nerves of steel, nerves he was hoping he still possessed. He'd need a good lawyer as well, could hardly think of representing himself. The old maxim of a lawyer who represented himself having a fool for a client was drummed into every new law school student. And it was only now, as he was attempting to reinvent himself, that it occurred to him his plan had serious flaws. What was he going to do with the boy once he won his case? Well, that was some ways off. He already had the name of a company who did DNA testing. He would persevere one step at a time.

Tyrone's kitchen was now equipped with a new drip coffee maker and there was ground coffee, some of it in the freezer beside the frozen Pizza Deluxes.

His refrigerator was packed with half and half for the coffee, fresh blocks of Parmigiano-Reggiano, Romano and Pecorino cheeses, fresh basil and other herbs he couldn't identify, homemade Italian meat sauce, firm zucchini, eggplant, spinach, onions, and spicy Italian sausages gleaming wetly in transparent casings. A new grater hung from one of his kitchen cupboards and the counter held a bowl of bright red Roma tomatoes that had been thoroughly prodded and examined for defects at the grocery store.

There was also a plastic bag of fresh ciabatta rolls on the counter, while olive oil and garlic, pasta and coffee filters filled the cupboard space to the right of the stove.

Within ten minutes of their excursion into the nearest respectably sized town for groceries, the resident had sniffed out the local Italian bakery and deli, something Tyrone had never bothered to do himself. Once inside, Rafe had an animated conversation with the owner, a slim, comfortable looking blonde-haired woman wearing a spotless white apron. They'd talked about the best way to make meat sauce for pasta — don't brown the meat, always use fresh tomatoes, pure olive oil, crushed garlic, basil, salt, pepper, a few red pepper flakes, slow cook for as long as needed, serve over fresh pasta — and the joys of a simple pasta dish made with fresh tomatoes, olive oil, garlic and basil.

Then, ignoring Tyrone's presence, they switched to rapid fire Italian and talked at length and with even greater animation, while she pointed out her Italian ready-made dishes among the deli meats and cheeses behind the cold display.

The young resident was so fully absorbed in the discussion of food and food preparation, that it made Tyrone suspect his first career choice might not have been medicine. Possibly intense family pressure had swayed him to follow in his father's footsteps.

Looking at all the food on display was beginning to make Tyrone's mouth water, so he turned his back and explored the pastas, biscotti, cans of Italian tomatoes, spices and herbs, gnocchi, buns and breads displayed on the shelves.

They left the store loaded down with packages in brown butcher's paper tied with a string. It was only when the resident appeared to be heading towards the liquor store, one Tyrone was well acquainted with, that Tyrone put his foot down. Rafe looked at him once, said nothing and changed direction.

When the resident wasn't tending his patient, he and Tyrone spent their time together eating Italian food, drinking home-brewed coffee and not discussing Juan Carlos's prognosis because, in Tyrone's opinion, optimism was preferable to reality. They talked about everything else.

"You have a girlfriend?" Tyrone asked on the fourth morning.

Rafe bent his head for a moment, piling his eggs on a piece of ciabatta roll with an enthusiasm at odds with his sudden scowl.

"So?" Tyrone persisted, like an old uncle.

"Well," the resident said. "Sort of."

"How can you sort of have a girlfriend?" Tyrone pressed.

"Our parents have been friends forever. She and I have been, well, paired off or something since we were born. My parents love her."

"And you?"

Rafe continued to eat without speaking.

"Aha," Tyrone said.

"She's a great person," Rafe muttered. "My mother keeps hinting how much she's looking forward to grandchildren."

Before he had a chance to reply, Tyrone heard the sound of a loud motorcycle outside.

He got up quickly, heading for the front door, about to make a blunt statement as he flung it open.

Henryk was sitting quietly on his bike. Sheba lay loosely harnessed behind the sidecar bars looking just as weary as the biker. For a moment neither of them looked up. When Henryk raised his head, Tyrone was shocked. Henryk's eyes were dark sinkholes.

"A fine time to show up," Tyrone said. "After making off with the dog."

Henryk made a small amused sound and gave Tyrone the finger before getting off the seat.

"How is he?" Henryk asked.

"Do you actually care?"

"I left you in charge, mister smart lawyer, did I not?" Henryk said, moving heavily towards the front door, Sheba at his heels. Once inside, he headed straight for the stairs with Rafe and Tyrone close behind.

The three men and the dog crowded into the Rose Room to inspect the unconscious gambler.

Henryk looked over at Rafe. "No change?"

"I've been sedating him. But I think his fever's breaking," Rafe said. "If his temperature comes back to normal that'll be a good thing."

"Please God, make it so," Henryk said, although Tyrone was certain he never took the time to believe in God. "You telephoned Tess?" he asked Tyrone.

"You've got to be joking."

"I never joke about serious matters."

"You're the one with her phone number. You might have called her yourself instead of disappearing."

"I was busy," Henryk said curtly.

"Busy with what? Taking the dog for a ride?"

Henryk pointed to the bed. "Busy with finding who was responsible. I needed dog's help. I did my job, now why did not you telephone?"

"I just told you, I didn't have her number."

"You know where she lives. You could ride over and bring her back."

Tyrone opened his mouth and said nothing.

"A pies ci morde lizał." Henryk swore. "We must call her now."

"There's just one problem," Tyrone said. "I have no phone."

He had absolutely no memory of what he did with it after he last used it.

In the end, Henryk drank a cup of Rafe's coffee, grunted at all of Tyrone's questions and comments, pulled himself up and set out noisily without taking the trouble to explain himself. At least he left the dog. Sheba did not appear to notice his desertion. She inhaled the dog kibble Tyrone brought in from the bag in the barn and then looked up eagerly for more.

At five o'clock the next morning, she growled to be let out and then sat waiting expectantly by the front door. When he didn't get up fast enough, she climbed the stairs and nosed him until he gave in. He felt insulted by her selfishness. At ten o'clock, just as he was starting on his second cup of Rafe's coffee, he heard the unmistakable roar of a motorcycle and hurried out to check.

Henryk was back with a passenger in yet another sidecar. This one was maroon with a gleaming leather seat. Tess climbed out and tossed her helmet on the seat. "Take me to him," she ordered Henryk. "Quickly, quickly please. I can't believe you never told me."

She gave Tyrone a nod when he spoke and walked past, hanging on to Henryk's arm, too preoccupied for niceties.

Upstairs, she ran her hands lightly over Juan Carlos's bandages and wrappings; she felt his face. "How bad is it?" she asked Henryk.

She looked radiant as she unzipped her jacket, her cheeks pink from the recent ride.

"He'll live," Rafe said. "Today was a good day. He was pretty traumatized, but — today was good. He'll live."

"Who are you?" she asked almost belligerently.

"His doctor," Henryk said. "The one saving his life."

"Raffaele Marino," Rafe said, stepping closer.

"Oh. Raffaele?" Tess said, her head down and turned slightly.

Tyrone assumed she was paying attention to all the clues she told him about the afternoon in her kitchen, listening to all the invisible signs she listened for.

Rafe didn't speak. He merely took her outstretched hand and kept hold of it without letting go.

"Marino?" Tess spoke to the silent young man, with the barest hint of playfulness. "You are a sailor?"

"A resident in medicine, actually," Rafe said, holding her hand intimately in both of his.

"A resident with the name of Marino? How strange," Tess said, her cheeks suddenly pinker than before.

Rafe said, "All right, a sailor then, a family of sailors."

"That's more like it."

"Home from the sea," Rafe said.

In the charged atmosphere, Tyrone took a look at the young man. He was clean shaven and in the green scrubs he usually wore when tending Juan Carlos. His medical skills and knowledge were impressive — they were in constant evidence. But up to then, in Tyrone's view, although highly skilled and competent, he just seemed to be a young man — dark-haired, hard-bodied and focused — but one not yet fully grown into his future self. All of a sudden, he looked more seasoned, darker, more driven. Like one of those striking doctors on popular TV shows. Tyrone could almost picture the self-confident, empathic and mature man he was going to grow into. It was remarkable how pheromones had a way of clarifying things.

He sneaked a glance over at Henryk but the biker was already on his way out of the room.

[20] Inside Outside

For the next few nights, Tyrone slept fitfully on one of his living room couches. Henryk slept on the other under the double window he insisted be left open, snoring often. Tess slept upstairs in Tyrone's queen bed after he'd changed the sheets to some white ones made of Egyptian cotton he'd kept but never used. A few of the bits and pieces left behind by his second wife. Tess touched the finely woven sheets and pillow cases and almost smiled at him.

Rafe slept on an inflatable mattress on the floor of the Rose Room next to the patient and Sheba was supposed to sleep under the patient's bed. Rafe complained she constantly and deviously attempted to insinuate herself onto the inflatable mattress when he was asleep, thinking he wouldn't notice. On the first night of this arrangement, Tyrone, passing by on his way to the bathroom, saw Rafe trying to roll Sheba off his bed. By the second night, Sheba craftily claimed half the mattress and on the third night she appeared to have won the war and was sprawled, snoring, beside an unresisting Rafe, relegated to one small corner, too exhausted to notice. It made Tyrone think all that was needed was for the feral cat to sneak in one night and cozy up to the duo. He wondered what would happen if he conveniently left the back door ajar sometime.

Juan Carlos seemed to be coming around shortly after Tess's arrival. It appeared he really was on the mend just as Rafe predicted.

As the days with his odd assortment of roommates dragged on, Tyrone went out often, pulling on his leather jacket and walking outside in his untended orchard and farther, to the mellowing fields and woods. Even the kennel dogs didn't annoy him as much as they used to. They seemed more distant somehow.

It was on those remote and lonely walks that he allowed himself to think again about the past. At least it was a change from being ambushed by it in the dark.

The memory of it always started out the same. One moment he was walking past an open office door on the way to his own office, the next he heard Leah's voice — her laughter, actually. He walked in on her without knocking. She was there with that smug idiot. It looked like they'd been having an intimate conversation. Tyrone watched them for a moment, lost for words. Then he headed straight back to his office, reached for the mickey he kept in the bottom drawer of his oak desk and untwisted the cap. He took a swig straight from the bottle. A sin, he supposed, if he were to consult a true Scotch whiskey aficionado who would demand a tumbler. The hell with that.

She came to his office immediately, thinking, no doubt, to throw him off the scent. "I came by to see you," she said brightly. "You weren't in, so I was just talking to David."

"Talking to David, my ass," he said.

They hadn't slept together for well over a month, maybe even two by this point.

She was wearing a white square-necked dress that accentuated her ass, making her look dark, desirable even a little dangerous. It was times like these he was terrified of her.

"What else were you doing with David?" he said loudly.

"What are you talking about? I came to see you and you weren't in."

"So why did you have to go there?"

"I can't talk to anyone else when you're not around?"

He knew something was very wrong, he sensed it. Next door she had seemed to be talking so freely. She never talked like that with him anymore.

"Might as well have been shtupping him," he said.

"You're drunk," she said with disgust. "An ugly, foul-mouthed jerk."

Her eyes were full of contempt and yet he was beginning to feel aroused.

"I know guilt when I see it," he accused her, liberated from caring who heard or who saw. At the same time he wanted to reach out, suddenly yearning to touch her, be absolved for all his transgressions, whatever they were.

"I came to tell you something," she said, stepping out of his reach and looking him squarely in the face. She crossed her arms as if to put further distance between them.

"Why go to him then?" His voice was too loud. He couldn't seem to let go of his suspicion.

"He's a friend. This has nothing to do with him."

"You could have called. Did you call him so he'd know you were coming?"

"I just told you. This has nothing to do with him."

"*What then*? I come back to the office and you're there rubbing knees and god knows what else."

Hearing his own angry words as if from a distance, Tyrone was vaguely aware of how the whole confrontation was going to hell in a handbasket and yet he couldn't help himself or let it go. His colleague was younger, more Leah's age, and he couldn't get the picture of how intimate they looked together out of his head.

"I came to tell you —"

"Tell me what? Coming here for an excuse to see your so-called *friend*?"

"No. You know what? This isn't a good idea or a good time. We'll have to save it."

"Oh, so you can visit your *friend* again?"

"You really are something else."

"When's a better time then?"

"When *I* decide," she said.

When he thought about it later, she had seemed strangely calm, as if her mind was already made up. He could hear her heels on the wooden floor as she was leaving. It was the one other thing he remembered. Her heels and how easily things might have gone another way.

Once she was gone, he followed his usual pattern, fortifying himself with another swig or two to calm down. He was not an impulsive man, not given to spontaneous physical expressions of either love or anger, but this time he took a step that tipped the balance. Still feeling jealous, unsettled and irrational, he flung open his door and made his way down the hall.

Reliving his memories, Tyrone didn't notice how far he had tramped in the woods past the edge of his fields until he broke out through the branches and pines into the small valley beyond his first hundred acres.

There was a broken fence here and a platform of old escarpment rock. It sloped gently upwards, punctuated by grasses, ferns and the occasional stunted bush. And in this landscape, two figures leaned into each other halfway up the crest. Rafe and Tess.

For a moment, Tyrone couldn't accept what he was seeing. The wind whirred faintly in his ears. They were usually so matter of fact inside the house in front of him and Henryk, like polite and cordial strangers, never sitting too close together or touching. It was hard to imagine the duplicity. In fact, everybody was unfailingly polite when they were all together, or when they couldn't avoid each other during the early mornings and late evenings, talking about the weather, the current health of the patient, the latest football scores that blared from time to time on the upstairs radio.

Here, now, at the beginning of September, Rafe was helping Tess up the slope, holding her hand, brushing something off her shoulder and simultaneously gazing at her while he appeared to be talking to her almost nonstop in a most intimate way. It was a wonder he wasn't wearing out her patience. Her head was down and she gave the impression of someone who was listening intently, if not to him then to whatever was under her feet — a sharp crunch of hard mud, dried out after the last rain, or the snap of small twigs, or the feel of wild grass. Tyrone averted his eyes. When he next looked they were kissing with such urgency and passion it seemed to have come out of nowhere. It stuck in Tyrone's throat. The picture was so clear the former professor felt he could just about see Rafe's tongue pushing into her mouth.

He stood frozen until they fell to the ground and then he backed away, heading quickly back to the farm. By the time he walked out to the paved road at the front gate, he felt depressed. And then he saw Henryk, riding towards the house from the road at great speed.

Not wanting Henryk to suspect anything was amiss, Tyrone changed direction and tried to rush to the front door before Henryk got there. He was too late. The biker came roaring up beside him and then kept pace politely. Tyrone turned his head and gave a brief nod, which was not meant to be encouraging. Henryk left the bike under the oak beside the limo, engaged the kickstand and walked through the front door with Tyrone. With so many comings and goings in the house, no one bothered to lock up anymore.

The former professor made his way to the kitchen, intending to look busy rushing about making coffee so as to limit conversation, but there was a problem. At the scarred kitchen table, more terrible than anything he could have possibly imagined, sat Audrey reading a newspaper and drinking a cup of coffee, which appeared to be freshly brewed. She was wearing the same large purple top she wore the first time they'd met. Some sort of shapeless brown cover-up rested over her shoulders because the house, owing to Henryk's obsessive demand for fresh air, was as usual, cooler than outside. And worst of all, Sheba was at her feet.

Tyrone felt his breath deflate. With all the comings and goings, disappearances and reappearances, he had entirely forgotten to go next door and report on the dog. In truth, he hadn't totally forgotten, he just kept putting it off, telling himself he would go at a more convenient time.

"Well hello, Professor," Audrey fixed him with an acerbic look. "And where have you been keeping yourself?"

[21] Hidden Waters

Tyrone cleared his throat, considering his options. Before he could think of anything to say, Henryk came to his rescue. "Good dog," he said, pointing to Sheba. "You will forgive me. I needed to borrow her."

"And who might you be?" Audrey asked in a softer manner.

"A lover of dogs, same as you," Henryk said. "A desperate person. We were very far away and she came with me."

Audrey reached down to pat the animal and made a point of examining her sleek coat and looking into her dark brown eyes.

"At least you took good care of her," Audrey conceded.

"Yes," Henryk said with irritating smugness. "Certainly."

"You kept her a long time, though. Why so?"

Henryk raised his eyes to the ceiling in a laughably dramatic gesture. "Finding lost souls," Henryk said. "Our patient. You of course know about him?"

Tyrone had been listening to this charade and trying to remember if there were times Henryk had tried to hoodwink him in the same way. He was about to open his mouth to comment acerbically that the dog was gone a long time after the patient was found. Just then the lost soul upstairs chose to let out a pitiful moan. The three of them kept silent, watched the ceiling for a moment with serious expressions and then resumed the conversation when it appeared the patient would not join in again.

"The lovely young woman was over to ask if we owned an armchair she could borrow," Audrey said. "So I came along to see what was what."

"Pardon?" Tyrone said.

"She wanted to borrow an armchair for her brother to sit in," Audrey said with exaggerated slowness.

Tyrone was surprised. He couldn't imagine what had motivated Tess, and more importantly, what Audrey was up to. Why was she so curious to come to his farmhouse after what transpired between them? And what about her duplicitous husband who knew damn well the dog was untrustworthy and yet had said nothing, waiting no doubt, for Tyrone to lose her so they could blame him and maybe even escalate the fight in court.

"I walked back with her and Sheba," Audrey said almost as if she were following his train of thought. "I thought it would be neighborly-like."

"You mean she came to you alone with the dog?"

"Of course, she came alone with the dog. Sheba knows the way."

It was then his uneasiness made him imprudent or else it was the fear she would turn on him for not returning Sheba

190

sooner. For all he knew she might be thinking he was never planning to return the dog. "I understand Sheba failed her test as a seeing eye dog," he said.

"Failed her test," Audrey snorted. "Who told you that?"

He affected a cough to give himself time.

"I know it was Wills. That man just has to announce everything to the world with his sick sense of humor."

"What? No. No," Tyrone said hastily. The last thing he wanted was another altercation at his house no matter how justified.

He forced an ingratiating smile. "What brings you here?"

"Once I got here we got talking about how we would bring my armchair over for her brother so he could sit in it, comfortable-like, and the young man here, someone called Rafe, I think, looked so pale and ill I thought they should go for a walk. So I shooed them out — for fresh air, I said, even if what he's got will take more than fresh air to cure — and here I am."

"Well," Tyrone said uncomfortably.

He looked over at Henryk who was staring out the window, as if he wasn't part of the ongoing conversation.

Audrey finished her coffee and got up heavily, supporting herself on the table. "Well, I better be going. Thank you for the coffee and the conversation."

"And what about —" Tyrone gestured towards Sheba.

Audrey ignored him and turned towards Henryk. "How well do you know the young lady?" she asked.

Henryk inclined his head.

"She spoke about you," Audrey said. "She said you saved her brother in some way, that you all saved him. But you — the way she spoke about you — well, never mind, it's none of my business."

Audrey suddenly looked almost embarrassed.

Tyrone wondered if she had deliberately thrown a little dart aimed at Henryk and then regretted her impulse to pry. She was an alarming woman.

"Okay then, bye, Sheba," Audrey said.

"You mean you'll let her stay here?" Tyrone heard himself saying the words from far away.

Sheba was lying under the table, her head raised, eyeing Audrey with benign interest, as if they were equals.

"Look at her," Audrey said. "Does it look like she's going anywhere?"

"The patient upstairs —" Tyrone said humbly, taking a page from Henryk's act, wishing to appear grateful without saying too much.

"We are most grateful," Henryk interrupted. "You must understand how grateful. She sits with him always. Hardly ever leaves."

"Ah," Audrey said, thinking it over for a moment. "She's not really a guard dog, you know. More like a dog who hunts socks and shoes." *And garbage*, Tyrone wanted to add while Henryk nodded his head and said, "True. But appearances count for something."

A look passed between her and the biker that puzzled Tyrone at first. A few minutes ago, she seemed unclear about Henryk's position and now she and Henryk were sharing a silent understanding, a dog lovers' secret handshake, even though they'd just met.

As she glanced up at Tyrone on her way out, zipping her shapeless brown jacket over the purple top, he caught the faintest look of amusement in her sharp eyes.

The minute the door shut behind her, he turned on Henryk

"Were you ever going to come straight out or just keep it to yourself?"

"There was nothing to tell," Henryk said stubbornly.

"It seems there was enough so my nosy neighbor now knows we need a guard dog. Although to call that dog a guard dog is a gross exaggeration. You call that nothing?"

Henryk hit the table with his hand and then he sat down abruptly in Audrey's vacated chair. "I cannot change the world," he said. "Only fix things a little."

"Just exactly how did you fix them? I don't understand. And what about that resident who fixed up Juan Carlos? How does he fit in?"

"Where, exactly, do you think I found him, mister smart guy professor? You think I was beating bushes for doctors? I was not. I found him leaving hospital emergency room."

"Very comforting. So, what did you say? What made him come with you?"

"Nothing," Henryk mumbled. "He just came."

Tyrone pounced, waving his finger. "Ah-ha. You must have known something."

"Save your interrogations for someone else."

A. K. Blackman

"Are we in danger or are we not?"

"Little danger."

"What?"

Henryk held his thumb and forefinger close together. "Very little."

"So what did you say to him? I want to know."

"You want to know? And will that make you better man, my dear professor? Or will it change the way you view world?"

"It may change how I view you."

"Ah, of course. You are anxious to understand people."

"I want to know what we're up against. It's my house after all."

"Very well," Henryk said, abruptly. "You want to know? I will tell everything. This is how it happened."

Rumpled and distracted, Henryk nevertheless looked like a tough character, a hard, crafty man to beat. At the kitchen table, he leaned on his elbows and gestured for Tyrone to take the opposite seat. If he was suffering over Tess it didn't show. For a moment Tyrone wondered about the young lovers and how that scenario would play itself out.

While the afternoon wore on and the light mellowed, Henryk spoke at length and with deadly softness, not allowing interjections or interruptions, holding up his index finger when Tyrone opened his mouth.

"I explained what was necessary. He said, why should I do it? I said, because it is your Hippocratic Oath. He said, I already fulfilled my Hippocratic Oath for twenty hours at the hospital emergency. I don't need any more oaths. I said, think

194

of it as case study, your very first attempt to save patient by yourself. He said, is this illegal? And I said, only a little, but then only fool would ask question like that and I think you are not a fool. Man I want you to see is man who made mistakes but I swear to you he does not deserve to die and he has sister who needs him. Why does she need him? he ask. Because she is blind, I said so very patiently. What does she look like? he ask. Is the life of a man going to depend on how his sister looks? I said. In this case absolutely, he said, because I am very tired. I became agitated with such arrogance. You unfeeling North American product of dogs, I said to him, I imagined I was through with Russian army long ago and here I find such opinions again, now are you going to ask questions until he dies or come with me? So, you see, mister professor, that's how story goes."

"Why him?" Tyrone asked curiously.

"Because I watched them all and he came first."

Tyrone started to laugh. "Fate. Circumstance. Lucky him."

"The rest is another story."

"Try me," Tyrone said.

"Excuse?"

"Tell me the other story."

"It was about your car."

"What?"

"No shit, I promise you. Juan Carlos give it to this guy for his gambling debt and transmission went. Kaput. No more transmission. No more car. No more paid gambling debt. What did I tell you? I said don't give him anything."

"You said don't give him money."

195

"Same difference."

"So, who is after him? The Sicilian mob? The Asians? Gamblers Anonymous? Who?"

"Only two very drunk people he owed money to. That is why he is alive. They all hurt each other before he collapsed."

"Did you fix it or are they still after him? They track anything, I'm told. For days. They never give up."

Now it was Henryk who laughed. He hit the table with his hands and put his head back.

"It's not so funny," Tyrone said, tempted to wipe the smile off Henryk's face.

"Us with the dog and they with —" Henryk couldn't speak, instead he tapped his nose and sniffed, caught in another irritating paroxysm that left him gasping. "How primitive are we all?" he managed, just as the startled lovers walked in the door.

To the former professor's way of thinking, Henryk seemed to have forgotten that, primitive or not, a man almost died and they might all be in danger, but when Rafe and Tess came in the door Tyrone decided the distraction was almost welcome since it was obvious they too were arguing.

The young resident looked grim, holding the door open while she swept through.

"What is wrong with you?" Rafe said to her back.

There was some dirt and grass blatantly stuck to the back of her jacket which neither of them had bothered to brush off.

"Stop it," she said furiously. "I asked you not to talk about it anymore."

"Why not? Just give me one good reason."

"Because I asked. That should be a good enough reason if you meant the things you said."

"That makes no sense. You are totally illogical."

"I have my reasons. Just because you don't understand them doesn't mean I am illogical. Tell him, Henryk," she said turning wildly in the room. "How we all have to give up something but quietly, without making a goddamn fuss."

"Tess, my dear," Henryk said, clearing his throat.

"If you won't tell him, I will," she said furiously.

"What is there to tell?" Henryk appeared to be making a conciliatory effort. "You are being very dramatic. A misunderstanding only. A perfect misunderstanding, that is all."

"Did you hear that?" Tess turned to where Rafe was standing, tuned to his breathing or his small noises, perhaps even the creaking of his bones. "I am both illogical and prone to perfect misunderstandings! Men don't stop to think when they come out with such stupidities. Your turn, Professor," she turned. "Anything else you want to add?"

She was relentless. Tyrone realized he had always been drawn to passionate women, displayed a fatal preference for them, maybe because he lacked such passion himself. Possibly why his second wife, the shrewd accountant, seemed so safe. As usual it made him bold in Tess's presence.

"Yes," he said, seizing the opportunity. "I want to add a number of things. The first one so obvious to everyone else but you, or perhaps it is obvious to you but painful. This young man is a young man and therefore probably not so mature." Tyrone held up his hand for silence as Rafe opened his mouth.

"One thing is obvious to all of us, even to Audrey, a stranger, I may add, who was waiting here for you. His reaction to you is obvious."

"Crazy," Tess said.

"From the first moment he saw you," Tyrone said, trying to dispel the image of them on the ground.

"Stop it," she cried. "Henryk, make him stop it."

"Henryk's the problem," Tyrone said. "Maybe even the solution. But just what is going on?"

"Nothing is going on," Henryk said quietly. "I am sixty-two years old today. So, it is my birthday."

There was silence. The quick beats of an unexpected pause. Tyrone was about to leap in when Tess beat him.

"Oh Henryk." She turned towards the biker. "I forgot. I am so, so sorry. With everything else, my head has floated away as usual."

Screwed away on the escarpment, Tyrone thought. And then he gave himself an imaginary slap.

She walked slowly and reached out to hold Henryk's arm, caught in the same dance again, the urgent sexual collision with Rafe apparently forgotten. Once again, Tyrone witnessed the flowing and yearning he'd seen in her kitchen what now seemed so very long ago. The former professor glanced over at the young man. But Rafe was at the counter making more coffee and slamming cupboard doors trying to find sugar.

"As usual? On laundry line, outside?" Henryk spoke to Tess with soft, intimate humor, looking at her gently with his old-young eyes. "Your head is hanging up with clothes pegs in the wind."

His square face was suddenly the hard face of a much younger man.

"Yes," she said, smiling. "Exactly so. How funny you remember."

Henryk smiled at last. "Some things," he said, "are too terrible to forget."

[22] Agua Caliente

"I have decided," Henryk announced the next morning as he poured himself the dregs from the coffee pot. Tyrone kept his composure. "Another revelation?" he asked pleasantly. "Perhaps you remembered something else you never thought of telling me?"

"Hey?" Henryk looked puzzled.

"Never mind," Tyrone said.

He was sitting in his office nook, in front of his computer, browsing the news headlines rather than reading anything in depth because he was thinking about something else. Henryk's night on the neighboring couch had been restless, though miraculously, this early morning, it didn't show. It was Tyrone who was reflective and puffy while Henryk was clear-eyed, with the swagger back in his step, a man ready to take on the world again.

While listening to Henryk tossing and muttering during the night, Tyrone came to a surprising understanding that in turn kept him awake. He'd assumed solitude was all he was good for. At three in the morning he began to see things differently. He suddenly realized he was coming alive as a result of the house invasion by this odd assortment of misfits. At four in the morning, caught up in the circular obsessions of his first marriage, he started to puzzle about what made him place the motorcycle and Spanish lessons ad. And then he started thinking again about Leah and his ongoing mission, which kept him awake until six. And at precisely six in the morning, Henryk got up, clomped around and dressed noisily, making sleep impossible.

As Henryk sat in the kitchen sipping his coffee without saying another word, Tyrone became curious. "What have you decided?" he asked.

Henryk stared at him boldly. "I will go to Mexico with you," he said.

"What??"

"Yes. That clearly was the purpose of the riding lessons. Now you need someone to travel, help with motorcycle et cetera, et cetera. We go together."

Tyrone's radar was on full alert. This must be the consequence of Henryk's restless night. Even though the biker was pretending to be oblivious to everything going on in the house, it was clearly getting to him.

He looked over at Henryk and shook his head. "I'm not going to Mexico."

"You will need someone to help with motorcycle," Henryk repeated, as if Tyrone hadn't spoken.

"I'm curious," Tyrone said. "Why do you want to go?"

Henryk was silent. Noting his silence, Tyrone felt compassion for the man. Compassion and a certain anxiety that made him realize how close he was to understanding Henryk's need for escape.

"Besides, if I were going to Mexico, I plan to take my car." Tyrone found this new idea enormously appealing especially when he saw the look on Henryk's face.

"You're joking, of course?" Henryk said.

"No. On thinking it over, I fail to see why I can't get my car back."

"Because they beat him up. Because they want working car. Because there were two of them with tire irons and I did not wish to get dog hurt. Because I promised working car and then I escape. They do not know where I am. They do not know where Juan Carlos is unless he chooses to go gambling. Now do you understand? You still want to ask for this car back?"

"The law is the law. I have the registration. I'll explain it to them when they're sober," Tyrone said without a trace of irony.

"Ah. *Mać psa,*" Henryk said disgustedly, pulling back his hair roughly and pacing the kitchen floor until Tyrone started to laugh.

Once he started he found he couldn't stop. Every time he looked over at Henryk's thunderous face he pointed a finger and laughter overtook him again.

After his exchange with Henryk, Tyrone left the house in a good mood. As he walked through his fields, he whistled an old Sergio Leone tune from *The Man with No Name*, a famous spaghetti western he had been fond of long ago. Passing the wild bees' nest and heading for the woods and the escarpment rock, he felt kindly towards them as they flew and buzzed about.

He found himself thinking about how people in those old spaghetti westerns were always looking for a place called *Agua Caliente*. Someone would ride up to someone else and say, *"Are you going to Agua Caliente, señor?"* And no matter what the answer, nobody ever got there. Agua Caliente was a code, a promise of something no one ever reached. It was odd that westerns, with all their gory and graphic details, could inadvertently be linked to allegory in this way.

Just before he came out of the woods into a clearing he thought he heard a short yip or growl, followed by a kind of thrashing and thumping noise and then a loud curse. "Damn it to hell," Tess's voice came from beyond the trees.

Tyrone ran the rest of the way clear of the woods and saw her halfway up the hill, sitting on an outcrop of grass, brushing off her black pants.

Before he could do anything, she started to cry. He would not have thought it possible that she felt so much despair. Her face was in her hands and she was sobbing. This was not the Tess who was so assured in her blindness she almost made it seem like it didn't matter, the apparently whole and happy Tess who even treated Henryk's defection as if it didn't break her.

His first impulse was to carefully back away but that felt wrong. He had no clue what he could do to comfort her.

"Are you okay?" he called up.

Sheba was sitting by Tess's side looking on with interest.

"What?" Tess turned and tried to quickly brush her tears away.

He gave her time by walking slowly towards her.

204

"Are you okay?" he asked again when he was closer.

Her cheeks were wet.

"I'm fine," she said. "Just humiliated."

"Let me help."

"No. No. I don't need any help. Thank you."

"Well then, let me walk with you."

"I won't be very good company," she said. "Though Sheba here is splendid company, aren't you, girl?"

The dog allowed herself to be patted, stood patiently while Tess got her bearings and then kept pace with them, close to Tess, as they continued up the incline towards the flat platform of shale rock.

Tyrone was careful to give her room. He was acutely aware if he were Henryk or Rafe she would be keeping close.

"So," Tess said finally. "What do you think?"

"About what?"

"I am not being clear. That exchange between Rafe and me yesterday. You are an outsider and one capable of observation. What is your opinion?"

Tyrone did not feel flattered at being called an outsider. Especially now when he was trying so hard to understand where he fit in.

"What are you afraid of?" he asked.

"Is that a question? You must know I am afraid of everything. Every morning I wake up afraid. There are days I have no hope at all."

She put her head back in her hands, hiding her face.

"Please," he said helplessly. "Please."

"Do you know — I could see until I was almost eight, then something started to happen — it happened so very slowly and then one day no matter how hard I tried to open my eyes and how hard I rubbed them I saw nothing. Ever again."

"I'm sorry," Tyrone said.

"At first I didn't believe it. I just knew my sight would come back. I prayed every night and morning as hard as I could. And then I began to think I did something bad. I was being punished for something and I asked God to forgive me. I said I would do anything He wanted if only He would tell me what I did wrong."

Tyrone wished he had something to offer, but he couldn't think of anything.

"They sent me to a special school. I didn't want to leave my mother but she said I had to. She said it was best. I prayed to God again. Of course, God was silent. What could he say to an eight-year-old? 'Mama,' I said. 'I am asking God to help us, but I can't hear him, he doesn't talk to me,' and that is when she told me something I have always remembered.

"You are silent." Tess turned towards him. "I will tell you what she said. She said, '*Mi hija*, He doesn't talk to anyone.' And then when Henryk came he tried to help. It was too late. He liked my mother, did you know? He said she was special. And over and over I wanted to know why I was blind but nobody answered. Do you know what it's like to be blind? You have to trust, you have to force yourself to do things even if you're scared. And then what do you suppose it's like for anyone to have a relationship with a blind woman? There's always going to be something wrong."

"How did it happen?" Tyrone asked. "Do you know?"

"Ha! They kept changing their minds — the doctors we went to — so I didn't understand what they were talking about."

"What about now?

"Yes, I think so. Does it matter? Do you want to know?"

She was right, it wouldn't make any difference to her current situation, but there was no way to exit gracefully. "Yes, of course," he said.

"I'll give you the short version. After going through a bunch of possibilities, leaving my mother totally confused, they settled on infiltrative optic neuropathy."

He kept silent, waiting.

"It means they're not really sure," she added. "But they think it was some sort of bacteria or virus that attacked my optic nerve — both of my eyes if you can believe it, both of them."

"Not easy," he said.

"No. And then what about …"

"What about what?"

"Never mind," she said. "It's not important."

"I saw you together," Tyrone admitted. "You and Rafe. Right about here."

He was embarrassed. "I'm sorry," he said again. "I don't know what made me say that."

"It's okay," she sighed. "Did you see me crying before? I feel like such a wimp. I was hoping you missed that at least."

"Yes," he said quietly. "I seem to have a lot to be sorry for."

"I hope you didn't stay too long … when Rafe and I … I mean …"

"Don't worry. But envy is a terrible thing. You of all people must know it."

She took a few steps with the dog, held her beautiful face up to the silent sky and sighed.

"I don't know what to do," she said.

[23] Dragon's Blood

O ver the next few days Tyrone got up early and would have left the house, except he had nowhere to go. He ended up sitting in his kitchen study nook, drinking coffee he finally learned to brew properly and scrolling through news stories on his old computer. *The Globe and Mail, Toronto Star, National Post, New York Times, Washington Post, USA Today* and even the *Miami Herald* were all subject to his critical scrutiny. He was becoming a news junkie.

He had always been a Luddite, even when the internet started making a bigger splash. As the nineties raced full speed towards the year 2000, he congratulated himself for not relying on the quirks of computers and the vagaries of unstable bits and bytes flying over cyber space. And given his contrary nature, he made his students learn how to search the physical tomes of case law as opposed to doing it the easy way on-line. Even though they grumbled about the comparative ease of on-line searches from the comfort of home, he was not dissuaded. But now, he had to admit the internet might have a useful purpose after all, especially as a lifeline to the outside world.

A. K. Blackman

In the mornings, the household ritual was becoming predictable. Henryk would run heavily up the stairs to check on Juan Carlos, who kept asking to sit up in a weak, petulant voice. Tess would enter the Rose Room to hold Juan Carlos's hand, murmuring reassuring words of comfort and hope whose effects lasted only for the duration of her visits. Rafe, who was still spending nights on the Rose Room floor fighting for space on the inflatable mattress with Sheba, would poke his head up from the sheets to make sure, no doubt, that the visitor was someone with prior approval, and then, checking all the drips, fluid bags, blinks and squeaks delivered or diverted by each separate unit attached to the patient, he would roll himself in a ball and go back to sleep for another twenty minutes. Compared to the dog, who appeared well-fed and rested, Rafe looked more hollow and wild each time he came up for air.

Afterwards, the inhabitants of the house would all come downstairs to help themselves to Tyrone's coffee while the recovering patient was loudly demanding the priest be removed from his room because even though every bone in his body was hurting he wasn't going to die just yet.

"For God's sake, can't you give him something to stop his hallucinations?" Tyrone said to Rafe.

"I've been gradually reducing the morphine," the resident said. "He'll snap out of it soon."

"Not soon enough," Tyrone muttered.

"Who are you?" Juan Carlos shouted at Tyrone one afternoon. "*Va te*. Get out. Leave me alone."

Remembering how he washed this man when he thought he might be dying, Tyrone kept silent and left immediately as Rafe unhooked him from the catheter and various drips. Then, together with Rafe, he carried Juan Carlos downstairs in spite

210

of the man's half-hearted protests and placed him in Audrey's old chair in front of the kitchen's French doors.

Wills had brought the unwieldy chair over one morning in the back of his truck. It took three of them to confine it after Henryk was debilitated by the flying leg rest which was not tied down properly. The seat cushion had strands of dog hair and several large unidentifiable stains. To make it look more inviting, they covered it with an old turquoise blanket Tyrone found among his possessions.

While bathing Juan Carlos in the Thousands Island motel room, Tyrone was surprised at the solidity and musculature of the gambler, despite his purple skin and flaccid muscles. It was not something he would have guessed the very first time he saw him at the diner wearing his loose fitting blue suit. Now he was surprised at how light he seemed, as if he had shed invisible burdens.

The first day he was propped up downstairs, Juan Carlos settled into a stupor and then dozed, growing abruptly quiet. Tyrone, driven from the familiar comfort of his kitchen nook where he might otherwise have sat all day, paced restlessly around the house while Rafe stayed in the kitchen with the patient, sipping coffee.

Henryk drove off on his motorcycle and Tess, loosely bundled in a light jacket, went to roam the fields and woods with Sheba.

Not knowing what else to do with himself, Tyrone went upstairs.

His room was no longer his room. Tess's clothes were neatly folded on a chair and her brushes and toiletry bag were on the dresser. The Rose Room next door, in addition to the bountiful roses, now had a sickly smell which permeated the whole upper floor. There was a large garbage bag on the bathroom floor containing a detritus of medical tubes, gauzes and drip bags. The only uninhabited room was the third bedroom, a blue room, painted a dark shade and fittingly crammed with all the remaining odds and ends he hadn't known what to do with. He opened the door and stood on the threshold.

The room was dim and smelled stale. He took a moment to orient himself, to decide if he really wanted to stay, and in that moment, apart from the cardboard boxes full of law school texts and lecture notes, among small Persian carpets, dressers and coffee tables, he saw what he must have known he would see.

Leaning against the wall was the never-opened parcel Leah left for him in their old apartment so many years ago. After he came home from the hospital, he found the parcel on the dining room table. Though well-wrapped, he could tell it was a painting.

When he first saw it, he was afraid it was the painting of the Kiskadee Tree, the one she'd shown him, full of oblivious birds and a snake crawling up to get them. One of those weird and terrible paintings she was producing while pulling away from him. He couldn't bear the thought of it and chose to leave the parcel unopened all these years. And yet could never bring himself to throw it out.

The room grew darker as clouds covered the sun. He flipped on the light switch and bent down for the package. Taking a deep breath, he ripped through the old brown paper. It was wrapped too well. At the third layer, he saw it was not the painting he had suspected — not the bird and snake Kiskadee

Tree — it was the other accursed tree, the one she'd shown him before the very last time they made love.

He remembered the time. Was that why she'd chosen it? Months after she let him see the Kiskadee tree with the insidious snakes, as he labelled the painting to himself, he was back looking at another canvas.

"You gave up law for this?" he asked, in one of his provocative moods, convinced he was being reasonable. It was the last time he was in her studio at her surprising invitation. "Aren't you wasting your talents?"

This was a moment, he now understood, when there might still have been time, a chance. Only he didn't know it. She seemed to be making an effort, a concession, by letting him into her studio.

"Wasting my talents? That's very funny, coming from you," she said.

Her wide eyes were serene, her dark hair freshly washed, as if she were already planning an afternoon with a lover.

Without another word, she stood back from her newest painting, as if asking him to look at it once more. She'd painted a short, twisted, supple trunk and a spreading green canopy, covered in blue-green rosettes and red berries. "See," she said. "Flowers and berries. All seasons of life at the same time."

"A miracle," he said.

"Yes," she said. "Today is the day for miracles. I'm calling it the Dragon's Blood Tree."

"But what does it *mean*?" He said. "What is the logic behind it?"

She herself appeared to him as a miracle, limber and somehow unattainable. The word that came to him then was lush. He almost felt dizzy.

He was the professor, after all, the academic needing to stand apart and dissect things — to see why and how they ticked. "That is how you destroy things," she said as if reading his thoughts. "You can't pull things apart without destroying them."

And then, to his surprise, she slowly unbuttoned her dress and stepped out of it while her eyes never left his face. He remembered it vividly, the light on her skin in her brilliant eerie studio. Her breasts were full and delicate as white roses with stemmed purple hearts. He had never felt such heat in himself, the desire for her beyond his control. Drinking was his refuge, but it was only an excuse. What he really wished for, he realized just then, was that she would never leave him. He wanted to be both tender and urgent, the way he'd been when they first got together. She held his face in her hands, wrapped her legs around him and wouldn't let go for the longest time.

When the heat between them died away, he lay weak and disoriented on the floor, while she propped her head on her elbow. "I can't fight you anymore," she said, giving him the impression she was tired beyond words. "There is something about the two of us — something I can't explain. You appeal to my dark side. I want you to be — no, that's not it — I am the bird. You are the snake. There is something in me that finds this both repellent and irresistible."

"Do you actually know what that means?" he asked, wanting to appear in control again.

"Oh, yes," she said. "Absolutely."

His hands were trembling. He yearned to touch her hair, smooth the lines in her face. Instead, he got up and pulled on his pants and socks. Deliberately shedding what he saw in himself as weakness, he started to wonder if perhaps he should have been more careful, used a condom. He continued to think they would remain together as he wished, nothing would change. The last glimpse he had of her, she was sitting up and the damn tree floated over her naked shoulder. And then he left her studio and shut the door, not wanting to entangle himself in emotions he couldn't control. He might even have whistled on the way to his office.

On viewing the tree once more after such a long time, he noticed right away she had added the title and other details, an afterthought, or perhaps something she meant him to remember. He stared at the additions, a lifetime after they were painted, too preoccupied to hear anyone coming up the stairs.

"Hello, Lawrence," Tess's voice startled him.

He looked up to see her standing at the doorway.

"Is something wrong? Why are you breathing that way?" she asked.

He cleared his throat and then shook his head, wanting her to leave. Instead, she came farther into the room and crouched beside him, giving off cool air and the woodsy smell of grass and leaves. She reached out and touched what he was touching, running her hands along the frame and then touching the canvas with her fingers, feeling the whorls and bumps the dried oils had made.

"A painting," she exclaimed. "Tell me about it."

He wanted to say it was none of her business, but he couldn't do that either. He sat on the floor quietly, and when he spoke it was without his usual defenses. He told it to her as if it was a story. A story of a couple pulling away from each other, a man who was so unaware and a woman who started to paint weird trees.

"This one is called 'Dragon's Blood,'" he said, feeling foolish.

He described the Dragon's Blood tree to Tess the way he first saw it. The green umbrella canopy, the vividly surreal blue-green rosettes and gleaming scarlet berries meant to denote more than one season. How weirdly menacing it looked in spite of there being nothing he could put his finger on to justify the impression.

"That's all?" she said. "Is that what's upsetting you?"

"No," he added, quietly. "It's about something that wasn't there."

He let her trace the outlines of the tree and then put her hand on one branch in particular. The branch was twined around a knife, sawing through itself at the trunk, severing itself. Fat drops of blood, the weeping blood of dragons, were falling to the ground. On another branch sat a tiny dragon sat with its head firmly under one scaly wing.

"So?" she said.

"Don't you see?" he said. "She left this on purpose. Meaning to torment me."

"Maybe it's you who don't see. Maybe she was trying to get through one last time."

"Right now that's not how it looks to me," he said.

It was not dragon mythology that disturbed him. Once he finished opening himself up to Tess, he was aware he had not told her everything. There was a time when he was close to his brother, when Spenser looked up to him. He used to visit his brother with Leah when Jessica, Spenser's daughter, was going through a dress-up period — a toothpick-sized delicate dragon queen in gossamer tutus who tried sweeping him into her lair and ended up ensnaring Leah instead. From early on, with every visit, Jessica and Leah would spend hours in Jessica's room, plotting dragon tales, Leah drawing everything that came to Jessica's mind. It probably all started then, Leah's whole craziness, her wish to punish him for not wanting children, her vindictive rage. But he was too oblivious to notice, focused on other concerns — the disciplinary committee, his desire to always do things his way, his need for a drink even though he was sure his drinking was under control, the fact that his brother was always out of Scotch every time they came to visit.

In spite of everything, there they were, the two girls, happy and glowing with dragon tales, while he and Spenser were friends. He didn't have many friends. He had colleagues, rivals, competitors trying to outrace him on the academic ladder, but no real friends unless he counted his brother.

"She was wrong," he said to Tess. "She was absolutely wrong. She didn't need to cut herself off like that. That was totally unnecessary."

"Of course not," Tess said, in a voice whose nuances revealed to him she both saw and didn't see what had worked to destroy him.

[24] The Case of the Reluctant Wife

While he was still at the faculty, one particularly slow summer when the semester was over, Tyrone planned to write an overview of specific legal positions in the history of law. Not a particularly weighty one, but one to teach his students to think about wider issues.

He was a man who needed constant activity and now that there was a hiatus, he was bored. In addition, he'd already attended one, no, two, committee meetings where they accused him of being too iconoclastic, told him he needed to follow the set curriculum and not his own preferences. They hadn't mentioned anything about drinking, but he was aware it was also on the agenda. He needed something to redeem himself.

In his paneled office with the tall windows giving out to a summer campus of grass and trees bordered by a stone and iron fence, he combed law case books searching for relevant materials. He'd even broken down and let the librarian direct him to some on-line resources.

He wanted to start with the obvious and branch out — make sure his students understood that those in the legal profession were only there to defend the laws in existence as best they could, not make them. They had to interpret in the context of what was already there. Pretty mundane stuff. But it was precisely the mundane that needed to be scrutinized and examined. You couldn't take it for granted — as if it didn't bear questioning. What if the law was wrong? Or at least wrong for the times and mores? Then what? Where was the leeway?

Some laws could be fluid while others remained fixed. Was this logical? Was there a sound reason for it? Was it even just? Could the crime of murder lead to hanging in the eighteenth century and acquittal in the twenty-first? Of course. Everyone knew that. Those were both legal and ethical questions. It wasn't enough just to know the rules, his students needed to think them through, debate them. Impatient with polite parroting of what they thought he wanted to hear, he sought to push them to extremes, even argue from extreme positions and see where it got them. He asked questions not necessarily expecting answers but wanting to see where they could lead. He was convinced students needed to be challenged and argued with, no matter how exasperating he sometimes found their arguments. The faster they could think on their feet, regardless of the topic, the better they'd be. Those were the days he was at his bloody damn best.

One afternoon, when the Scotch bottle and the building in which he sat were both nearly empty, he was leafing disconsolately through dusty old law volumes, reluctant to go home and face Leah. Even though he knew he should be doing something, a lethargy would overtake him each time he thought about it.

While looking at case law in the sixties where adultery was the one compelling reason for divorce, he glanced outside to see Leah walking beside David, his colleague and rival, as he suspected, for Leah's affections. They were strolling along the concrete sidewalk beside the tall wrought iron inner gate where they stopped, facing each other.

Tyrone got up in order to peer closely through the panes of his tall, somewhat dusty window. Leah was wearing high heels and a long straight summer coat made of some light flowing material, a vivid scarf around her neck. She was saying something while gesturing with her hands. Shortly after, she smiled and kissed David on both cheeks before they parted, each going in a different direction.

Tyrone sat back down to the law book in front of him but had lost the will for it.

He looked at the themes in the outline on his desk. The issues he meant to cover. Never mind how a particular judgment came down, Tyrone was planning to say to his class. What do you think has changed? What might we learn from this as pertains to the law? Does the law follow social mores? If a wife was unfaithful then versus now, how are things different? In law, should adultery be cause for divorce?

The personal nature of his obsessions was not covered or resolved in any of the law journals or case studies before him.

He couldn't bear to sit still. What the hell, he thought, he needed a break. Slamming the law book shut, he put on his jacket and made his way to his favorite bar down the street.

At home that night, while Leah played with the food on her plate during a mostly silent supper, he said, "Why don't you come down to my office sometimes and we can go for lunch."

"Did you hear me?" he asked again when she didn't answer.

"I heard you," she said. "I don't really like going downtown anymore. Too much traffic."

He raised his eyebrows. "Oh?"

"And besides, I've stopped drinking," she said before she got up to leave the room.

He found himself simmering with mistrust, but unable to articulate his anger. Perhaps some atavistic instinct in him was telling him how easily things could get out of control. The ethical part of him, the clear-sightedness underlying his willful blindness, was aware he had to be careful. The state of his marriage was not good. And then, a week later, to add to his mounting suspicions, he came back to his office and found Leah and the guy he suspected was her lover, head to head in an intimate, if not entirely compromising, position. Nothing would convince him he hadn't been justified in punching the jerk out. Even now he kept telling himself he had absolutely no regrets.

[25] The Devil's Kitchen

In the morning, Tess was running her fingers along the rim of the saucer and then up and along her cup and back again.

"Just don't keep ignoring what I'm saying," she stated. "The painting your wife left you has already begun speaking to you. Maybe you're just afraid to be a different man?"

"I don't really know how to do this," Tyrone said. "The past is the past. It's a waste of time."

"The past is never a waste of time. Don't you remember? If you can't learn from history you're doomed to repeat it, whoever said that."

"It's attributed to Santayana," he said. "But I prefer Stephen Hawking who said something to the effect that studying history is mostly studying the history of stupidity."

"Ouch," she said. "Is that too close to home?"

He resented her insinuations. "Aren't you presuming just a little?" he said.

"Lawrence," she said, reaching out to touch his arm. "This is what I think. I think you have been avoiding change for a long time."

"You sound like a lawyer with an agenda."

She laughed. "Maybe you're right. I am going to let you have the last word but watch out, we're not finished."

"With your problems or mine?" he asked dryly.

The young resident and Tess were still barely on speaking terms. The only food left in the house seemed to be frozen pizzas. Remains on the cutting board left carelessly on the counter attested to the fact someone had raided the freezer and then overcooked a Pizza Deluxe.

Just then there was a thumping on the stairs and a cheerful voice, one that Tyrone hadn't heard in quite a while. It was making light of the fact that it was necessary to limp down the stairs holding on to a *cabron*, a goat, who would not believe he was perfectly mobile by himself. Rafe's voice in turn made some equally impolitic reference. In between the exchange, Tyrone heard a thump, a soft "shhhit" in three languages and more footsteps working their way towards the kitchen followed by the scratchy nails of a dog.

Tess, smiling warmly, stood up from the table and clasped her hands.

Tyrone had not counted on Rafe and Juan Carlos disturbing his thoughts just yet. He rose from his chair and watched as the resident, supporting a limping Juan Carlos and trailed closely by Sheba, carefully made his way across the floor. The procession was complete when the feral cat, who materialized inside the house every night, came slinking in after Sheba. Tyrone had been meaning to check out how the creature was getting in so inexplicably and yet consistently. He suspected Sheba was to blame in some way.

"Good morning," Juan Carlos said cheerfully. "I hear we're going to Mexico in a limo. Of course, I am coming with you."

"Who said anything about Mexico? Nobody's going to Mexico," Tyrone stated.

"It's my limo too." Juan Carlos signaled for Rafe to help him sit in the Audrey chair. "It's there because of me, so of course I can go."

Tyrone saw him as a self-absorbed man with the propensity to both court and cheat death without paying attention to the toll on those around him. He would be damned if he was going to do anything more for him.

Pandemonium ensued. Three people speaking loudly over each other. The noise bounced between tiled floor and wood ceiling and reverberated off the walls. For a moment Tyrone saw the humor. Here were people ostensibly desperate to part, with the possible exception of Juan Carlos, who might be remembering the need to skip town for different reasons, and yet they were plotting a flight to Mexico together. It made him forget his thoughts about not wanting solitude.

He whistled through his fingers and made a piercing sound which affected even Sheba who pushed her way under the kitchen table, flopped her head down on her paws and magnanimously allowed the cat to settle on her back. Watching the cat's astonishing presumption, Tyrone lost his advantage.

"Oh, Lawrence," Tess said before he regained his thoughts. "You have been so very good to us and we haven't even thanked you properly. Look at my brother. It's all thanks to you. I thank you from the bottom of my heart. I will never, ever forget what you have done and neither will Juan Carlos, isn't that right *Carlosito?*"

Carlosito, bandaged and not quite healed, looked away. Tyrone wondered if he was experiencing a flashback, something that reminded him of the reason he was now bandaged and not quite healed. While Tess, who was standing beside Juan Carlos, gave her brother a light tap on the shoulder.

"Well?" she demanded.

Juan Carlos sighed. What was left of the bandages, together with the scar on his face, made his eyes appear sharper than ever. He was leaner than he normally might have been, and weak, yet maybe something was different.

"Spanish lessons," Juan Carlos said quietly.

"You weren't much of a teacher," Tyrone retorted.

"True. But your car wasn't much of a car." Juan Carlos smiled.

Tyrone couldn't be sure if there was anything left to say or if it had all been said.

"I'm going outside," Rafe said.

Tyrone decided to join him.

He found Rafe standing outside under the bare oak beside the stretch limo, unshaven, looking dour. His hands were in his sweatshirt pockets and he was kicking at small stones. Too preoccupied with his thoughts, he didn't notice Tyrone until they were close enough to stand together.

"You okay?" Tyrone asked.

He was a good two inches taller than the compact young man, who was nevertheless quicker and more resilient.

"Sure," Rafe said, without looking up. "Only a few more days now, four, tops, and I think he'll be okay to travel. Tess can take him home." His tone of voice was somber.

"That's wonderful," Tyrone said with false heartiness.

He was certain from what he had seen that Rafe was nowhere near as intimate with the human heart as his more observant but currently annoyed love interest.

"How old are you anyway?" Tyrone asked. At the moment, despite Tyrone's vision of a more mature man when the resident first met Tess, the young man looked no more than twenty. Maybe it was the tousled dark hair, careless clothing and the occasional awkward swagger.

"Twenty-eight," Rafe sighed. "Is that the problem? I could have sworn it was something else."

"I don't know anything about a problem," Tyrone lied. "I was just curious."

"Well then, what do you think?"

"I think you need to get back and finish your studies, young man," the former professor said abruptly

"That's not what I was asking, *old man*."

Tyrone opened his mouth to protest and then thought better of it. "Fair enough," he said. "Then tell me, why're you here? Why are you wasting your time?"

"Wasting? You think this is wasting? Hippocratic oath. Remember?"

"That doesn't answer my question. You looking for something else to do?"

"No — that's just it. I don't know anything else, but —"

"Forget the buts. Go. Finish. Drive back in the limo and get on with your life."

"This whole thing felt like I was doing something with my life, it was real. I was actually making a difference."

"You and the dog?" Tyrone smiled at the memory of the resident and Sheba vying for space on the mattress by Juan Carlos's bed.

"Yeah, the dog. Sure. And then —"

"Yes," Tyrone nodded. "And *then*. So what are you going to do about it?"

"I don't know," Rafe said. "I'm making it up. Weren't you planning on going to Mexico?"

"No," Tyrone said. "You heard me. That's gone." In saying it, he realized it was true.

Mexico was something to hope for. A place more exotic, more perfect then humdrum reality. He could tell them all, Rafe included, that you couldn't cheat chaos and the tendency for most things to fall apart. But he didn't think they'd listen.

"And what about Tess?" Tyrone tackled what was not being said.

"She just needs time," Rafe said. "I'm not giving up."

In the wake of so many floating pheromones, in the deep cocoon of his living room, accompanied by Henryk's snores, Tyrone had started dreaming of someone other than his first wife even though he couldn't see the face clearly. He had the impression of someone tall and strong, a hood over her hair. He didn't know the meaning of the dream. It made him uneasy.

He said, "You're going to have to do better than that."

"That's so typical — all this crap advice people like you hand out that means nothing."

People like him? What did this entitled young dick know about anything? "Well," Tyrone said, feeling curiously sad. "You can think of it any way you want or you can smarten up fast and figure out what matters. Up to you to decide."

[26] Last Stand

Juan Carlos was getting stronger and feistier by the day. In what appeared to be preparation for a possible escape plan to Mexico to evade the complications awaiting him in Canada, he demanded food, mineral water and exercise equipment.

Tyrone cornered Rafe just before he was planning to drive back home in the stretch limo.

"What's your opinion?" he asked, trying not to make it sound like he was anxious to get rid of the patient.

"Be more specific," the resident said, looking distant and serious. Things were still not going well with Tess.

Tyrone sighed. "Okay," he said, "I was just trying to get an idea of what I could expect once you're gone. Will he be here much longer?"

"He can go now if that's what you want. He'll be okay."

"So how should I...."

"You're tired of being the good Samaritan?" Rafe smiled. A genuine smile Tyrone hadn't seen for some time.

"Yes and no," Tyrone said, making up his mind. "Let me ask you a favor before you go."

Over Juan Carlos's protests that he needed more substantial exercise equipment, Tess and Henryk went out on the motorbike with sidecar to look for five-pound ankle and wrist weights. "You will work yourself up to ten pounds when we say so," Tess said with surprising firmness.

In the meantime, between restless sleeping bouts, Juan Carlos ate food like a starving man, exercised both feebly and vigorously, depending on his mood, and complained constantly about how slowly things were progressing.

Tess now catered to him day and night, to the disgust of both Henryk and Tyrone.

"Can't he do that himself?" Tyrone said. "Putting the dishes in the sink?"

"Just another day when he will be stronger," an exhausted Tess muttered.

"Stronger? If he ate any more he would qualify for sumo wrestling. He needs to move about more."

"Any day now," she said brightly.

"Look. And I don't mean this unkindly, but when the food is gone, which is any time soon, he will have to learn to cook. I don't have Raffaele's cooking skills," Tyrone said.

He had prevailed on Rafe to lay in some food along with instructions just before he left them. It was the first time in a long time he saw Rafe nearly happy. Food and its preparation made him come to life, like nothing else had, not even the continuing care of his patient. Puttering around in the kitchen, putting ingredients together and leaving a mess for Tyrone to clean up had very nearly revitalized him.

Having watched the gambler working out in his room and then working his way down the stairs using his newly pumped arms, it was obvious to Tyrone that Juan Carlos was taking his time. And while the former professor sympathized, he wondered what was going on.

One afternoon, unable to contain himself any longer, he attempted an oblique discussion with Tess. Except, like most things having to do with her, it did not go as expected.

She was in the kitchen, neatly uncovering the last three casseroles in the fridge and sniffing them, trying to find the one most likely, in the olfactory sense, to make Juan Carlos strong. If she'd relied less on smell and more on squeezing his biceps, Tyrone thought, she would have seen the gambler had already reached that point by himself.

Uncharacteristically quiet, Juan Carlos was outside in a track suit, brooding and limping as a result of the cast still on his leg. His dark hair was long and he was unshaven but as he worked the wrist and ankle weights, he appeared more youthful and energetic every day.

"He's doing well," Tyrone said.

"Yes," she answered, distracted. "Will Rafe be coming soon to look him over?"

"Rafe? What has this to do with Rafe?" He knew he was being disingenuous. It had everything to do with Rafe. Maybe that's why Tess had not suggested moving Juan Carlos. She expected the resident to come back to the farm like a homing pigeon.

"He needs to come and look at Juan Carlos's leg. Take the cast off," Tess said.

"But he won't be here for another week at least. Don't you remember?"

"No," she said stubbornly. "He needs to come soon. Otherwise we cannot possibly leave."

"Who asked you to leave?" Tyrone said, taken aback.

"I can hear it in your voice. You are getting impatient."

"I most certainly am not getting impatient. Why couldn't you stay with Henryk?"

"Henryk?" she started to laugh. "That's the plan?"

"What's so funny?"

"I am just making a wild guess here, indulge me. I take it you haven't seen Henryk's place?"

"Certainly not," Tyrone said over her merry laughter.

"You understand Henryk's passion is motor bikes?"

"Yes."

"Take a guess. How many do you think he has?"

"Two? Three?"

Tess kept silent.

"Four? Five?"

She didn't say anything.

"Okay," Tyrone said. "How many?"

"Last time I asked, it was ten," Tess said. "And he only has space for four in the garage. So where do you think he keeps the rest?"

"Okay," Tyrone said. "Is that why you're not together?"

"That's a weird question coming out of nowhere. Or have you been planning to ask all along?"

"I've seen you and Henryk. And you and Rafe," Tyrone said quickly. "Remember? We did talk a little."

"I wasn't feeling so good about anything then. Me and Henryk. Me and Rafe. Holy shit. You are direct."

"Do you know what you're doing? And what about the man you said you are marrying?"

"I lied."

"I gathered as much. What were you expecting?"

"I don't know. Something. Nothing. It was stupid."

"So everything's fine now, is it? Between you and Rafe?"

"Me and Rafe? I thought we were talking about Henryk. I don't want to talk about Rafe."

"Why not? Absolutely nothing has changed."

"I've changed. I'm okay now so no need. I don't want to talk about it"

"Okay." He held his hands out in a gesture of surrender.

"So if we are being nosy, tell me, why aren't you still teaching?" she said in the silence.

"Ahhh." He scratched his face making a grating sound.

She turned her face towards his voice. "Is that a dangerous topic as well?"

He didn't want to deal with topics dangerous or otherwise. In his role of professor, he always assumed he could ask questions but was not obliged to answer them. "Look it up," he would say. "Come back when you have the answer." Of course, it had not worked with Leah. He cleared his throat. "Maybe we should go out to check on Juan Carlos," he said.

Tess shook her head. "I can hear him doing a bit of yelling just now. He used to do that when he was frustrated or working things out. And I hear some kind of rhythmic thumping. Is he by the trees working his feet? Don't worry about him, he's okay. But you — you're avoiding," she said.

He wasn't sure if she was laughing at him, teasing him, or serious. He kept silent, trying to figure out what to say.

"I punched out another professor in the office down the hall from me," he told her, feeling both ashamed and liberated as he said it.

"That's it? And they got rid of you for that?"

"Well, there was a little more."

"Aren't you going to tell me?"

"I broke his nose."

"Okay so you punched him out. You know your law. What if you were defending yourself? What if there was provocation?"

"There wasn't enough for what I did," he said. "And besides I was already on probation."

"And?"

"And I threatened to kill him next time. They said I could have one more chance, only one, and I blew it." He didn't want to think about how far down he'd gone.

"An interesting story. Why did you punch him?"

"I convinced myself she was cheating on me, my wife that is. With him."

He had felt such satisfaction knocking the man down with his bare hands. He wasn't sure how much damage he might have inflicted if it weren't for the security guards who came to pry him off. And then of course there was the disciplinary hearing. *What kind of faculty do you think we are running? He has agreed not to lay a charge against you but you are already on probation. Is that clear?*

"And was she cheating?" Tess asked.

"Yes. No. I don't know."

"And what does that mean?"

"She was. Maybe not with him. With someone else. I don't know." He had absolutely no wish to go into his brother's betrayal, with her or anyone else.

"Ah," she said. "The things we don't know. How we torture ourselves with things we imagine."

"Nothing imaginary about it. It was with the last person in the world I would forgive."

"Okay. I think I see."

"Do you? Absolutely the last person in the world?"

"Oh, yes," she said. "We all have a last person in the world like that."

He didn't answer. Instead, he asked, "And what happened with you? You and Henryk, I mean."

"I am thirty-two years old," Tess said. "And Henryk is now sixty-two?"

"Yes?"

"Henryk was always concerned about the age, I think, though he never said so. Except I was happy and so was he. That part I know. Anyway, when you're blind, there are obviously things you don't notice and other things become more important."

"I've heard that. We are too visual and not perceptive enough."

"Well, all I have are my perceptions and we could have managed, you know? There could have been a happy ending except Henryk took part in a motorbike-riding competition and nothing was right after that."

"Now that is strange."

"Yes," Tess said. "Can you believe it? He won. And his name and photograph were splashed all over the papers. It was an international competition. Not Daytona, something very special somewhere else."

"Someone saw him?" Tyrone said. "The Russian army? The ex-KGB?" He wanted to keep it light.

"His wife," Tess sighed.

"Oh my."

"His wife back in Poland and his two daughters. He was away so long they all lost track of each other, or he didn't care to be in touch with them or something happened. I don't know. The end result was they were in touch and that is when Henryk didn't show up at my place anymore. He had, it appears, found a conscience."

Tyrone kept silent. A thought came into his head that suddenly made more sense than the tale of a wife back in Poland. But then it left him as suddenly as it came.

"After some time," Tess continued, "he came back and said the strangest thing to me. I think it was after he saw his daughters, or maybe even his wife, we never talked about it. Maybe he never saw them, only talked to them by phone or maybe they wrote. I don't know. Probably that is the way they first got in touch with him. I could hear how hard he was trying not to show things in his voice."

Tess touched her chest for a moment, smoothed her short hair. Her eyes were wide and were gazing — if they could have been gazing at anything — outside the kitchen windows straight at Juan Carlos moving his arms about with agitation and talking to himself or perhaps the trees.

"He said," she whispered, "he said, 'My fifty-year-old wife — this was a while ago, you understand — my fifty-year-old wife is old and tired taking care of relatives.' I said, 'of course,' or something like it, only intent on what it was I wanted, not thinking of his wife and daughters at all. I think he knew because then he said something else. He said, and I remember this so well because it cut me up. The fact was he could say it and I didn't want to hear it. He said, 'My wife. You know the wife we are so casually talking about? She was once beautiful too.' And then he left. Just walked out. I felt bad about it. I have to tell you it took me a while to know how wrong I was because he never came round like he used to anymore. Only once in a while and only if I needed something, but not like before. And I sat feeling sorry for myself, thinking he was brutal to stay away like that, going over and over things in my mind until I accepted what he said was true. So, you see, it is a very boring and usual story. Nothing to be sad, nothing to cry or be sorry about. And besides it was so long ago."

"But you did cry," Tyrone said gently, wanting to say, *for more than Henryk.*

He knew it wasn't that simple, couldn't help thinking everyone felt guilty about something; it went back to his training.

"Oh, yes, I cried," Tess admitted. "Now it just makes me tired."

"I meant Rafe."

"Rafe?" she said. "What has Rafe got to do with it?"

"Yes, Rafe. The young man who thinks he loves you. In our family, we are cursed with never letting go of something once we get hold of it. The last time you cried it was about Rafe." And even as Tyrone said this, he felt a pang for the brother he would never forgive.

"I've told Rafe it's impossible so to stop thinking about it. There's the age thing anyway."

"I don't believe you. Age is a non-factor for you but it should be a factor for him? I think there is another reason."

She put her head down between her hands. Outside, Juan Carlos was waving his arms about and wordlessly admonishing the tree trunk in front of him in his incomprehensible pantomime. Expanding his horizon to the woods, he threw his arms up to the sky. It looked like he was yelling except he made no sound. As Tyrone was concentrating on the gambler's antics, Tess suddenly sat up.

"Someone is at the door," she said.

[27] Tumbleweed

The woman at the door was blue-eyed and blonde, wearing a long black leather coat. A silk scarf around her throat matched her eyes. She balanced delicately on small leather boots. From his second marriage, Tyrone was well versed in the accoutrements of taste, money and an expensive head of highlights. Nevertheless, he stared blankly.

"Lawrence Tyrone?" she said, as if he should know her.

She was beginning to look familiar yet he still couldn't place who she was. "Yes?" He said.

She held out her hand. "Karen Resnick. Remember me?"

"Oh."

He couldn't think of anything else to say and didn't remember her being so put together and groomed, but then of course that had been another time and she was in another frame of mind. He looked behind her for a car, wondering where her boy was hiding. Her black SUV was there, under the oak, with no boy in sight.

"I left Bry with — well, with someone," the widow of Rattlesnake Point said, looking at Tyrone with her clear blue eyes. "I would have called but you have no phone and I wanted to talk to you."

A direct woman with something on her mind. Now that he was past the mental block he saw what confused him in trying to place her. She reminded him in a darkly-through-the-veil way of his second wife. It wasn't so much a point-by-point resemblance as an overall effect.

"Well?" Karen Resnick said, crossing her arms in front of her and taking a small step back in her fashionable boots.

Her lips were coated in something shiny. Jarred from his contemplation, he found his voice and his manners.

"Please come in," he said.

As Karen Resnick followed him into the house he made a point of looking back at her when they entered the kitchen.

Ever since his second divorce his reactions to women were unpredictable. After feeling numb for such a long time, he found himself both uncomfortable and excited by this turn of events. Now he wondered with a measure of clinical interest how much Karen Resnick, in her resemblance to his second wife, would manage to stir him further. He allowed himself a quick check of her firm body and then fixed his eyes on Tess.

"This is Teresa Mendes Garcia de Arroyo," Tyrone said.

If Karen was surprised at seeing a woman in casual clothes settled in the kitchen, it didn't show until she started to talk.

"I was nervous," she said confidentially to Tess. "So I dressed up. I always do that when I'm nervous."

"I know how that is," Tess said.

"Coffee perhaps? A glass of water?" Tyrone asked.

He continued to watch Karen while not looking at her directly.

She settled back with her water, looked over at Tess who was sitting with her right ear slightly closer to the visitor than her left. The area around the new coffee maker was untidy with spilled coffee grounds and dirty cups. Her gaze moved out the window and rested on the hopping and vocalizing semi-crippled athlete addressing the trees outside. From behind the trees an ecstatic and hyperactive dog was joining in the fun, jumping and chasing something invisible with sharp yips.

"Oh," Karen said, drawing in her breath.

"My brother," Tess said, interpreting the sound. "What do you think?"

"Interesting," Karen said. "Why do you ask?"

"I like your voice and you aren't wearing a ring."

"Ah," Karen said. "I thought you might be blind. So that's why you held both my hands."

"All the clues we can get," Tess said. "And how did you know?"

"I have a boy who's hypersensitive," Karen said. "He listens and touches things like you. He also tastes and smells."

"Except he's not blind," Tess said.

"No," Karen said. "He's just got other — ah — problems."

Tyrone coughed. He felt as if the two women had instantly reached a level of understanding that excluded him. He stared thoughtfully at the antics of the dog and man outside and then he rapped the table. Karen had, after all, come to talk with him.

"You wanted to talk?" he said to her.

Caught up in her exchange with Tess, she looked over blankly.

"Is this a private matter?" he asked as an afterthought.

The widow hesitated. "Not really private," she said. "I understand you were his friend."

Tyrone didn't know how to respond. Denial would appear churlish or at best a lame excuse to avoid responsibility for whatever she had in mind.

"Poor Lawrence," Tess broke in. "Everybody wants something."

"What do you mean?" Karen asked.

"He is our Don Quixote, don't you know?"

"And who is that?" The widow sounded sulky.

"Ah, I have annoyed you," Tess said. "Someone in Spanish literature who went out in full armor with a sidekick to try and do some good in the world. I forgot you don't learn about him in your school system. There was even a play about it. And he sang about an impossible quest or an impossible dream. Or maybe it was both." She hummed a few notes to prove her point.

"It's okay," Karen said, a hint of defensiveness in her voice. "I am the daughter of grocers. Possibly if you said he was Mr. Potato Head out to save the world I might have caught on."

She gave a low chuckle, looking annoyed.

Tyrone suspected Karen, in spite of her professed lack of formal knowledge, would catch on quickly to undercurrents and complications given the chance.

But Karen had other things in mind. "I need help," she said.

Tyrone's first thought was fate was paying him back for the rash decision he had made to buy a motorbike. At the same time, he felt wide awake at the thought of a challenge to keep him going. By long force of habit, he didn't ask what do you need help with, or even, why do you think I can help you?

"What," he said, "is the problem?"

The problem, Karen explained, had to do with her dead husband. Her husband had been instrumental in setting things up before his death, not wanting to let go of his certainty about Paul Desroseau's guilt. And now there were repercussions for her and her young son.

She claimed she was sure her husband did not foresee his own death and therefore could not be held accountable. Tyrone thought otherwise. Even if Resnick were alive, he should have foreseen his own vulnerable family ties whether he lived with them in the matrimonial home or not.

Tyrone wondered about the real reason she was coming to him for help.

He asked, "This man, Desroseau, approached you?"

"Yes. The guy came right up to me and said it was my husband who tried to have him convicted for murdering his boy. He was trying to scare me, I think. He said Brian was on some rampage with mistaken ideas but he forgave him because he was so obviously wrong." Her shoulders rose and fell. "And then he looked around for Briney and said, *I understand you have a kid. Make sure you keep him safe.*"

Tyrone had been waiting for her to say something intelligent or at the very least give him some hard facts that could prove indictable.

"You do understand what you're saying is pretty weak? Let me rephrase that — it's so weak it would be thrown out of court. He could have just meant it exactly how it sounded."

"But he killed his kid — and now he's threatening me."

"Hold on a minute, you obviously know something no one in the judiciary is aware of. You're telling me you know, that is you have proof, he killed his kid?"

"It was the way he talked to me, the way he looked at me, insinuating something. I can't put it into words, but it was there," she said with resentment.

Tyrone threw up his hands. "He was found innocent; do you remember? The Crown appealed and the charge was overturned. It went all the way up to the Supreme Court. Do you think the doctors and the coroner and every other person who testified was in collusion?"

"Brian thought he was guilty," Karen Resnick said as if it proved everything.

"That proves nothing. That's what the courts are for."

"Guilty people get away with things all the time. The police catch them and then their lawyer or some crazy fluke lets them go free. Is that justice?"

Tyrone knew exactly where she'd heard that and more of the same. And though he knew it was how it worked sometimes, he had spent too long teaching the rule of law as opposed to vigilante justice to back down.

"No matter what you think, he was found innocent. You are going to have to do better than that. If you feel you are in danger, why can't you go to the police?"

"They can't spare any more men," she said. "They say they're going to have to pull out."

"Wait. Hold on a minute. What do you mean? Pull out? Can't spare more men?"

"They were keeping an eye on him."

"Let me understand this. Doing what?"

"Driving by his place so he knew they were watching."

"Harassing him, you mean."

"It was a favor to Brian, if you must know. What's wrong with that? The courts were wrong and he got away, so they were keeping an eye on him."

"And now they're pulling out, you said?"

"They said they have nothing to go on and no more men to spare. The guy knows where we live, Briney and me. I'm scared."

"This must be hard for you," Tess said. Tyrone was so focused on overcoming his frustration while trying to understand the dimensions of the problem he'd forgotten she was there.

"Yes," the widow put her hands to her face. "It seems we're at a stalemate. The guy knows where I live. He told me the police are harassing him and he wants them to back off. He says he was found innocent and they're spooking his girlfriends and stopping him when his taillight is out, stupid things like that. He says they regularly check to see if his girlfriend's kid is strapped in a car seat. Brian's friends on the force say they can't do much else, especially if they get too busy with other crimes. They said I should get help and keep their phone numbers handy at all times. And that's where they said you might come in."

"Me?" Tyrone said. "What do they think I can do?"

"You know the law. Maybe you can think of something that will make him go away and leave me alone."

"If the police back off, like they plan to do," Tyrone said, beginning to see what this was really about, "then you'll be okay. Isn't that all he said he wanted? What more do you want?"

"Revenge," Karen Resnick said.

"Revenge for what?" he tried to keep his voice down. "Why would you possibly want to endanger yourself?"

He was aware of what she would say before she said it.

"My husband," Karen Resnick said, "was a man who acted on his principles. A good husband and father. Until this thing happened. It's what made him leave our home to pursue what he thought was right. I loved my husband. I want to honor what he believed in. None of this would have happened if it weren't for Desroseau."

"And what about your son?" Tyrone said. "Don't you care what happens to him?"

"Of course I care!" Karen Resnick suddenly yelled at him. "Why do you think I'm here?"

"What do you think I can do?" Tyrone said, putting his hands out in surrender.

In a logical world, he wasn't entirely sure what she wanted revenge for.

"Brian would still be with us if it weren't for that man," she said. "You know the law, you may have connections who can help us. Or at least that's what I'm hoping."

He was both astonished and speechless at her self-delusion.

"Well then," Tess said in the growing silence. "If you have finished, I have something to say."

Juan Carlos limped into the kitchen through the entrance by the study nook in his new tracksuit, his face looking almost healthy. It took him a while to notice the silence. Tyrone observed Karen Resnick's doubtful look with interest as she watched the tall limping man.

Tess in the meantime leaned forward. "How strong are you feeling?" she asked her brother.

"What?" Juan Carlos was looking tolerable, but not anything like the fearless, macho defender Tess made him out to be in spite of his facial scar. Tyrone hoped that, along with the injuries to his body, Juan Carlos's brains had not been beaten out of him as well.

"You've been working out, right? How strong are you?" Tess, unaware of how her brother was presenting himself, kept on track.

"He can't do it," Tyrone said impatiently. "He hasn't the skill or the will."

"Can't do what?" the invalid asked mildly.

"We have a problem," Tess said.

"He's not the man," Tyrone insisted.

She turned, exasperated. "Are you judge and jury?"

"In this case I am."

"Tell him anyway."

"Tell me what?" Juan Carlos sat beside Tess and put his hand on her arm, touching her gently. He looked over at Karen and moved his head in a silent question.

"We've been rude," Tess said. "Karen, meet my brother, my very strong and stubborn brother, Juan Carlos."

"Hello," Juan Carlos said softly. "Karen, right? I didn't hear you arrive."

His jawline was dark with the scruffy unshaved look photographers and film producers favor for their their male stars when they want to make them look sexy and laid-back. This casual carelessness didn't appear to impress Karen Resnick. She crossed her legs, crossed her arms and stared back at him.

"Hi," she said.

"Now what is it I can't do?" Juan Carlos turned to look at Tyrone.

Contrary to the arguments he had made just a few minutes earlier, the former professor was silently revising his opinion. He was beginning to have doubts about Karen Resnick's mental stability while at the same time he was seeing something different about Juan Carlos. In spite of all the convalescent stages he'd gone through and the crazy pantomimes in front of the stand of maple and birch trees, or perhaps because of all that had transpired so far, Tyrone was beginning to see another man. He no longer appeared as a pale, dark-haired, ne'er-do-well gambler and con man. If the former professor were to examine his motivations more closely his change of mind was by no means altruistic. He was thinking he would no longer have to feel responsible for the gambler.

"They've been arguing about you," Karen Resnick spoke.

Juan Carlos aimed a thousand-watt lopsided smile at her. "An unusual situation. I am such a good patient. I cannot imagine what they were arguing about," he said.

For the rest of her visit, Karen Resnick did not seem thrilled with Tess's efforts to introduce Juan Carlos as a body guard for her and her boy while Juan Carlos appeared indifferent. So nothing was settled.

After she left, Tyrone was left alone in the kitchen with Juan Carlos and his own doubts that were intensified by the casualness and humor with which the man referred to his one and only stint as a body guard.

"Only once?" Tyrone asked. "What happened?"

Juan Carlos laughed. "We went gambling. The one thing I lied about on the form they didn't check. A gambler guarding a gambler from gambling." He threw his head back, enjoying himself as Tyrone kept silent. "Well, the two of us thought it was funny," Juan Carlos said.

Tyrone couldn't let it go. "What do you do besides gambling?" he asked.

Juan Carlos stopped laughing and watched him for a long time without speaking.

"I'm serious," Tyrone continued when it looked as if Juan Carlos was not going to answer.

"You're serious?" Juan Carlos said. "What do you know about Mexican food besides guacamole and nachos?"

"Pico de Gallo?" Tyrone suggested. "Tortilla soup?"

"That's only the basics," Juan Carlos interrupted. "There's the more esoteric Mexican cooking that North Americans don't know. Pozole, Cazuelitas, Sopa de sesos, Caldos, Sopas secas, Chayotes con almendras, jamon, queso y huevos. That's what I do. I can cook up a Mexican feast."

"In Tess's kitchen, those were your meals?"

Juan Carlos nodded, still looking wary.

"Then why —"

"I'm making plans, new plans," Juan Carlos surprised Tyrone by saying. "Maybe this time…." He trailed off.

As Juan Carlos leaned forward on his arms at the table, possibly planning a rosy future. Tyrone thought about the serendipity of having two men in his house with cooking skills. What were the odds? For a fraction of a second, he considered asking Juan Carlos whether he might give a demonstration but closed his mouth and settled back once he observed him more closely.

[28] Dump Trucks

A week later, Rafe, looking far more relaxed and alive than when Tyrone last saw him, returned in the limo and parked in his usual spot on the brown earth under the oak. It was a fine morning in late September and he was a hurricane of fresh air as he bounded about the farmhouse.

Within the space of five minutes the resident cased the foodless kitchen from counter to fridge to freezer. "What the hell do you eat?" he asked as he fed ground coffee to the coffee maker. Tyrone sighed and shrugged, hoping this would elicit another shopping trip closely followed by a half day of cooking in the Italian style, since Juan Carlos was not making any efforts to cook in the Mexican style just yet. They'd been subsisting on salads, pizzas and Chinese take-out from one of the few restaurants that delivered to his area. It was strange. Two different men whose passion was cooking ending up in the same house, and still the fridge was empty except for indifferent left overs.

"Tell me, how do you stay so fit?" he asked the resident. Watching Juan Carlos working out, he'd been thinking he needed to engage in some activity other than dreaming of elusive Italian feasts, eating pizzas and going for walks around his acreage but wasn't sure what. He wasn't ready for a paunch just yet.

"I play pick-up basketball whenever I get the chance. Why?"

"Basketball?" Tyrone examined Rafe's admittedly fit, but compact frame.

"Yup. Growing up, I used to play hoops with my brother on the street. I'd never make it to the big leagues — I'm no Magic Johnson — but I'm fast and I'm sneaky. I love the game."

Tyrone eyed him with suspicion, remembering the fiasco with the vacuum cleaner, then he shrugged, reserving judgement. Catching a glimpse of Tyrone's incredulity, Rafe just smiled, not caring to prove or justify himself any further.

Once the resident found out that Tess and Henryk were out, time of return unknown, he lost all interest in food and conversation and took the stairs two at a time to talk with Juan Carlos.

Tyrone moved stealthily to the foot of the stairs in an attempt to hear what was going on. He suspected he wasn't yet privy to the latest news.

Hearing only muffled conversation and feeling ridiculous for loitering, Tyrone climbed up.

"Who are you calling?" he asked suspiciously when he entered the Rose Room and saw Rafe holding a cell phone to his ear.

"Someone you know," Rafe winked, a business card in his hand.

"Can you narrow the field a little?"

"Someone blonde and female who lives in the area and is in need of help."

"When?" Tyrone said, putting together what he imagined had gone on behind his back.

"Right now, because Juan Carlos here has decided to help her. In his former role of bodyguard, that is."

Tyrone felt ambushed. He berated himself for not being more vigilant. Instead, he had been too entrenched in arguments with himself about the widow's frame of mind and Juan Carlos's competence. In the meantime, Juan Carlos, Karen and, no doubt, Tess, took the decision out of his hands.

The gambler was standing by the mullioned window in his room overlooking the oak-sheltered parking lot. Dressed in a new pair of dark grey sweats, he looked almost handsome as he worked his arms with hand weights. Various other arm and leg weights were neatly stacked in the right-hand corner of the room. He looked fit enough though somber. Tyrone thought he was a man considering what he may not have had the inclination to consider before. A previous life that included driving off in someone else's car, losing the vehicle in a game of five card stud or maybe Texas Hold 'Em and being subsequently beaten almost to death because of his lack of self-control and the cars' mechanical faults.

He focused on Juan Carlos. "You really think you can help her? You mean it?" He asked.

Juan Carlos nodded. "Yes, to everything," he said.

The opportunity was too good to miss. "What about Mexico?" Tyrone asked.

"Mexico? Are you *loco?*"

"No," Tyrone said. "I seem to recall you wanted to run away to Mexico."

"Ha-ha. You too?"

"I was most definitely not running."

"You don't even know Spanish!"

"Is that my fault?" Tyrone said. "And besides, I have no car."

"Is not your fault?" Juan Carlos mocked him.

"Look," Tyrone said. "I know what you're thinking, but no."

"Okay. I love this. What am I thinking?"

Tyrone spread his hands out in a gesture Juan Carlos could have made. "And there is only one Spanish teacher in Canada? In Guelph? In Milton?" He mimicked the gambler's voice. "And there is only one car?"

"Pues, claro que si." Juan Carlos shrugged. "You have an extreme clarity of thought, just like my sister. Me, I have a job waiting, as you know."

"No, I didn't know — but I suppose I do now." Tyrone said feeling a familiar jab of irritation.

When Karen Resnick arrived, she parked under the large oak behind the limo. From the living room, Tyrone could just barely see her boy bouncing up and down on the passenger side and yelling out the window. He was about to turn away when he thought better of it. No matter what he felt about the kid, maybe he was mistaken about Resnick's widow. Maybe his conviction that she resembled his second wife skewed his thinking and made him dismiss her real concerns. What if she truly was in danger and he would be responsible if anything happened to her or the boy? What if Juan Carlos failed to protect her in the same way he failed with his first and only bodyguard assignment?

He opened his front door and approached the SUV as Karen got out, biting her lip.

The kid somehow got hold of the door handle and the car door flew open. As if uncoordinated or unable to control his movements, he tumbled out and struck the ground with a smack that surely must have hurt. Steeling his ears against a frenetic shriek or wail, Tyrone waited. The boy got up slowly, smaller than ever in his jacket. And it was this moment Tyrone would remember for a long time. The same little boy who was so irritatingly wound up and unaware got up from the ground, limped for a moment, yet did not utter a sound. What Tyrone saw was a look of resignation. A moment of clarity most kids that age never have to face. It was then Tyrone made an impulsive decision.

"Would you like to see a surprise?" he asked the boy, whose eyes were once again the opaque eyes of a small hell raiser.

"Huh?" the kid mumbled, crushing the ground with his sneaker as if trying to get back at it. Possibly there was nothing that could surprise him.

"Can I give him something?" Tyrone felt obliged to ask Karen Resnick determined not to let the kid get the better of him.

She nodded.

"Okay," the kid said, holding his hands up in front of his eyes and making a loud irritating engine sound.

"I have to bring it down," Tyrone said. "You wait here."

He climbed the stairs to the blue room. In the half light, the room was cool and fresh. Perhaps the cracks in the caulking could no longer be ignored before another heavy winter. He walked past the picture of the Dragon's Blood tree leaning face forward against the wall and went straight towards his intended goal: one unopened box piled among many others in the corner. The box he picked out was dusty from its sojourn in the room. He carefully wiped off the dust with his sleeve and looked at the shiny red dump truck encased in cellophane. He had bought it along with all the others and then lost his nerve. He just kept buying a damn assortment of toy trucks and cars after he had so painfully dried himself out, promising himself he would have them ready for when the time came to be with his son. Dump trucks, fire engines, sixteen wheelers, SUVs and sports cars that raced over metal rails. It was easier to buy them and pretend he was doing something while he kept delaying and delaying. There were lots of actions he could have taken both in and out of court. What a procrastinating fool he was.

At Karen Resnick's SUV, he handed over the red dump truck in its pristine cellophane box with the bright bold lettering without a word. The boy dropped to the ground, appearing to be made entirely of elbows, knees and boneless ankles as he ripped at the box.

"WOW!" he shouted, not looking at Tyrone but at the tree Juan Carlos sometimes abused.

"What do you say?" The widow tried to take hold of the mangled carton.

"Wow," the boy said more quietly and wouldn't let her wrest it from him.

258

"Bry, look at me. No. No. Stay still for a minute. Now look at me. What do you say?" Her firm grip strained her hands.

"Thank you," the boy shouted and danced away under the oak clutching the box.

He finished ripping it open, littering the ground with pieces of bright cardboard.

Tyrone felt Karen Resnick watching him as he watched her boy. He heard her sigh and wanted to say something kind or even reassuring but could only nod his head.

When Juan Carlos and Rafe came around from the back, it wasn't clear what they were doing since Tyrone hadn't heard them go out. Neither of them was breathing hard or sweating so it couldn't have been a trial jog to see how far out of shape the gambler was. He had started jogging, fast walking, really, as soon as his cast came off. The first few times, accompanied by Tess, he only made it half way up the driveway and had to stop, his hands on his knees. The two young men seemed friendly with each other and at ease.

Juan Carlos went in and carried his possessions downstairs, placing them by the front door — his hand and ankle weights together with the duffle bag containing his few clothes.

The three of them, Juan Carlos, Rafe and Tyrone, waited in the kitchen drinking Rafe's coffee for another half hour making small talk. Karen was visible outside the kitchen nook with the kid who was running around in crazy circles on the trampled grass and around the trees. Tess and Henryk were taking their time returning.

Finally, Juan Carlos looked at his watch, knocked on the kitchen bay window to catch Karen's attention and then called out to her before walking outside through the front of the house carrying his possessions. "Tess will know where I am, she's got my cell," he said, shaking Rafe's hand and then embracing him.

Tyrone stood outside by the oak, watching the departure, feeling unbalanced. At first Juan Carlos approached him with an outstretched hand, then he examined the former professor more closely and embraced him as well before climbing into Karen's SUV. Tyrone, who was unused to such male displays of emotion, felt awkward and stood there stiffly. He temporized by giving Juan Carlos an awkward pat on the back.

"Hey," the gambler said softly in Tyrone's ear, "I know what you did for me. I won't forget it."

As the widow drove around the oak with Juan Carlos beside her, the kid squashed his nose against the side window in a grotesque manner with not a trace of the confused and resigned small child Tyrone had imagined for just that single moment. Then, at the very last instant the little hell raiser quietly held up the fire-engine-red dump truck and plastered it against the window for Tyrone to see.

[29] Best Laid Plans

Once the others had gone, Rafe settled in the kitchen and prepared to wait for Tess. Tyrone wished the resident would stop making romantic errors and think his life plans through. He told himself it would be best not to mention Tess, safer to talk about Rafe's future plans once he finished his residency.

"So, you're hanging around waiting for Tess," Tyrone said once the coffee was poured. He swirled the milk around his cup and then attempted to give it a quick stir with his finger.

"Coffee or frozen pizza," Rafe said as he quickly rifled through the fridge, freezer, and kitchen cupboards in his controlled, precise style.

"We can always go shopping," Tyrone said hopefully.

The young man laughed and sat down, saying, "look, she keeps backing off. Do you know the problem?"

"No. Yes. I think so."

"And I thought you knew everything."

"There are issues," Tyrone said, using a phrase he learned from some of his youngest students. The older ones were often more settled. There were so many issues with the youngest ones who got into law school way too early by virtue of their academic brightness and stellar marks coupled with immaturity. Girlfriend troubles, parent troubles, sleeping problems, computer disc problems, database problems, sex problems, all labeled the same way. "No more issues will be accepted as an excuse," he finally proclaimed to the class at large in order to put a stop to the nonsense. But then he was forced to deal with them one at a time as the more inventive ones brought in increasingly wilder excuses.

"What *issues*?" Rafe said.

"Look," Tyrone said. "Not to rub it in, but haven't you noticed? She can read your voice. If she touches you she can feel your muscle tension. You may think I'm exaggerating — I probably am — but think of her as someone with super powers and you won't go wrong. And besides, didn't she say something to you about Henryk?"

"Just that they've known each other for a long time. What am I supposed to do about it?"

"Talk to her. Pay attention to what she tells you," Tyrone said, feeling pleased he could skate around the topic without really giving anything away.

The resident held up his hands. "You're making as much sense as she does. What the hell is this about?"

"Ah," Tyrone said with relief. "I think I hear the motorcycle roaring around the front. Shall we go out to greet them?"

While Rafe cornered Tess, Tyrone tried to stay out of it and asked Henryk to go riding in an attempt to divert the biker. Henryk, coffee cup in hand, refused to be diverted and silently watched the contentious proceedings between Rafe and Tess through the living room's front windows.

Under the large oak close to where the limo was parked, Raffaele Marino, a soccer star rising to the occasion, was kicking a tire with no great enthusiasm while Tess spoke. It was a fairly long speech on her part, complete with hand gestures. Rafe listened, arms crossed, not looking as if he was following any of Tyrone's careful advice. Once she appeared to have stopped talking, he stomped over to the limo, tore open the door, slammed it shut and drove away, looping around her and the oak, across the brown grass on the other side and back onto the driveway. Tess, having felt something under her feet, bent down to pick up the ripped pieces of cardboard Karen's boy had torn from the fire engine box and then stood motionless, holding them in both her hands.

In what was left of the day, Tess went upstairs to pack her clothing.

Before she and Henryk drove off in the motorcycle with sidecar and left Tyrone alone in the now empty, suddenly way too empty, house, he felt compelled to take her aside.

"How about a quick walk before you leave?" he suggested. "I want to show you something."

"Isn't it a little late to be showing me something?" she said sourly.

"All right. I want to talk."

"About what?"

He couldn't bring himself to say about what. He had visions of her taking off without listening. "About your brother," he said.

They walked through the orchard and over the wild untended field with its fallen and trampled grasses and then onto the path through the trees. He tried to give her his arm but she asked him to find her a walking stick and used it to tap her way forward. Other than warning her about trees, bushes and boulders in the way, Tyrone deliberately didn't say much until they climbed the incline and were walking over the shorter grasses on the flat part of the escarpment.

"It's not about my brother, is it?" she said.

"No."

"Well, aren't you going to say anything else?"

"I'm trying to figure out how to say it."

"I'm waiting."

"Okay."

"This is a novel way of discussing things."

"What?"

"You say you want to talk, then you get me to say your piece."

"Sorry," he said.

"Why is it important to you?"

"Let's just say I have become sensitized to people who throw things away. God help him, he loves you, and by 'he' I mean Rafe, not Henryk, and you, well, I've seen you together. I think I could share his feelings, but you're stopping yourself."

"And this bothers you?"

264

"Yes. I think you're doing it for the wrong reasons. Some misguided loyalty to Henryk. Can't you see? Henryk has made his decision. Why can't you move on?"

She stopped suddenly. "How can I just leave him like that? He is so unhappy,"

"He's already left you. And you told him you were getting married!"

She sighed and poked the ground with her stick. "Oh, that," she said.

"Exactly that. It makes no sense."

"Since when do obligations of the heart make sense?"

"You make no sense."

"Well then, we will all have to be confused a little longer."

They walked back in silence. Tyrone opened his mouth a few times, trying to work out his next argument, and then closed it again. Logic hadn't much worked with Leah either and logic was all he had at the moment.

After Tess and Henryk were gone, piled onto the motorcycle with sidecar and waving as if nothing had changed, Tyrone was left standing at his front door all alone, wondering what more he could have said or done and why he felt so unsettled. In the empty house, he noticed Sheba and the cat were missing. Intently focused on keeping track of visitors and loose ends, he hadn't perceived their absence until now. The stillness was doubly noticeable.

And so, after being alone for no more than a nanosecond on the wheel of time, Lawrence Tyrone suddenly had enough of solitude. Even though he might have wished for it when his house was full of messy, intrusive strangers, he stopped wishing for it the instant they were gone.

Part Three

[30] The Other Side of Unsociable

The living room was gloomy in the morning light. Tyrone turned on the Tiffany lamp and read another three pages of the Roosevelt biography he was working his way through. He examined the book's thickness in his hands and calculated it would take him ten years to finish at the rate he was going. He dropped the book on the coffee table where it lay along with ten other books of differing sizes. A few of them were by lawyers. He bought the lawyer books wondering whether at some point he might go back to practicing law. A one-man firm, fighting for right against might. In truth he was no longer sure anything was mightier than the sword.

Every three weeks Tyrone had to make a personal appearance at his local library to check out "The Bee Keepers Bible." He'd renewed it so often he could no longer just do it on-line and, as a result, had gotten to know one of the librarians quite well. She was a quiet lady with short, grey hair and a wide smile that appeared whenever he showed up. In keeping with her tolerant nature, she never asked him why he didn't just buy the damn book. If she had asked, he wasn't sure he could have given a satisfactory answer.

He fantasized about a more leisurely, less distracted, version of himself tending the hives. But then, he thought, he was fifty-three years old and maybe it wasn't time to give up on the wider world just yet.

And in that wider world there was still a loose end — the gambling girl — the one who by a strange fluke, turned out to be the daughter of one of his former law students. He convinced himself he needed to justify himself to the man or at least follow up.

Mulling this over on the way to the computer in the kitchen nook, he stopped for a moment to wonder whether it was silence or boredom that made this a priority. No, he decided, in this instance he was merely following up on a legal problem because the girl was underage. Tyrone shook his head. What was her father thinking or, more to the point, not bothering to think?

Signing into the Law Society website in order to look up the list of members, he was pleased to note they still hadn't taken away his privileges. The website contained some of the information he wanted about his former student, Sidney Katz.

To do or not to do? To go or not to go? Since there was nobody to argue the pros and cons of his intentions with him, he decided he would think them through by taking the longish walk to his mailbox at the end of the driveway. As he walked and talked to himself, there was no one to contradict him — his best arguments were for going ahead with his plan.

At the mailbox he found two letters along with a fistful of marketing brochures. Why real estate agents went to the trouble of advertising themselves to people living in the middle of nowhere was always beyond him. They were no doubt working with developers wanting to make huge profits. He shoved the brochures back in the mailbox, but he hung onto the letters.

One was addressed to him personally from Spenser. It had Spenser's company name and address in the upper left-hand corner. The other envelope, addressed in smaller, less obtrusive writing, was from Spenser's daughter, Jessica. She wrote, *Please open* on the back of the envelope in her childish script. He had no idea how long it had taken the letters to get to him, addressed and readdressed valiantly by Canada Post. The postal code was wrong. He held both letters in suddenly icy hands as he walked back to the farm.

His bedroom was once more his own. Keeping the Rose Room door shut now bothered him so he kept it open. The bed in the room was made up with a colorful, quilted bedspread, a small, hand-hooked rug lay on the wooden floor, light filtered through the flounced curtains and the smell of sickness was gone. It almost looked inviting. He could still picture Rafe and Sheba maneuvering for position on the inflatable mattress they shared on the floor. The only door that remained tightly closed was to the blue room which contained the painting of the Dragon's Blood tree and all those dusty packages of toy cars and trucks.

The stairs squeaked, the floor boards were uneven, the walls were cracked. The farmhouse was beginning to look noticeably old and tired. Sheba was gone, the feral cat with her. He'd become used to their company. They were fickle, untrustworthy creatures.

Still, no matter how hard he tried to distance himself, the letters he was holding threw him. It was not lost on him that the two people he would have most trusted were now married to each other and unavailable to him.

He wrested his Hudson's Bay jacket off its hanger and set out for the farm next door. Years ago, the jacket was a birthday gift from Spenser, who said at the time that Tyrone needed something brighter than dark suits and coats to survive the dreary winters. "Trappers and voyageurs, think of it," Spenser announced. "Trading beaver pelts for blankets and now there's a jacket."

"Looks just like a blanket," Tyrone said, secretly appalled at the distinctive stripes of the jacket on the cream background that made it look exactly like the blanket it was meant to represent. As young boys, he and Spenser used to play explorers, *coureurs de bois*, woodsmen, intrepid voyageurs, running wild over the fields and woods behind their house on dangerous missions which they planned and fought over, taking turns wearing the Hudson's Bay blanket like a cloak. Then their mother died and Spenser cried so much that Tyrone had very little memory of the rest of the year. All he remembered was that it was the worst year of his life.

As he trudged out his gate encased in a jacket he wouldn't have been caught dead wearing a number of years ago, Tyrone felt determined. Alone on the paved road running past the country farms and houses, he wondered how many beaver pelts he could trade for Audrey's goodwill. He was hoping she would not turn him away. At the moment she was the only person he knew within miles.

As the wind blew past him and he breathed the air into his lungs, he wished he was just starting out on the riding lessons with Henryk. He shook his head. That wasn't going to happen, no point wasting time. He walked faster. It would still give him great pleasure to punch out his brother. And yet, what could the traitor be writing to him about?

[31] The Truth in Earl Grey

At the circular entrance to Audrey's farmhouse, Tyrone stopped, tempted to take a page from Juan Carlos and take a few swings at the trees. After watching the gambler, he wondered if they were both addicts, but his addiction he speculated, was to not admitting he had any.

He knocked. Audrey looked startled when she answered the door and saw him.

Instead of purple, she was wearing a large brown top that matched her small sharp eyes. What he was very sure of, standing there on her threshold, was he was wired up.

A long time ago on a visit to his brother he was coerced into reading stories to Jessica, five years old at the time. "Do you want to be right or do you want to be friends?" Jessica raced around the room, parroting the words in a story about an insufferable girl badger and shrieking with laughter. He thought his niece was acutely disturbed and wanted to explain to her that not being right had serious repercussions in a court of law, but Leah was enchanted.

He now resolved to take a page from the story, no matter how deeply flawed it was or how much trouble the kennel dogs might cause him.

"Hello." He smiled at Audrey. "Will you talk to me?"

"Well," she said with a sour look. "I guess you haven't come about a trailer. Maybe not even about a dog. What brings you round again?"

He waited for the dogs to start their cacophony of displeasure.

The silence from the kennels was absolute. He made a point to show her he was listening. "You've given them away?" he asked, hopefully.

She grinned maliciously. "Not a chance."

For some reason, he was encouraged by her feistiness.

"What then?" he said.

"Sheba has straightened things out for you."

"You're putting me on. A dog?"

"A dog? Hah," she mocked him. "Haven't you learned anything?"

"It appears not," he said mildly, biting his tongue.

"The dogs have just eaten and Wills has taken them for a run outside the kennel. It's always a treat for them. You looked strange there for a minute. Are you okay? I was joking about Sheba, although she is very capable. You want to come in?"

He dipped his head and followed her to the kitchen, confused at how fast she changed direction.

Given a choice between an old jar of instant coffee and a pot of fresh tea, he chose Earl Grey with milk. Rafe had spoiled him with his meticulous coffee-brewing skills. The tea set came complete with red flowers, gold rims, an immaculate tea pot and a cream and sugar.

"And how is the young lady?" Audrey asked while pouring tea into flimsy china cups.

From the look of her, he would have guessed she might have preferred thick chipped mugs rather than the porcelain she was holding in her fleshy fingers.

"The young lady? Gone," he said, not meaning to sound abandoned.

"Mmm," she said, taking a sip of tea. "Everybody's taken off on you, have they? And what about the injured man? Her brother? Where is he?"

"Gone," Tyrone said resentfully.

Being friends versus being right was a tough call. He was reminding himself that this woman, with her small sharp eyes, possessed a mind like a vise. She could probably squeeze out every bit of information she desired. There was no way he was going to sit in her kitchen and bare his soul, especially not about Spenser and the letters he hadn't yet opened. He tried to drink his scalding tea quickly so he could excuse himself with dignity.

"And what about that nice young man, the doctor in training?" Audrey kept her sharp stare on him as they sipped. She seemed determined not to let up her interrogation. Egged on by her brashness, Tyrone was thinking of a retort. "The one who is truly and hopelessly in love," she said before he had a chance to come up with one. "He should be careful — beware of betrayal and disappointment."

He opened his mouth but couldn't reply. Clearing his throat, he tried to recover.

"I'm not sure what you mean," he said.

She reached over and swirled the remnants of tea leaves in his cup, deftly upending them onto his saucer. "Ha!" she said, "I have the gift. Let's look at your tea leaves."

"You do parlor tricks?"

"Oh my." She ignored his tone as she studied the meaningless patterns.

"You're struggling with something from earlier on."

"That could be anyone."

"I said it to you. I want to be sure, give me something you usually wear."

He raised his eyebrows, then shrugged and handed over his watch, a slim gold one he used to be very proud of. It appeared she was just as deluded as he first surmised. Even more bereft of reason than Karen Resnick. He should have known better. She weighed his watch in her hand, holding it lightly, then examined the dregs in his saucer once more.

"I usually both feel and see — not always — often enough. Don't look at me like that. Ha! A woman. These leaves suggest a woman — your wife? — this woman was very important to you and something happened. I see pictures here in this group of leaves. There were pictures. These pictures have something to do with her, perhaps? But I also feel a great deal of anger for someone who used to be close to you. A relative? A male? That's it. You're angry. You blame him for something. Yes. I see bars. That's strange. You haven't been free of this. Something happened recently, something has changed. A change has come for you and you have to decide what to do about it. And there's something else, I see letters that will bring news to you and it might not be the news you are expecting. Yes, there will be letters with news and they will change everything. So, tell me, how was that? Could I have said it to anyone?"

"Nonsense," he said. "Generalities."

"This isn't hard stuff, you know. You can just nod, yes or no, I can take it," she replied.

He looked away, thinking of his anger and what she said about pictures and letters. He wanted to forget about the letters. It was all so vague, yet almost close enough to be worth staying in her good graces. He wouldn't be revealing much if he nodded a curt yes.

"Ah. Okay." She smiled. "Well, that's something. I won't go any deeper. It makes you uncomfortable. So, what happened with all those misplaced people running around your house?"

And what about your disruptive kennel dogs? was his first thought. He mentally slapped the thought away, having gained some sense. "Can't you just read more tea leaves and watches and get the whole picture by yourself?" he asked drily.

"I take getting used to," she said with a big smile, as if she'd read his thoughts. "Wills will tell you and you can believe him. But you gotta know you can't listen to everything that man says, being in his own world half the time and all, and the other half being stubborn about everything else. Me, I'm a good listener. I have to be. Dog owners have secrets like you wouldn't believe." She handed his watch back to him. He would have missed her wink if he had taken his eyes off her for a second.

Every time he thought he had her pegged she confused him. Like Tess, she seemed to veer towards unexpected positions and unpredictable paths when he wasn't prepared.

The way she changed topics in her offhanded manner to get you to trust her probably meant she could have been a sharp courtroom lawyer in another life. He reminded himself to be wary, although he was beginning to suspect this late in his life that he had a tendency to misread women.

She stood up with him as he got up to leave, pulling down her large brown sweater over her hips and trying to brush off stray dog hairs.

"Was there something you came for besides tea?" she said.

For the first time since he'd arrived she appeared slightly unsure, as if she hadn't just read his tea leaves and didn't know him at all.

"You were right a while ago. I came back about your dog." It sounded lame but he did miss Sheba.

"The dog again? Nothing about her in the tea leaves."

"Maybe the tea leaves are wrong about dogs."

"Okay, let me take another look."

He made a face as she reached down for his cup and pretended to study more random patterns floating around the saucer in a small puddle of leftover tea.

"Ha! Wait. This represents a man. Perhaps someone you knew. An acquaintance? Also, a young girl? Does any of this make sense? Is there a man you know? See, right there, the two are very connected. Definitely a man and a girl. Is it possible this is about a man you know and a young girl and something about them that is connected to you?"

She could have been talking about Spenser and Jessica or any other combination of men and young girls for all he knew.

His mind was functioning again, reclaimed from his previous confusion. He was certain whatever she said was random, there was nothing true about it, except he knew someone once whose mother could read people in impossible ways. He always thought of it as a parlor trick and he wasn't at this stage prepared to give Audrey the satisfaction of believing she had divined anything remotely accurate. He saw this as an excellent opportunity to use the information he gained during his internet search. He opened his wallet and took out a piece of paper on which he had written a name and a phone number.

"Amazing. It just so happens that I am thinking of calling someone I know who has a young daughter," he said. "Of course what you said could have applied to anyone in a number of ways. Anyway, I'll give you some points for your tea leaf reading. May I use your phone?"

He called Henryk from Audrey's kitchen phone while Audrey bustled about, cleaning up the tea things in a show of indifference to the conversation. The kitchen was mostly old though homey, with old counters, old fixtures and a porcelain sink where she was rinsing the cups and saucers and laying them out carefully on a threadbare tea towel.

Henryk sounded hoarse and in a bad mood.

"How is Tess? Did she get home okay?" Tyrone asked.

"Yes," Henryk replied curtly.

"What happened between —"

"Please," Henryk interrupted. "Mister smart person. I am sixty-two years old and getting older. What is your business?"

"You keep telling me your age as if that explains everything!"

"And what will you say to my wife, my sixty-two-year-old wife? What will you tell her after forty years?"

Tyrone hesitated, wondering at the craziness of the conversation, in fact the craziness of the whole day, including the visit with Audrey.

"I apologize," he said. "That's not what I was asking. You misunderstood."

"I misunderstand nothing. Do you hear? Nothing. I know exactly what you mean, mister lawyer, when you try to ask questions in sneaky way."

Tyrone was thinking it was a fine time for Henryk to start feeling guilty but all he said was, "Okay, none of my business."

He wanted to say a lot more. *Why then did you leave your wife? And what about keeping in touch? This loyalty and conscience thing is very touching but you have developed a very late case.* He bit his tongue, using every effort to stop himself.

"I will give you a name," he said instead. "And you can tell me if you recognize it."

"What are you talking about?" Henryk said.

"In Orillia, that day. My student? The one with the gambling daughter? Remember? The one you followed home and interfered in her life?"

"You should not be so eager to disturb those hornets again," Henryk said.

"That was before I knew who it was. Are you listening? Is it Sidney Katz?"

Henryk whistled into the receiver. "Very good, mister professor. You are, I would say, unique."

"Unique?"

"Most assuredly. Did I hear correctly? I interfered?"

"Yes," Tyrone said. "Up to a point."

"My head is already full with aches," Henryk said.

"No, no, no," Tyrone broke in. "This will be easy. I promise."

[32] Young Girl's Field Guide to Bullshit

As Henryk and Tyrone headed along the highway again, north to Orillia, Tyrone was beginning to think of it as old times. It was early November. With luck, the weather would not start pelting them with freezing rain or snow. From behind the plastic visor of his helmet, the sky looked bright. He whistled a Kingston Trio version of "Greenback Dollar," a song from his camp days, into the oncoming wind. He and Spenser performed it with a few of their own embellishments as guitar-playing hobos during a summer talent show the year before their mother died.

He tapped his fingers lightly against the handlebars as he whistled, thinking about the guy in the song who only wanted a song and a guitar in his life, thinking how Spenser used to look up to him and how they often kept each other company even as they squabbled and competed. And then he reminded himself this was the no-good brother, the betrayer, he was thinking about. He increased his speed, overtook Henryk and concentrated on staying ahead.

"Wait one moment," Henryk said when they reached Orillia. "I must think about road." He made hand movements this way and that with his eyes closed.

"You didn't look at the street signs?" Tyrone said.

Henryk shrugged, indicating this was of small importance. "Street signs?" he said.

"If you can't remember, I have an office address," Tyrone said.

"No, no, let us proceed to casino. I will know from there."

After half an hour of roaring up one street and then another using the casino as a starting point, Henryk pulled over.

"It was early morning," he said. "I was following car. Very fast car."

"And you tracked and found your way about in Russia?"

"I was much younger man."

"I see now why you needed the dog."

"Please. Dog was companion and not essential."

Tyrone was studying a map he brought with him. "If it weren't for that dog, we'd still be in the woods," he muttered. "Ah, here it is. His office. Follow me."

It was four o'clock. Sidney Katz was in court arguing a trial. A criminal case, the assistant assured Tyrone, eyeing Henryk with curiosity. Underneath his riding gear, the biker was wearing his vintage bomber jacket and red bandana. Tyrone asked him to wear those items so it would jog Sidney Katz's memory more quickly.

He remembered Katz very clearly once he put his mind to it. A student who could argue six sides of a two-sided argument. Someone a wrongfully accused innocent man or a criminal hoping to beat the odds would want to employ.

Tyrone settled into the leather couch in Sidney's plush, meant-to-impress office, pointing the other one out to Henryk who didn't seem to be in the mood to sit.

The assistant, a brash-looking young man, regarded them. "He may not be back for a while," he said.

"We'll wait," Tyrone told him. "Can we get a glass of water?"

"Perhaps I can help you?" the assistant said.

"I doubt it," Tyrone said, amused. "But just in case, which one of us do you think is the client?"

The clean-shaven, short-haired young man pointed at Henryk without hesitation. Henryk, apart from the theatrical clothing, was also sporting a grey five o'clock shadow along with his colorless ponytail. He could have passed for a pirate, a wider-faced, somewhat irritable Captain Hook.

"And what makes you think that?" Tyrone asked.

"Well ..." The assistant suddenly hesitated.

"Yes?" Tyrone said. "Feel free to speak."

"You were doing all the talking," the assistant said. "So, I assumed ... okay, I don't know."

"Indeed," the former professor said. "You just realized something because you're basically clever."

"Yes," the young man nodded, brash once more.

"Lawyers ask questions. Never make assumptions."

287

"Yes, sir." The assistant nodded. "But what —" and then he stopped, a dismayed look on his face.

Coming through the door was a dark-haired young woman in black leather. Her hair was short and spiked. She had a nose piercing, an eyebrow piercing, and five earrings in each lobe. Her lips were painted almost as black as her fingernails. On her feet were black-laced leather boots, the high kind a Goth dominatrix would wear. Tyrone could also see a tongue stud because her mouth was open. Her eyes were skewering the assistant.

"Where the hell is he?" she demanded.

The only thing about her that was familiar was the voice and short leather skirt. She had apparently hung on to both of those during her transformation.

"He's —" The brash assistant was flustered.

"He promised to be home, damn it. He lied as usual."

"Ali, please," the assistant said. "He got tied up in court."

"Don't give me that!" she yelled. "He knew I was going out. Call him from here."

"I can't. You know I can't. That's why you're supposed to check in first."

"Well, I'm here now. And I'm gonna go to court and see what the fuck he's up to."

"Hello, Alison," Tyrone said pleasantly.

She gave him a quick glance and then narrowed her eyes when she saw Henryk.

"You!" she hissed.

"Here we are," Tyrone said quickly. "I have a proposal."

"Fuck your proposals!" she yelled. "The last one banned me from the casino."

"This one is much better."

"Fuck you."

"We'll babysit until your father comes home."

"Fuck y — what?"

Tyrone shrugged calmly. "We'll babysit."

"What are you? Some kind of perverts?" she asked suspiciously.

Tyrone got up and held out his hand. "I'm Professor Lawrence Tyrone."

"Yeah, so?"

"Your father was one of my students."

"You're Lawrence Tyrone?" the assistant said.

"You know this guy?" Alison turned to him.

"A legend," the young man said. "By the way, my name's Mark Russell."

"Mister Russell," Tyrone said. "Tell this young lady we're harmless."

Mark Russell opened his mouth and then closed it. He considered Tyrone and then Henryk, warily. "I can't do that," he said, looking embarrassed.

The former professor laughed. "Very good," he said to Russell. "You're learning your lessons."

"That's just fucking great," Alison, hands on insubstantial hips, said sharply. "And how is all this mutual admiration going to help me?"

"Well," Tyrone said. "I do hope you brought your little girl with you and you didn't just leave her at home. I'm glad you asked. I want to talk to you."

When Sidney Katz walked in his front door he heard his granddaughter shrieking with laughter. Once he came into the kitchen, even though he looked tired, he took in the situation with one sharp glance. He did not appear surprised at seeing the two men. One of them was sitting on the floor with Caledonia, who was overexcited and overtired. The man was rolling marbles, playing the old alley game. The other man, an offensive biker Sidney remembered meeting months ago under disagreeable circumstances, was seated at the kitchen table.

Never a man to react quickly, Sidney bent down.

"Hello, Professor Tyrone," he said, inserting his finger between the diaper and Caledonia's tiny waist to see what was what.

"Ah, Sidney, hello," Tyrone said pleasantly. "What a lively family you have. We're babysitting."

"Yes, Mark told me you were around," Katz said.

This was not the vibrant brash student Tyrone last saw years ago who went out of his way to take on any argument. His hair was thinning. His skin was washed out. Yet if their presence made him apprehensive it didn't show.

"She's uncontrollable," he said, getting right to the point.

Caledonia put her thumb in her mouth and smiled up at him.

Tyrone rolled another marble. "I am assuming you are not talking about the munchkin here," he said.

Katz didn't answer; he rubbed his face and sighed.

"We had a very interesting conversation, by the way," Tyrone said.

"With Alison?" Katz showed far less interest than Tyrone would have liked.

"Yes. Your daughter tells me a lot of young women here compete to have babies. She says she's in good company in the teenage baby-making capital of Canada and it's all your fault."

Katz frowned and folded his arms across his chest. "How can it be my fault? Was it me who ran around and got pregnant? She's always ready to blame someone else, just like her mother."

"We heard another story," Tyrone said.

"Oh, yeah?"

"We heard you neglected your duty of care."

"What?"

"She's your daughter," Tyrone said, amused and, in a dark way, content that the law student who gave him so much trouble was now struggling with troubles of his own.

"Just what the hell is she talking about? I feed her, put up with her crap, support her and give her everything she wants. Did you see her car? Her clothes? What's she got to complain about?"

"Bad advice."

"What bad advice?" Sidney said, pulling himself up in full fighting form.

"Didn't you and your wife tell her she should keep the child?"

"What of it? She agreed."

"What did she agree to?"

"To — that it would be better to keep the child. My wife said she would regret giving it away later on."

"What else?"

"We would provide a home for them, all the comforts and someone to take care of the kid when she was in school."

"Anything else?"

"What else is there? She dropped out of school!"

"Sidney, Sidney, Sidney," the former professor said, enjoying himself. "You're smarter than that."

"I can't just let her run around on the loose and drop out of school. She's got to understand there's consequences."

"What if she wants to go out sometimes?"

"Same thing. If she goes back to school it'll be a different story. And besides, I'm working! She's got to appreciate I can't be there all the time."

"And what about Mrs. Katz? The very lovely and very bright Melissa Jones. I remember your wedding."

"She's ... she's in Toronto," Katz said. "Better opportunities."

"And yet your daughter chose to come and live with you?"

Katz looked uncomfortable. Tyrone was pretty sure there had been a contest between the two parents and the daughter was the prize. And yet, Tyrone knew the mess had started long before that.

He remembered Leah sitting beside him at Katz's wedding, bright with mischief, glowing with happiness because she had just decided to leave law and devote herself to painting full time.

"It won't last," Leah whispered to him while the bride and groom were firmly exchanging non-denominational wedding vows with their seven-year-old out-of-wedlock daughter acting as flower girl and ring bearer. She looked normal then, like any other little girl. No wonder he hadn't recognized her at the casino.

"How long?" he whispered to Leah. "A day? A month? You've got to have a better prediction than that."

"Day? Month?" she scoffed. "Wrong focus."

"What's the right one then?"

"They're both too ambitious."

"Ambitious? That's a reason? They have a child."

"Think about it, Tyrone." Leah often called him by his last name. "Think about it," she said. "When you both burn with ambition what gets lost?"

"Okay, what?"

"Compromise," Leah said just before the people in front turned around and shushed them.

"Sidney," Tyrone happily took what he considered a golden opportunity to lecture his former student. "Let me point something out. Your daughter says her mother was too strict, made all these rules and then left her alone. She also says you don't give a damn, and I quote, 'there are no fucking rules,' and *you* leave her alone. In spite of her youth I think she has understood something fundamental. Is anything being made clear to you in this picture?"

"What am I supposed to do?" Katz said. "Her mother was unwilling to stay home at night."

Amazed, the former professor waited. It appeared Katz, the student who argued every side of the equation and even found unexplored territory, had come to the end of his argument. A point of view which would have had him strung and quartered by every current female practicing law. Tyrone raised his finger to give him a lecture and then thought better of it. Since when had a lecture ever helped the willfully blind?

"You're disappointing me again, Sidney," Tyrone said mildly.

"Just spit it out," Katz said irritably.

"She doesn't want somebody else taking care of her child at night. She wants family. She wants you."

"She'd go out every night if it were up to her. I've tried everything. Just what the hell do you expect me to do?" Katz ran a hand through what was left of his hair.

"Compromise," Tyrone said, feeling regret and shame.

"Compromise?" Katz looked startled.

"That was an answer, Sidney," the former professor said, almost feeling virtuous, almost feeling as if he were once again in front of his class. "Not a question."

[33] Brilliant Plan

Tyrone called Audrey from Sid Katz's kitchen. At first, possibly mistaking him for someone else, she appeared bad tempered, as if she had no memory of their brief exchange and subsequent understanding in her own kitchen after he spoke with Katz. Then the former professor found his stride or else she exhibited one of her incomprehensible mood reversals. He asked her a few questions and they had a long conversation about dogs, timing and her spare bedroom. While she dictated, he made a list on the back of a napkin and hung up sweating, feeling like he'd been walking on eggshells.

In an initial spirit of compromise, he and Sidney traded vehicles for a time unspecified, Tyrone's Harley Street Glide for Sidney's black BMW. Sidney, who used to ride motorcycles to law school in his earlier, more adventurous days, studied the bike with what appeared to be his first show of excitement.

"Don't forget what we talked about," Tyrone admonished Sidney just before leaving his house.

Sidney gave him a look that suggested he was having second thoughts, which was not reassuring. Tyrone reflected on how much life dulled bright and brash young students over a ten-year period.

"What happened to you, Sid?" he asked, before thinking it through. "If I remember correctly you never used to be so cautious."

Dressed in his tailor-made suit, leather shoes, Egyptian cotton shirt and silk tie — successful lawyer garb if there ever was such a thing — Sidney continued to stare at him as if he were contemplating some strange witness in court.

Once he was behind the wheel of Sid's car, Tyrone sank into the soft leather and kept switching radio channels, trying to find some music he could at least recognize. After a few go-rounds, however, he stopped, not wishing to wake the little girl strapped into the child seat in the rear on the passenger side. Wrapped in a warm blanket and wearing pink fuzzy pajamas with feet, Caledonia at first whined in a tinny little voice and hiccupped as Sidney was strapping her in. Then she settled, treating the car seat with the familiarity of a second bedroom. Corkscrew curls squashed flat on one side, she was sound asleep, thumb in mouth. Her favorite toy, Alley Cats, a homemade stuffed cat in striped pajamas, had fallen from her hand. Next to the mangled cat was a duffel bag full of bottles and clothes and on the front passenger seat, beside Tyrone, was a super economy-size box of diapers for toddlers.

Tyrone was astounded when he first saw it.

"How many of these do we need?" he said.

"Healthy kid," Sidney answered. "You will take good care of her, that's a promise?" he said.

"You've talked to the woman yourself. She's just up the road from me," Tyrone said, thinking it was a little late for Katz to have second thoughts especially after he'd jumped at the solution so eagerly.

Back on the highway, Henryk rode in front of Tyrone. Trying to make good time they sped into the night.

Soft snow was tumbling, circling and drifting as they approached Audrey's driveway. The front door flew open and Audrey hurried outside without a jacket, followed more slowly by Wills. The man looked confused. He peered over at Tyrone with a raised eyebrow.

"Let me." Tyrone got out of the car as Audrey tried to push past him to the rear seat.

He was unsure how seriously to take Sid's pronouncements about the necessity for a child's slow introduction to strangers. Still, with Sid's words in mind, he blocked Audrey's approach and fumbled till he managed to unhook the car seat himself. Breathing from the exertion, trailing straps and snaps, he staggered into the house with the whole damn thing, including the sleeping child. Audrey and Wills crowded him from behind with the rest of the small-child paraphernalia from the car.

At this point, in keeping with his usual abrupt departures, Henryk took off with a wave and an irritating rev of the bike engine. He disappeared into the country darkness before Tyrone had a chance to react.

Hanging on to the car seat complete with child, Tyrone examined the house suspiciously from the entranceway as if he were a health inspector. Other than a faint whiff of dog, it smelled fairly fresh. He fixed his eyes on Audrey by the hall light as she came in after him. As far as he could ascertain, she was clean with no visible plume of dog hairs, even though she was back to wearing the voluminous purple top.

In her familiar car seat bed, Caledonia slept on, her tiny bow mouth restless for a moment under her small thumb.

"Ahh," Audrey said, trying to wrestle the car seat from Tyrone.

"Wait a minute," he said.

"If you'll let go, I can put her to bed," she said impatiently. "She'll be fine, I promise."

"You're sure?" he asked, wanting to maintain control.

"Of course," she said. "Now go on. You can go home now. Everything will be fine."

He could see she was trying to mask her annoyance, even though she flashed him one of her toothy smiles.

"You're sure you know everything?" he said. "Maybe I should stay here for a while, just in case she wakes up."

"What for?" She eyed him. "Are you familiar with grandchildren? Children, even?"

"That's not it," he said stubbornly.

"Then what?"

"I feel —" he groped for unaccustomed words "— responsible. And then there's the dogs."

"What's wrong with the dogs? They're in a separate part away from here, so there's no problem."

To his surprise, Audrey was not treating his worries as an excuse to feel insulted. She must really want the child. "Responsible for taking her away," he said.

"Ah," she said sternly. "Is this all above board?"

"Her grandfather knows," he said quickly. "I told you. That's his car. But —"

"But? You said she needed short-term care. Fine. Now tell me about her mother?"

"She's young," he muttered.

"Son of a gun," Audrey brightened. "The young girl in the tea leaves. What haven't you told me?"

The former professor pointed at Caledonia. "The mother's having a hard time coping."

"And taking away her child will teach her to cope, you think?"

"No," he admitted. "The grandfather thinks it's best this way for a while. What would you suggest?"

"Now is a fine time to ask me," she said. "Wills! Where is that man? He always disappears when he thinks it's getting tough. Wills?"

There was the sound of slow footsteps coming down the stairs.

"There you are," Audrey said accusingly. "Will you take her upstairs? I need to have a talk here."

"Yes, ma'am," Wills said slowly. He was wearing a T-shirt and old baggy jeans and looked like he had just been shaving. There was a towel around his neck. His eyes were narrowed.

"Oh, come on," Audrey said more softly. "It's only a little kid. No need to be afraid. Think of it as a baby calf or something."

He sighed and took the car seat easily, showing surprising strength for such a scrawny looking man. The passenger in the car seat opened her eyes suddenly. "There now," he muttered. "Go back to sleep, doll, will you do that?"

The doll glared at him suspiciously, opened her mouth in a huge yawn and closed her eyes again, a deep frown on her face.

"All animals adore him," Audrey said without irony. "It's just me who sometimes has a hard time."

Wills looked over at Tyrone as if expecting more answers. Tyrone surmised that perhaps Wills was planning on interrogating Sheba for a better understanding.

"Now," Audrey said to Tyrone as Wills climbed up the stairs with car seat and passenger. "You'd better tell me what you've got us into, because I'm telling you now, I'll have something to say if I don't like it."

[34] Alley Cats

Two days later Tyrone was in his kitchen nook at the computer, sifting through the various news sites, a cup of instant coffee by his right hand. His nearly new coffee making apparatus was clean and unused. He had decided it needed too much maintenance. Cleaning it was a nuisance and so was feeding it. Instant coffee was a much easier undertaking.

Just as he was taking a last indifferent sip, a car came careening around the back of the farmhouse onto the brown, cold grass in front of the nook. It was a car he thought he recognized. Nevertheless, he got up to check for Sidney's BMW car keys on the kitchen counter. They were still there. This was some other car. He glanced at his watch and surmised it had taken Sidney less than two days to cave in and part with Tyrone's address. The man was unreliable when it came to personal matters.

Sid Katz's daughter, complete with black lips and spiked hair, came bounding out of the car and pounded on the French doors of the kitchen while peering in. His instinct was to get away as quickly as possible.

301

She saw him through the wide glass panels as he was attempting to back out of sight.

"You'd better let me in, you asshole!" she yelled. "You had no right! My father's a scuzz. I'm going to break in if you don't open up."

He waited, frozen, until he saw her searching the ground for something to carry out her threat.

Hurrying forward, he unlatched the door.

"Come in, Alison," he tried to say in a mild tone. "What took you so long?"

"Not Alison, especially not to you," she said furiously. "Where is she?"

"This is quite a change."

She marched through the kitchen towards the living room. He followed her.

"You think I'm just some stupid kid, don't you? You think you can just, like, do what you want?"

"No."

"Well then why'd you do it?"

"Think back for a moment to the first time I met you. You wanted to be rid of her."

Suddenly she was crying, wracked in a way he never expected. "That, that's … not…not … true. Why? You can't … you and my fucking father can't just … can't. Callie? CALLIE? Where are you? I'm here. Mummy's here."

The house was silent.

"Alison," he said.

She pointed a long black fingernail. "Don't you ever call me that!" she screamed. "Where is she?"

"What should I call you then?" he asked desperately, wanting to calm her down.

"Cats," she said venomously, mascara streaking her cheeks. "And I will scratch your eyes out if you don't tell me where she is."

"Katz?" he said. "Just your last name?"

"No, stupid. Cats. The ones with the claws. Callie? Callie? What the hell have you done with her?"

Small as she was, she rushed towards him with her nails. Holding her claws in a one-handed grip and trying to stay out of reach of the laced killer boots was all he could manage.

He struggled to get her outside, cursing her strength and too aware of the position he was in should she choose to accuse him of anything more disturbing.

"Help!" he yelled to the sky, the trees, the fields, the wild bees and anyone else who might listen once he wrestled and slid and prodded her outside. "Help! Help!"

[35] Fighting Girl

Her mouth open, ready to claw and fight to the end, Cats stopped when she heard Tyrone's ridiculous cries for help, eyeing him in astonishment.

"Just what the fuck are you doing?" she asked.

"I need help."

"Are you nuts?"

"No, I am not nuts. Will you listen to me if I let you go?"

"Yeah. Maybe."

"Which is it?"

"Okay, okay."

Suspicious, he tightened his grip. "That means you won't kick or bite or claw or scream?"

"I can scream any time in case you haven't noticed."

He regarded her thoughtfully. "I think you are a very smart young woman," he said, letting her go. "I wanted to help."

She rubbed her wrists. "By kidnapping my kid?"

"You know very well that's not, well, I guess it could appear that way but … but you are probably aware your father is the legal guardian of your child."

"Legal guardian? What the fuck? What's that got to do with this?"

"He can decide on a caregiver, among other things, and that's just what he did."

Tyrone was conflicted about giving her the full implications of Sidney's guardianship and about his little lie. He didn't want to trigger another scene, this time over something he had no hand in engineering.

"You only said you'd babysit till my dad came home. I trusted you!" Her face was shifting again.

"Wait," he said quickly. "Just hear me out. Will you do that?"

"Just tell me where she is."

"I promise. But your parents are in a mess."

"So?"

"They were such promising students. It just goes to show."

"That's a stupid thing to say."

"No. No. Really. It just goes to show being smart doesn't always mean you're right. I want to help you. I mean it."

He didn't know where that intention came from, only that it sneaked up on him. It seemed ironic to think he wanted to help others when he hadn't been able to help himself. He wondered what someone else might make of his crusades and the habit he appeared to have developed of jumping right in with both feet. The idea was not as horrifying as it might have been in the past as long as it diverted him from thinking about Leah and Spenser.

Not privy to his thoughts, Cats moved restlessly. "Will you fucking just tell me what I want to know? I know all about you."

A momentary impulse to comment philosophically on her statement overtook him, something like, how can any of us know each other truly? But he could tell she would not take this kindly so he opted for something direct. "And what exactly does that mean?"

"You were a drunk, that's what. That thing Russ said about you being a legend? You got kicked out for being a drunk and kicking ass. So don't tell me about being smart or ... or any other shit like that. Trying to preach about casinos and stuff and then taking my kid. You think you're so *smart*?"

"Maybe you can be smarter," he said quietly.

"Where is she?"

"Come," he said, "let's walk this way and I'll tell you."

"Fuck that. Tell me now or I'm not going nowhere."

Tempted to correct her double negative but resisting the impulse, he said, "we're already walking towards her."

[36] The Trouble with Callie

With difficulty, he managed to convince her he was telling the truth. She followed him, looking at once sullen and apprehensive. When they finally made it to the neighboring farm, Audrey answered the door with Callie trailing after her.

Cats rushed forward. "Come here, baby," she said.

"Mummy," the little girl whispered, pointing to the bedraggled cat she was dragging on the floor. "Mr. Cats sleeping, don't wake him, please."

The young mother dropped to her knees. "Did you miss me?" she asked.

"You went away." The little girl's mouth twisted in a hard pout. She reached out a hand and hit Cats on the leg.

Audrey moved her large frame quickly towards them, looking Cats straight in the eyes without seeming to notice her in-your-face outfit. At the same time, she reached out to touch Callie, moving her hand gently over her curls. "Remember, sweetie, no hitting," she said. "How do we tell people we're mad?"

Callie just shook her head. Cats began humming a tune and taking dancing steps around the floor, until the little girl joined her. Together, faster and faster, they danced down the hall, laughing nonstop.

"I'm sorry I couldn't call," Tyrone said sheepishly over the commotion.

"It's okay," Audrey said, moving her eyes expressively in the direction of the dancing enthusiasts. "Someone else called."

"Oh."

"Were you ever planning to get a phone?" Audrey said.

The two girls were chasing each other. Cats's shrieks were louder than Callie's.

"Okay," Cats puffed, projecting herself in front of Audrey. "We're ready to go."

"Certainly," Audrey said immediately. "I'll get her things."

Tyrone opened his mouth, but Audrey, looking sideways, gave him such a fierce glance that he shut it again.

"Come upstairs for a sec, hon," Audrey said to Cats, putting a hand on her shoulder. "This must be so hard for you, you poor soul."

"Well," Cats said, in a belligerent manner.

"And you came here all by yourself," Audrey continued, not paying attention to Cats's tone of voice. "And these men, thinking they know better than you. What a good mother you are. It must be very tough, at your age, to have to do all these things by yourself and everyone criticizing. In my books, you are very brave and I admire you."

This was too much for Tyrone, who opened his mouth once more. He was stopped, not because he was checking his impulse but by two extraordinary things. Callie, sucking her thumb and watching the proceedings, came over to slip her tiny hand into his as Cats put her head down, apparently crying. And Audrey, Audrey with the gimlet eye, gathered Cats up in her substantial arms and patted her back, murmuring, "There, there, dear. It's okay. I understand. Cry all you want, you're safe here."

But that wasn't the most extraordinary thing. The most extraordinary thing was that Cats, sobbing, put her arms around Audrey's soft neck and was holding on tight.

"Mummy crying," the urchin, imaginatively named for a region in Ontario or a Cape Breton song or a group of islands in the South Pacific or even for nothing at all, said with great interest.

"Yes, I believe she is," Tyrone replied, unable to determine whether the tears should make him feel relieved or wary.

In the meantime, Callie let go of Tyrone and ran over to her distraught mother. "Don't cry, Mummy," she said.

When no one paid attention, she raised an angry hand and slapped Cats's backside. "Don't cry, I said," the little girl yelled.

"Oh, my," Audrey peered down over Cats's shoulder at Callie. "We've got our work cut out for us, don't we?"

[37] Onwards, But Where?

Surveying a cold rainstorm swirling over the ground outside from his kitchen nook, Tyrone kept putting off calling Sid or returning Sid's car. It would be good for Sid to remember the freedom of his old motorcycle days for a while longer. Those were the days when Sid was more concerned about getting into Melissa's pants than in one-upping her.

In truth, the thought of being forced to ride a motorbike in foul weather while blinded by freezing rain or pelting hailstones or suffering irreversible frostbite in every extremity kept Tyrone firmly attached to the BMW parked in his driveway under the bare oak. He kept the car and got in the habit of locking his front door, walking down his drive and then heading north along the paved side road to Audrey's place. Months ago, he would never have believed such a thing was possible. The fact that she agreed to take care of a headstrong child who hit, bit or stomped to get people's attention was an important consideration.

"What's up?" Audrey said, carefully pouring tea into her delicate cups.

Callie was busy at her feet alternately playing with Mr. Cats and hitting him. "No, darling," Audrey said patiently. "Just tell him you're mad at him. No biting now. That's right, sweetheart, say you are very, very, very mad. Now what does he say?"

Callie whispered something Tyrone didn't hear because he was just crunching into one of the chocolate biscotti Audrey had arranged on a plate in front of him. Having painstakingly retraced the drive he and Rafe first took, he found the store selling homemade Italian goodies and belatedly brought a glass jar of biscotti as a gift for Audrey. Once there, he was reminded that the Italian husband-and-wife team who owned the store also made frozen, ready-to-heat chicken and eggplant parmigiana, lasagnas and various linguini, manicotti, and spaghetti dishes. These meals were now all heaped in his freezer beside six cartons of frozen Four Cheese Pizza Deluxe.

"That's right, darling," Audrey was saying complacently. "Now you tell Mr. Cats you forgive him and he can be your friend."

Duty completed for the next nanosecond, Audrey cautiously took another sip from the flowered cup. "So?" she said, turning towards Tyrone. "What are you going to do about Henryk?"

"Never mind Henryk," he said irritably. "I haven't spoken to him for a while. What are you going to do about Sidney Katz?"

"Oh, that's all taken care of, didn't I tell you? He's all for it. The arrangement. He was so happy he offered to pay even more. I said, no, this isn't for the money. Do you know why she calls herself Cats?"

"Ask another one," he grumbled.

314

"Not what you're thinking, definitely not. She asked me what kind of parents would name their kid Alison, a.k.a. Ali, when their last name was Katz? I said, I didn't know, maybe she could tell me. She said, stupid parents, that's who. I said maybe they were busy. She said they were busy being stupid." Audrey's wrinkled face broke into a smile. "I can't help it, I like that girl."

Audrey, whose own daughter was pursuing an important career as a forensic accountant, had no troublesome grandchildren of her own. Cats, in her current Goth incarnation, could either see or pick Callie up on weekends and Sid no longer had to duck his daughter's rages, at least not the ones having to do with Callie. Sid was grudgingly thankful, Audrey had a ready-made grandchild, and Cats was happy enough for the moment and agreed to go back to school. Tyrone wondered how long it would last.

"Maybe she'll study to be a lawyer just so she can outsmart her parents," he said.

"Hmmm." Audrey poured more tea. "Now what about Henryk?"

Tyrone could have sworn he hadn't told her much about the dilemma faced by Henryk, Tess and Rafe. Every time she talked about them he wondered where she got so much information. She was capable of weaving a whole story out of the thinnest threads.

"So, what's on your mind?" she asked, with what he was beginning to think of as one of her deliberately sympathetic yet nonchalant looks.

He was by then very familiar with those looks. She must have perfected them over many cups of tea and tea leaf readings. They belied the fluid curiosity in her sharp eyes.

315

He often tried to stifle the impulse to say what he was really thinking.

"You're very nosy," he said.

She let out a loud laugh, startling the child at her feet. "No, sweetheart," she caught Callie's hand. "No hitting. Give me a hug now, okay? That's my girl."

"Dogs and children," Tyrone said. "You have the gift." He wondered if he was sounding sanctimonious and if she would pick up on it.

"Comes from a long line of farmers and carny folk all mixed together," she said complacently.

"You can't help being nosy, then."

"Think of it more as human curiosity. Ask Wills if that man ever stops helping his sister and comes home."

"Very well. I think your human curiosity is mixed with a sharp observation."

"Hmmm," she said, scooping up Callie in a flamboyantly large gesture and holding her to her ample chest.

The child shrieked with laughter at a pitch that made Tyrone want to hold his ears.

He sat back in his chair and looked around him. There was a sense of warmth and safety in Audrey's kitchen, a place he now realized he came back to as much for Audrey's sharp company as for the unexpected feeling of home. He didn't quite know what made it seem like home. It certainly wasn't her cooking. Rafe had her beat in that department. She was more likely to boil some hot dogs than to make a pasta dish and serve bread dipped in herbed olive oil. Whatever it was she did or was, she made it easy to keep coming back. Maybe it was because, in spite of her firm opinions and uncertain temper, she asked for nothing.

Contrary to his first encounter with her, her generosity in lending Sheba to him was a case in point. The woman was a paradox. Her delicate china tea cups so at odds with her large presence. No matter how annoying she might appear, he enjoyed her acerbic opinions and down-to-earth observations. When she had something to say it was never dull and she often made him laugh. It always surprised him. A friendship like this was not something he would have cultivated in his other life.

Caledonia was suddenly fast asleep, her head resting on Audrey's purple shoulder. Audrey for once was completely silent. She rocked Caledonia absentmindedly, looking supremely content. He thought, it was because of him and his meddling that a little girl and a woman who needed her ended up together.

"Do you think I meddle?" he asked.

Audrey stared at him. "*Now* what are you going to start worrying about next?"

"I don't worry," he said.

"Henryk *this* and Tess *that* and Rafe *here* and Juan Carlos *there* and the widow and her brat up in the air and it's up to me to fix *everything* or worry about it till I drive myself crazy. And then of course there's the lawyer and his daughter, who I'm not really sure I approve of because she looks like a Hell's Angel warmed over and the crazy lady with the dogs next door who I have to keep coming to check up on. And those dogs, those dogs — don't worry, I know exactly what you think of the dogs — does that mean she can handle *kids*? I really think I need more *proof*, a better case study, so to speak. And oh, pardon me, did I say I drive myself crazy? No. No. I drive everyone around me crazy. Now does that address your concern?"

"No need to exaggerate," he said stiffly.

"Oh, pardon me. Did I say I drive everyone around me crazy? Well, better them than me. Well, at least the dogs got used to me."

She was laughing at him, large shoulders shaking in her purple sweater. Callie, head sideways, mouth open, clutching a handful of Audrey's pilled sweater in her little fist, remained dead to the world. "Now," Audrey said. "Seriously. What are we going to do with the loose cannonballs?"

"You said *we*? They're not your problem."

"No? As long as I have to keep listening while I feed you cups of tea, I might as well put in my druthers."

"That's an expression I haven't heard in a long time."

"It was my mama's. Get used to it."

"Why would you want to get involved? None of it is your problem. I feel maybe it's been an imposition. Everything." He had been gazing at the sink as he spoke, unwilling to look at her directly. "Even the kid there — do you want me to try and find someone else?"

The kitchen tap was softly dripping in a small, precise rhythm. The silence prolonged itself and she said nothing. When he met her eyes, he saw she was angry. Her jaw stuck out.

"Don't you dare," she said. "Don't you even think about it."

"What are you talking about?"

"Don't you even think of taking this little girl away from me."

A mother bear could not have been clearer. The light, when it hit him, might well have blinded him if it was physical instead of mental.

"Your daughter," he said.

"We're estranged," Audrey said, looking down at Callie's head of baby hair on her shoulder, her shrewd eyes quickly hiding whatever she wanted to keep to herself. He saw a stray tear making its way down her worn cheek. She made an awkward attempt to brush it away but it was replaced by another. "I had a grandchild."

"And your daughter won't let you see her?"

"No," she said. "Worse than that. I used to take care of her. And then we had a … a disagreement and my daughter decided she wanted someone else to take care of her. A neighbor who lived down the street. That was in town. There was a fire and — I can't talk about it. Let's just say there was a fire and my Lilibet died. We sat all night at the hospital and she died and I blamed my daughter and we haven't spoken since. I didn't speak to her, and now she won't speak to me, so I've given up. It's too painful to keep trying. And I don't want to talk about it anymore."

Tyrone, who had gotten a taste of Audrey's temper, could almost see and hear the direct accusations she might have made. Then he had another thought. What would happen when Audrey was obliged to let the child go? What would she do when they told her Callie was no longer coming?

"Stop right there and don't be looking at me that way with second thoughts. I will be very good for this little girl," she said.

He nodded his head and they sipped tea in silence until his cup was empty. Cradling Callie with one arm, Audrey got up to turn the kettle on to boil more water.

"I think you should call Henryk," she said, her tone of voice normal over the sound of the kettle.

"What for?"

"Maybe you can act as a mediator. Maybe you can counsel them or something. Who knows? You're the one with the law degree."

He thought for a moment. Obviously, Audrey didn't want any counseling herself but was willing to offer it to him and anyone else willing to listen.

"Why are you so interested?" he asked.

"I'm just giving you a little push."

"I don't need a push to call Henryk."

"And what about the gambler and the widow?"

"One thing at a time," he cut in, still troubled by what she revealed about the death of her granddaughter.

She moved her chin towards the kitchen counter. "Alrighty then, there's the phone."

[38] Dark and Light

For the first time in their short but intense association, Tyrone drove over to Henryk's place. Although this was his first visit, he'd formed a vivid impression of it based on Tess's description. As he settled back in Sid's leather seats, sipping a cup of coffee that fit nicely in Sid's cup holder, the forgotten pleasures of a comfortable drive were foremost on his mind.

The dark car gleamed from a recent wash which Tyrone supervised closely. First, scrutinizing how carefully the automatic mops, jets and hot waxes were applied as he sat inside the car, and then watching the attendants as they finished the job. The attendants pretended to ignore him or stared back at him with exaggerated patience. In his opinion, it was sometimes good to make people feel they were being watched. His students had always handed in better assignments when he focused on them and made them aware of what he expected. The difference between law students and car wash personnel was only a matter of degree, based on chance. He saw no reason not to use the same principles.

As the skies thickened and darkened, so went his thoughts. In the comfort of the warm and sheltered car he imagined if he were riding the motorcycle he would be freezing his butt off. And then, if he ever got farther south, maybe closer to Mexico, there would be the wind and the bugs splattering on his visor. He was no better than Sidney Katz, taking the easy route and giving up the excitement that came with uncertainty and a more adventurous, if uncomfortable, existence.

By the time he got to Henryk's place, following Henryk's haphazard directions and consulting a Perly's map, he was in a gloomy frame of mind.

Henryk met him at the door in old jeans, his pale hair in a knot at the back of his head, his hands stained and greasy. He held up his hands and moved his head, inviting Tyrone into the house. Tess had been uncannily accurate about the volume of motorcycles and parts lying about. Not counting the four she said were in the garage, Tyrone spotted what could have been three outside, discreetly tucked and covered behind a bare hedge, and three or possibly four more in the cluttered living room resting on drop sheets in chunky parts.

Other than motorcycles, the biker appeared to have a penchant for Old World furniture, dark brown and serviceable. Furniture to be sat in with little worry of stains or scuff or grease marks from the motorcycle debris. His kitchen was surprisingly clean and bright. The man who was into motorcycles was also into cleaning up when it came to food.

"Tea or coffee?" Henryk asked graciously, washing his hands with dish soap at the spotless kitchen sink.

They drank dark-roasted coffee poured from the pot and munched on some sort of crispy Polish treats Henryk said his neighbor made for him. Tyrone tried to figure out how to say what he wanted to say. A direct strike did not seem wise and might not meet with an open reception. The Polish treats were dusted with powdered sugar that had an annoying habit of coating everything, plate, fingers, mouth and clothes, which made it difficult to talk with dignity.

"It's about Tess," Tyrone said, trying to wipe the sugar off his lips discreetly and then lick it off his fingers. "You've got to let her go."

"Ah-ha!" Henryk almost shouted, waving his cup around to the point where Tyrone thought the coffee, following the physics of centrifugal force, would fly in an arc around the kitchen.

"That's it?" Tyrone said. "That's all you're going to say?"

"I am damn sure you have suggestions," Henryk said. "Go ahead, please, I am listening."

Tyrone knew he was in dangerous territory. In previous times, he might have been more polished, more evasive. Now he understood from his motorcycle lessons that when there was only one direction in which you were heading too fast, it meant there was nowhere else to go.

"It's about this business with her and Rafe," Tyrone said.

"Very true," Henryk said.

"And you," Tyrone said, at a loss. "Rafe and you."

"Of course. Please continue."

"It can't go on."

Henryk nodded encouragingly. "Of course not."

Tyrone narrowed his eyes. "You're doing this on purpose, aren't you?"

"What are you talking about, my friend?"

Tyrone forced himself to sit back. "Fine. We are both in the dark."

"Some more than others," Henryk said. "I will tell you what. We will help each other."

"And what exactly will you do about Tess?"

"I never had her, you must remember. But in your view, I will let her go, of course."

"You knew all along about this?"

"My friend, you are a very determined man, I have seen, except you do not have a telephone, so you are always behind when it comes to important problems."

"You've talked to her already, haven't you? Have you made her see she needs to move on?"

"You think it is so easy? You remember what I told you? She is her own person."

"What the hell does that have to do with it?"

"She is not someone I can tell what to do. No matter what you think."

"It's not what I think, it's what you need to do!"

All of a sudden Tyrone was distracted. The faint illusive thoughts that had kept nagging at the back of his mind hit him with astonishing clarity. Of course! How could he have missed it? His country sojourn was making him far too dull.

"Not Poland — Russia — that's what this is about," he blurted out. "Your family. They're in Russia. You left, they didn't want to follow. And now —"

But Henryk, whatever he felt, was not to be lured into talking about his personal life. He went on as if Tyrone hadn't spoken. "Remember the laws of backing up? To go one way, you have to do opposite."

"Please don't tell me you suddenly joined a Buddhist order. You're putting me on."

"No, my friend, I am very serious." Henryk regarded him with a poker face. "But first I will need you to do this other thing for me."

"Thing? What thing?" Tyrone asked suspiciously.

"Not complicated," Henryk said. "For you will be easy. Here is my plan."

[39] Suitable Man

Tyrone shaved carefully in front of the bathroom mirror knowing exactly what was needed to impress. It meant a visit to the Rose Room closet, where garment bags filled with designer suits were hanging like mournful black shrouds. Ever since he started keeping the door open, the room no longer smelled musty and he hoped the clean air had also managed to freshen the clothes. Shoehorning himself into the closet, he wrested out the necessary suit, shirt and tie.

Passing the full-length mirror at the end of the hall, he decided he resembled some underworld element with hollow eyes trying too hard to look respectable. The wild hair that hadn't seen the inside of a barber shop for a few months didn't help.

Once outside, he slipped on the treacherous ground in his thin-soled leather shoes. He wasn't sure whether the current mission warranted their ruin. On the other hand, if they were going to get old while they sat around doing nothing, he might as well speed up the process and introduce them to rain, ice and salt.

He buttoned up his cashmere topcoat before getting into Katz's Mercedes, which was spattered with salt, mud and dirty ice after a remarkably short time on Highway 401.

At the Milton police station, he circled the block three times arguing with himself. What was he thinking? This was not a Toronto police station located next to City Hall, where lawyers needed to wear fancy suits, arrive with expensive overstuffed briefcases and keep stressing their busy schedule to anyone within hearing distance. This was a station with arguably a different view on things. He stepped on the accelerator and drove away.

He fumbled around in the pockets of his unfamiliar clothing searching for spare change once he was in the phone booth. Finding none he tromped into the variety store on his cold, leather-clad feet and borrowed some. For once, rather than an amused remark about being back at his phone booth office, the only reaction he got from the owner was a silent raised eyebrow as he handed him four quarters from the till.

Back home, Tyrone stared at himself in the hall mirror. He didn't think he was ever going to dress this way again. There might never be any need to do so. He felt emotional when he put away his suit, tie, shirt and shoes and pulled on jeans and boots. There was no point trying to impress the Milton police with his fancy suits and cashmere coat so close to Brian Resnick's old haunts. They could smell bullshit faster than he could dish it out. His Hudson's Bay jacket, jeans and motorcycle boots would be good enough. Once he loaned the bike to Sid Katz, he wondered if the boots were unnecessary, but they kept his feet warm and he felt comfortable in them.

An hour later, at a local coffee shop close to the Milton precinct, he spotted a big black man named Des Brown, waiting for him and nursing a cup. The man stared at him with polite wariness. Tyrone knew that gaze from his previous life. Police officers had a universal look about them: friendly enough but taught to assume anyone could turn into a felon at a moment's notice, even wannabe bikers previously dressed in made-to-measure suits and shirts.

"Hello officer, thanks for meeting me," he said, as he stood at the faux-leather banquette.

The detective stared up without blinking.

"I'm here about Detective Sergeant Resnick's widow," Tyrone said more brusquely, beckoning the waitress over for a coffee and almost losing his balance as he tried to sit down on the unexpectedly low and soft bench seat opposite Brown. He struggled to keep himself from falling sideways. "You may be aware of the problems."

"And what problems would those be, sir?" Staff Sergeant Brown asked blandly. Tyrone wondered if the sudden gleam in his eyes was amusement or judgment.

"An injustice that Detective Resnick was hoping to put right."

"Important words. You are no doubt the lawyer?"

"Ah," Tyrone said, surprised.

"What are you after?" Brown asked.

"Peace of mind for the widow."

Brown stared at him and then settled back with his coffee. "Please explain."

"I know about the second trial that started it all," Tyrone said. "I was there by chance."

Brown blinked.

"I know how hard Detective Resnick took it when the Supreme Court upheld the verdict of innocence."

Brown said nothing. Tyrone wondered if that was the way he got suspects to talk. Drive them crazy with silence.

"Afterwards, I understand there was some sort of loose surveillance of the man, the former accused, that is," Tyrone said. "Because Detective Resnick requested it. A favor."

Brown sighed.

"Apparently, the surveillance was called off," Tyrone continued.

"You are informed to a point," Brown said.

"I wish I knew more."

Brown continued to regard him in a wary, direct way, without smiling.

"I'm here because the widow has seen the accused around her place. Once he apparently went to the boy's school and talked to him. Gave him a message to say hello to the mother," Tyrone said. And then he wondered if he had gone too far. The truth was he had some recollection of what the widow said, but no specific recollection she ever said this. He blamed it on Henryk for putting him on the spot without being able to talk to Karen Resnick again before this charade.

"Ah," Brown said, rubbing his forehead with a large black hand. His nails were clean and lighter around the edges.

"I want to help," Tyrone said. "But I don't want to interfere in case you have plans."

"We have a stalemate," Brown said. "We were doing it as a follow-up and we don't have the manpower. This is not something that would go over well in court. We need proof and there is none. Zilch. Nada."

"What if I get you proof?" Tyrone said.

"What kind of proof?" Brown said suspiciously, looking at Tyrone almost as if he were still wearing his made-to-measure suit and hand-dyed silk tie. A man who never left an office or knew where the real truth lay.

"I can look into it discreetly," Tyrone smiled, glad for his jeans and jacket.

Brown snorted. "Better make sure it's good," he said.

"I will, Staff Sergeant," Tyrone said. "If you help me with this thing, tell me a few facts, maybe we can both get what we want."

"Don't know about that," Brown said. "We're just hoping to tread water and keep our heads up. If you were to ask me, keeping our heads up means we're ahead."

[40] Almost the Kelly Gang

Tyrone was in Henryk's kitchen drinking tea, pondering Henryk's impassioned, and sometimes hilarious, views on what needed to be done to keep Karen Resnick happy, which would keep Juan Carlos happy, and which in turn, most important of all, would keep Tess happy.

Outside, the sky was covered in pale clouds and the wind had picked up, which would have made for unpleasant riding. Thank God he drove there in Katz's BMW.

For some reason which involved another long explanation, possibly something to do with Tess, Henryk claimed to only drink coffee in the mornings before noon and tea afterwards. The white refrigerator purred in the corner. The spotless sink and white cabinets gleamed. Initially, the former professor was afraid to walk across the tile floor to the bathroom in case he left footprints but Henryk, who kept glancing out the window every few minutes, seemed too preoccupied to notice.

"We have an address," Tyrone said.

"We will find him," Henryk said.

"You should have told me sooner. There's just the two of us?"

Henryk took a sip of tea. "You were incommunicado," he said. "Did you not once mention you have a cellular?"

"What does this have to do with my cell phone?"

"Think of what you have accomplished in business suit in such short time," Henryk said, his eyes drifting once more to the window behind Tyrone's left shoulder.

The former professor opened his mouth to boast that he had accomplished it in boots, jeans and a Hudson's Bay jacket. Before he had a chance, a great clatter, as if from hundreds of pistons intending to hurl themselves from the prison of their engines, could be heard full force through the windows behind him.

Henryk leaped out of his seat and headed for the kitchen door while Tyrone followed.

Three black forms came revving up to Henryk's back yard in full leather gear. With their helmets off, they were tough old-timers, greeting Henryk and recounting their adventures simultaneously. Tyrone had no idea from where they had materialized or how far they had ridden.

"BJ here," one of them said, a man with a trimmed head of white hair and possibly the neatest appearance, "rode his usual mile ahead and got stopped by one of your finest, a kid with a radar gun. When we caught up BJ here was explaining the virtues of a dual sports bike, an old dual sport, mind, and the kid let him off with a warning."

BJ wore a shy self-deprecating smile. He was bald with the tough appearance of a man who'd been recycled a few times.

"Beer?" Henryk asked hopefully, appearing to remember his manners.

"Don't mind if I do," the third man, the quietest of the three, said.

In addition to beer, coffee was now apparently on the menu even though it was past noon. Out of their leathers, they were men of varying presence and weight but of the same loudness. The well-groomed man, with trimmed white hair and Vandyke beard, was broad and tall. He held out his hand, introducing himself as Ed.

Henryk stopped rummaging through the stuffed innards of the fridge, turning his head. "Count your fingers, he is lawyer," he called out to Tyrone.

"Ah shucks," Ed said. "I was just about to hand over my card."

"What kind of law?" Tyrone asked.

"Accident. Mostly motorcycle accidents."

"There's a living in it?"

Ed laughed. "Invisible riders. Lots of them in the State of New York, it seems. Most people swear there was no bike there while they were making a left turn. It just suddenly appeared out of nowhere. A total fucking marvel."

"Okay," Henryk said. "The meeting will come to order."

Tyrone looked around. "Ah," he said uneasily. "Of course."

They argued strategy, told impossibly exaggerated and funny stories amid raucous laughter and seemed in no hurry to accomplish anything, while the former professor listened. Eventually they were all talking at the same time.

"Do I get a say?" Tyrone broke in using his booming lecture voice. Then he spoke more quietly in the ensuing silence. "What is all this going to accomplish?"

The plans they were formulating amid a growing number of beer bottles and a total unconcern for the rule of law could get them charged — there were no end of infractions the police could throw at them. Except they would be long gone, and he, Tyrone, would be the one facing the consequences and trying to explain himself to Staff Sergeant Des Brown. The fact that Henryk, who already looked like a potential lawbreaker, would be charged with him, was not reassuring. It occurred to him, belatedly, that he might have been let go from the Law Faculty, but they hadn't taken away his law degree and he was not in any hurry to let it go — especially as a result of some half-witted street justice carried out by three rowdy out-of-the-country bikers.

"We will show him what it means if he continues bothering Ms. Resnick," Henryk said.

"In spite of the fact that the police found nothing? He's done nothing so far." Tyrone said.

"That is not her story," Henryk said emphatically.

"You agree with this?" Tyrone said to Ed.

Ed looked down at his hands, non-committal. "Far be it for me to interpret the laws of your country."

The former professor looked around the table which was littered with beer bottles and empty coffee cups. He and Henryk were the only ones not drinking. Three pairs of shrewd eyes were weighing him, he was sure, making judgments about his worth and his resolve.

Henryk watched him carefully for a moment. "Okay. What is it you wish to tell us?" he asked.

Tyrone folded his arms. If it was going to be a game of one-upmanship, he held the winning cards. "I know where he lives."

After another bout of protracted arguing, what almost derailed the final plan was they expected Tyrone to ride pillion behind Ed, who owned the biggest touring bike, so they would all be a united brotherhood. A lone BMW escort did not fit the picture they wanted to stage.

Rather than wasting his breath arguing about yet another flawed idea, Tyrone turned to Henryk. "Didn't you teach me all you know?" he asked.

"Of course," Henryk said, scratching his ear uncomfortably, making Tyrone suspect that in all other circumstances the answer would have been an emphatic no.

"Then you will have to trust me on this from a legal point."

Henryk folded his arms across his chest, ready to argue.

Outside, it started to rain. A late November downpour flooding the roads.

"Besides, look outside," Tyrone said. "I am not getting myself killed just yet for some crazy plan. We can talk about this tomorrow."

Driving home through the downpour, windshield wipers flapping at full speed, he berated himself. He had allowed himself to become as sloppy as some of his former first-year students. A lazy work habit he would never have tolerated in

A. K. Blackman

the past, under the influence or sober. There was no excuse. Staff Sergeant Des Brown had promised him a transcript of all the trial proceedings and he wanted to get it as soon as possible before the bikers' actions got out of his control.

[41] Assumptions

The next morning the sun shone coldly on dry roads and highways. Not wanting another argument about riding pillion, Tyrone called Henryk at 8:30 from the phone booth, arranging to meet at the Milton Junction of Highway 401 in two hours. Henryk's mood seemed much more agreeable, perhaps because he thought Tyrone had fallen into line.

As he waited in the BMW for the ill-assorted gang on a verge just before the turnoff to the highway heading west, there was a sour taste in his mouth. It seemed to him he was spending a lot of time wondering how a great many things were going to end.

They came riding towards him in tandem, spread out on the inner lane. By the time they swerved into a U-turn and lined up behind him, revving their engines, he'd made up his mind.

"This is what we are going to do," he said, when he got out of the car to intercept them.

The house Tyrone drove up to was in a well-tended area of Milton. The sidewalks were clean and bright. The boomerang temperature was a sure sign the weather would remain ambivalent for the foreseeable future.

He knocked.

The man who answered the door was short and trim, dressed in dark jeans and a black sweatshirt and losing a battle with his hair. Twin peaks curved on either side of his high forehead. Not the brute they had all been expecting.

"Yes?" The man peered up at him shortsightedly.

Given the circumstance, Tyrone's plan was simple.

He would go in first, check out the man and the situation and give the signal while the rest of them waited down the road. If he lowered his hand they would back off. If he waved they would ride towards him. If anyone were to ask him it was a ludicrous charade. But even though it sounded juvenile, it was the best he could do to convince them — and especially Henryk — to fall in with his plans.

Having finally read the transcripts of the trial, the appeal, and the Superior Court decision, he had no intention of doing anything stupid. He was here simply to put his mind to rest about what happened and why. Brian Resnick's motivations were already clear to him.

"Paul Desroseau?" Tyrone felt strange coming face-to-face with the man for the first time. Giving him a name made him more human.

"What do you want?"

Tyrone heard the faintest French accent.

"A word?"

340

The Unexpected Journeys Of Lawrence Tyrone

The man glanced harshly at him and then peered up and down the street. "What for?"

"Unfinished business."

"Where are you from?"

Tyrone lowered his hand, turning to see the black crested riders, waiting at the brow of the hill in the hard, early light, revving their engines. He hoped they remembered what his signal meant.

"Ah *tabarnak*," the man said, having seen and heard them as well.

"I am here to talk about Detective Brian Resnick," Tyrone said formally. "I'm a lawyer and we need to get this whole thing settled before it gets out of control again."

"You don't scare me," the man said, pulling himself straight. "I have been through it all. I don't care who you are and I don't care who they are. I am going to shut the door."

Tyrone inserted his boot in the crack as the man pushed. "Listen to me," he said. "As long as the widow is saying you are bothering her, there will be no peace."

"Bothering the widow?" the man said, momentarily letting go. "Who told you that?"

"She did."

"I never bothered her. I felt sorry. I wanted to explain."

"Say what?"

"I was driving by and saw her, wanted to tell her I knew what it's like, watched her kid and made a comment. He was at the same school where my Yves used to go. And the next thing I know the police are everywhere, looking suspicious. Do you think I don't know my rights?"

341

"What did they say?"

"I don't care what they said. The fact is I was innocent, I was found innocent, and I am innocent no matter what you think."

"Well then why are you living around here? Why are you in the same area as Detective Resnick and his family? Why are you bothering his boy?" Tyrone said in frustration.

"Mister whoever you are, with your gang of hoods, is there some law that says I am not allowed to live in the house of my mother?"

This was not the scenario Tyrone had envisioned. The added lack of preparation on his part was not a mistake he would have made a number of years ago. But at the time he had eager students to do all the legwork. Now his back-up were grizzled bikers whose specialty was certainly not research into Canadian legal matters, court procedures, or unearthing suspects' backgrounds. Why this information was not in Des Brown's police file he wasn't sure. Of course everybody, himself included, was so intent on their own agendas he hadn't thought to ask the essential questions. The man had not followed Brian Resnick. Resnick followed Desroseau. No wonder Resnick's bungalow was so sparse. It must have been a recent acquisition.

"And for your information, I was not bothering her kid," Paul Desroseau repeated angrily. "I felt sorry for him. How he was. He was so high-strung I was trying to talk him down. That used to be my Yves too, only Yves was worse."

Tyrone took a deep breath and turned to face his clueless backup team, sliding a hand across his throat to turn off the ongoing racket and to shut them down.

Not immediately understanding his requirements, they revved louder. He slid his hand across his throat again and again in an exaggerated arc, grimacing as he did so. Finally, finally, after one more delayed piston, there was instant, blessed silence.

He held out his hand to Paul Desroseau, trying to make sure the boys could see it from the street. "Lawrence Tyrone, former professor of law and current farm owner. Can we start again?"

"Why?" Desroseau did not take the offered hand.

"Because, early on, I did something I told my students they must never do and that is jump to conclusions," Tyrone said. "I apologize, Mr. Desroseau. I think we have something to talk about."

Paul Desroseau thought for a moment, standing perfectly still. It seemed amazing that Desroseau's son had missed those genes entirely, if indeed genes were the issue.

"I appreciate what you are now trying to do," he said. "Truly. But you will be far more help if you explain my position to the police so they let me in peace. I do not want to be reminded of things anymore."

"How did it get to this?" Tyrone asked.

"My wife left me." Desroseau shrugged. "She said I didn't appreciate how difficult it was to deal with Yves, so I should get a taste of it for myself. That wasn't all. She said I knew everything anyway."

"Oh," Tyrone said, suddenly breathless.

"She said I just didn't want to know." Paul Desroseau said very quietly, with sadness in his voice.

[42] A Sound in the Forest

Tyrone drove up through the tree-lined path to Brian Resnick's bungalow and rolled down his window so he could hear better. The cold air flowed into the car, waking him up. After his inexcusable blunder with Paul Desroseau, he wanted to do it right. Karen Resnick's dark SUV was not parked in front. Instead, there was a small bright blue VW Bug resting on the icy gravel.

He glanced at his watch. One o'clock. He hoped someone was home and lunch was over.

Karen came to the door. She studied his face before inviting him in.

"I'm sorry," he said. "But—"

"I know. You don't have a phone."

Her back was straight, hips swaying, as if she was conscious of his gaze as he followed her in. A woman resurrected since the first time he saw her.

345

In the living room, something appeared different, although he couldn't have said what. The room looked fuller, brighter, more lived in. Toys spilled out of a yellow toy box at one end.

"Ah-ha," he said. "You bought new couches. Very nice."

In place of the one rundown old sofa facing the fireplace Brian Resnick made do with, there were two copper-colored love seats with soft yellow cushions, positioned on either side of the mantle.

She looked amused. "That's not all," she said. "Paint, rugs, curtains, furniture. You're very observant, aren't you?"

"Decorating is one of my strong points," he said.

She burst out laughing.

"How is your boy?" he asked in the eerily silent house.

"Juan Carlos took him swimming for the afternoon."

Alarmed, he mentally reviewed the proximity of any and all casinos but decided against being pessimistic.

"I have something to tell you," he said.

She beckoned. "Tea? Coffee? Come into the kitchen."

The kitchen hadn't changed, except there were far more appliances, boxes and dishes on the counter and in the sink. And Brian Resnick was no longer there. For a moment it seemed sadly empty.

"As you may know I went to see Paul Desroseau on your behalf," Tyrone said.

"Him!" she said scornfully. "I hope he starts running and never stops."

"That's going to be a tough one."

"Oh no, don't tell me there's going to be more trouble." She blinked rapidly. "I was so hoping it would all go away. Can't they put him in jail or something? What do we have to do to get them to reopen the case and have him leave us alone?"

"It's not that simple. There's something you need to know."

She stopped at the kitchen door and looked back. "What? Tell me!"

"I've looked up the court transcripts. Something I should have done a long time ago."

"Okay, so then you saw what he got away with."

"That's just the point. He didn't get away with anything."

"What are you talking about?"

"Slow down. I speed-read the entire transcripts, all three thousand pages, perhaps more. I lost track. I tend to agree with the judge and jury. He didn't do anything wrong."

"What are you talking about? He killed his kid. Brian always believed it."

"Brian could have been wrong."

"How dare you say that?"

"I dare because I read the evidence. The kid was so hyper he couldn't sit still. The mother left because she couldn't cope. The father tried to do his best but other than Ritalin, which he claimed just totally zonked the kid out, there was no help. And finally, the last time the father was bringing the child back to a special remedial program where he was boarded five days a week, the kid, Yves, took off on him."

Her look was hostile. "Why are you telling me this?"

"Took off headlong into an oncoming truck."

"Brian said he was lying about that. He pushed him."

"The truck driver confirms it."

"The driver didn't see what really happened. His line of vision was too high."

"The coroner found no evidence of wrongdoing."

"By the time the truck driver got out the bastard was right there, holding his son as if he cared."

"Maybe he did care."

"No, he didn't give a shit. If the mother hadn't left, he would have taken off." Karen was crying. "He would have taken off and left them."

Tyrone spoke deliberately. "But he didn't. And, in spite of everything, he maintains he cared for his son."

"What about all those other so-called accidents? What about those?" She spat the words.

"The school confirms the kid was very accident-prone. Some of those accidents happened at school when the father wasn't there."

He didn't want to get distracted by the thought that, secretly, the kid must have driven them nuts. In fact, they were about to give up on that lost, out of control boy, and hand him back to the father with great relief. "We didn't have the resources to handle a boy like Yves Desroseau," the principal testified.

"Your husband, Brian, was a good cop, but even good cops are human," Tyrone said gently. "I'll give you this. It does seem unbelievable the poor child was so hyper and accident-prone. In the end, the overwhelming evidence pointed to self-inflicted injuries. Not that he was bad and not that it was deliberate; the boy was wired differently and there was no help. Blame it on the system we live in. Blame it on the cut-backs which leave no place for such hyper or unusual kids. Would you like to see the transcripts?"

She started to cry harder. "Stop it. What are you trying to do to me? Why are you trying to upset me?"

"Because Paul Desroseau is not really the problem."

"Of course, he's the problem. I want him away from here. I want him gone!"

"He has no wish to hurt either you or your child."

"I thought you were supposed to be Brian's friend!"

"Wishing Paul Desroseau were guilty doesn't make it so."

"I want you to leave. Leave right now."

More than anything it was her initial look of happiness he regretted destroying. He was catapulted back to his conflicted feelings and memories of Leah accusing him of destroying all he touched.

She ran ahead of him to the front door and tore it open, flinging her arm out in a sweeping gesture. "You make me sick," she shouted, her face red.

"You don't have to do anything. Just think about it," Tyrone said, not sure whether he should pat her on the shoulder or try to reason with her some more.

"Get out! Get out of my house!" she yelled as he passed her at the door. She was trembling.

As soon as he stepped out, the door slammed. He could feel the vibration at his back.

[43] Bush Knight

On the way home, Tyrone was angry. Angry at Karen for being so unreasonable and angry at himself for not having succeeded in getting through to her. He hated failure.

As a means of distraction, he spent a day attempting to clean his place.

First, he lugged the vacuum out of the cupboard underneath the hall stairs. After a few passes around the living-room floor and carpets, he saw the layer of dust filming every piece of furniture and rummaged around the cupboard to find a cloth. Without a spritzer bottle to tame flying clouds of dust, he was soon sneezing, so he switched his attentions to the sofa cushions, meaning to shake them outside. It was at this point he found his cell phone buried where it had deliberately lost itself. He grasped it, a man starving for communication, thinking to call Henryk or even Sid Katz. The damn thing was deader than his career and more unwilling to listen to reason than Karen Resnick. And he couldn't find the charger he had gone out to buy no matter where he looked.

Determined to salvage something of the week, he dressed in dark slacks and a dark sweatshirt, pulled on his black leather jacket and got in Sid's car.

The sky was a gloomy pewter as he approached Henryk's house. Three familiar bikes were still lined up in the spattered driveway.

Parking the car, he made his way up the walk so engrossed in his thoughts he was startled when Henryk opened the door.

In the kitchen, the three men seated around the table were strangely subdued. This was a fraternity he probably would never understand. He wondered how easy it was going be to bring them over to his point of view.

"Well that worked perfectly," Henryk said. "The felon is walking free, the widow is hysterical and Juan Carlos is threatening to make you face him like a man."

News obviously traveled fast. Tyrone glanced around. Henryk was staring at him with an accusing look, BJ was examining his fingernails, Ed was profoundly interested in the bottom of his coffee cup and Zack was squinting down at his scuffed boots.

"I read the court transcripts, like I kept telling you I would," Tyrone said to the kitchen in general. "The Staff Sergeant, Des Brown, got them for me."

"And how will this help the widow with her problem?" Henryk seemed to be the only one speaking to him.

"Okay, you might as well know, none of this should have happened. It's a whole different story. I feel negligent in not reading the transcripts sooner."

Ed looked at him directly. "How so?"

"I jumped to the wrong conclusions without all the facts. Then I didn't bother going over them with all of you."

"Ha! Facts," Ed drawled. "Always gettin' in the way of a good story so no need to share."

Tyrone felt self-conscious at the implication he had underestimated them. "Crown witness was someone who claimed to have seen Paul Desroseau push the child under the truck. It was enough for an indictment. That and the history of injuries," he said.

Zach snorted.

"Listen to the man!" Ed commanded.

Tyrone continued. "It turned out the father was trying to prevent the boy from running under the truck. Coroner confirms there is no contradictory evidence."

"What about the witness?" Ed asked.

"Only saw the whole thing from a distance and from the rear. Defense lawyer made mincemeat out of her."

Henryk opened his mouth. Ed held up his hand to stop him.

"Boy had a history of injuries. Witnesses said he had poor self-control when it came to dangerous stunts," Tyrone said in the silence.

"So where does that leave us?" Ed said.

"It leaves us with a good cop, a smart, caring cop with personal problems and a personal agenda. And an accused who just might be innocent after all," Tyrone answered, sagging down in his chair.

It was sheer bad luck Brian Resnick was the investigating officer on the case, but Tyrone didn't want to say so out loud.

A case so very reminiscent of Resnick's own situation. Sheer bad luck. Or maybe not. What if it was something Resnick was in the process of working through? What if he were finally seeing past his own personal agenda?

Des Brown said one curious thing when he and Tyrone met again to discuss the transcripts over coffee and pie the day before. He said that a few days before he died, Resnick called him and suggested they could call off the watch. Since it was something the budget already dictated, Brown agreed without telling Resnick that it would have been called off anyway. Now when he thought about it, Brown told Tyrone, he felt it might have signaled a change in Resnick's frame of mind.

Tyrone mentioned all this to the boys in the kitchen but kept back what he had also avoided telling Brown. Cursed with an obsession to reconcile detail with detail, the former professor did not tell Brown about his last conversation with Resnick where the detective was still bitter about the outcome of the trial. There was no point. He was beginning to realize the heart could be as far away from public bravado as the moon was from earth. He had been content to leave it until the day he tried to talk to Karen Resnick where it all went to hell again.

"A hard place to be," Ed said.

"Why's that?" BJ broke in.

"Well, did you get what happened?" Ed turned towards BJ in an exaggerated way.

BJ sighed and regarded Ed without speaking. Tyrone surmised this was an on-going production that played out between them.

Ed smiled as if to prove Tyrone's observation was right on. "So now we have to talk to the — er — widow." His expression was deadpan.

"And say what?" BJ held his hands out, palms up.

Tyrone broke in before Ed could answer. "You have to say her husband was having second thoughts. That he re-examined the evidence. That he was going to talk to Paul Desroseau and apologize for his honest misconceptions and then he was going to come home to her. That's what you have to say." Tyrone knew he was being overly emphatic but he couldn't help himself.

"No shit?" BJ's eyes twinkled. "And those are the facts?"

"I don't know," Tyrone said. "But that's what you have to say. And I think Henryk here, especially because he goes way back with Juan Carlos, is the man to say it."

"All right," Henryk said loudly. "I will go and say it. I will tell them everything just as you suggest. But there is one thing I will not do. Do you understand?" He was looking at Tyrone.

"And what is that?" Tyrone asked.

"I will not speak with Tess. There is nothing to say. It has all been said."

"But has she heard it, my friend?" Tyrone asked. "Has she heard it?"

"I'll go," BJ said suddenly. "Might be better."

"You think?" Henryk looked relieved.

"Sure. New guy with no agenda. Just might listen to me."

"And you know what to say?" Tyrone asked.

"Darn right. Her husband wanted the guy to be guilty so he wouldn't let go because it reminded him of himself. And

355

then he called off the cop watch because they weren't being helpful. If he hadn't died he would have taken the guy out so she better admit it and move on."

"What?" Tyrone was horrified.

BJ's lips twitched.

"Don't mind him," Ed broke in. "He's got a very sick sense of humor."

"Very funny," Tyrone said. He stared at the man and wondered if he was a lawyer as well, a razor sharp one, who wanted people to underestimate him because it gave him an advantage.

BJ smiled. "I aim ta'muse."

"All right then," Tyrone said. "Tell me what the BJ stands for? I am hoping it isn't BS."

"Bush Jumper," Zack spoke for the first time. "He flies over bushes and ends up in one piece. He nearly creamed the guy who first called him that, but the name sorta stuck."

"Bush Jumper," Tyrone repeated.

"Yeah," BJ nodded his large bald head and dropped the act. "I'll try anything once. What's life without a little risk?"

[44] Unpredictability of Entropy

Tyrone drove west along Highway 401 in the comfort of Sid Katz's car. A car he was more and more reluctant to part with.

On this cold December morning he was on his way to see Tess, telling himself she was his toughest challenge, although he knew there was a much tougher one he was putting off with a growing list of excuses. He turned on the radio and tried to plan strategy.

Tess opened the door to him wearing red sweats and black ballerina slippers. Her skin gleamed, her hair shone. He could understand Henryk wanting either great distance or close proximity. There might be no other options between those two extremes.

"Lawrence," she exclaimed. "Here you are. Lunch is ready."

"I thought we were going out," he said.

He had dressed carefully in dark slacks, an old favorite cashmere sweater and his black cashmere coat and red scarf.

It was vanity, he knew, a remnant of the past. It was also a ridiculous effort since there was no way Tess could see him, but he went ahead anyway.

"No, no, Bea insisted on preparing lunch."

"Bea?"

"You remember? She comes to help me even though she really doesn't need to. She teaches piano. We met in dance class. We take it at the same studio. And then she said I needed someone and the someone should be her."

"Interesting," Tyrone said, his heart starting to beat a little faster. Or at least it was beating in such a way he could hear it.

In the kitchen, a woman was standing at the sink, her back to them.

"And here she is," Tess said warmly. "Bea, my lovely companion."

The woman turned and Tyrone let out his breath. His heart had been threatening to jump out of his cashmere coat and sweater and now he needed to give himself time to readjust.

"I think we've met before," he managed to say. He had always had a good memory for faces.

She smiled. "Perhaps."

He tried to compose himself. She wasn't the woman in some of the dreams he'd been having when he had his restless nights. This meant he wasn't becoming psychic, which his emerging awareness judged as a devious letdown. She had a freshness and cleanness about her, a clear smoothness to her skin and hair, but it wasn't her, although he couldn't help noticing Bea's lovely mouth. For just the briefest moment the name Roxanne floated into his head, but it hadn't been her either, he was sure of it.

"I know." He snapped his fingers. "It was months ago. You were heading towards this house in a coat with a hood. I was driving a motorbike. I saw you then." He saw her face again, the way it looked under the hood and remembered how mysterious and out of reach she seemed at the time.

"That is very possible," she said, unperturbed. "Would you like some bean soup to start?"

He focused on her more closely. She was taller than Tess, willowy, wearing a soft dress of an indeterminate rich bronze color or perhaps it had a fancier name in the fashion world. Her dark hair was pulled back in the way of ballerinas and she moved with grace. Her almond-shaped eyes looked golden. He forced himself to look at her carefully, with the eyes of a potential lover, saw her nose was elongated, like Leah's, and told himself he felt nothing.

"You take dance lessons?" he asked.

She nodded.

Oh that was clever. He congratulated himself on his grasp of the obvious.

When the soup was served and they sat down to eat, Tess took up the conversational slack. Chatting about her courses and professors, making comments about the boredom she was experiencing in tort law. He nodded often, sometimes forgetting to verbalize his responses, taking quick glances over at Bea, who glanced back with a small smile.

He couldn't understand what was wrong with him, hadn't been aware of the depth of his longing and could barely breathe at the extent of the confusion he was experiencing as a result.

"Yes." Bea was nodding at something and smiling at Tess. She glanced over at Tyrone. He wondered if she was reading his thoughts. "Yes," she said coolly and deliberately almost as if she were speaking to him.

During dessert and coffee, Tyrone sat in silence as the women talked.

"You are so quiet, Lawrence," Tess said mischievously. "I think Bea has bewitched you. Am I wrong?"

He swallowed coffee the wrong way. "Yes. No, no," he sputtered, trying to control his cough.

"Another conquest, Bea," Tess laughed. "You've confused him!"

Tyrone opened his mouth, trying to take his foot out of it. Sidestepping his awkwardness at the inability to be more gallant, he turned to Tess. "We need to talk," he said.

"Yes?" Tess bent her head to position her right ear in his direction. The secret smile had not left her mouth. "You have come here with a mission, I can tell."

"It's about —" he hesitated, realizing he had no strategic plan. All he had done was think about making one. He wasn't even sure what he wanted to accomplish. "It's about Rafe," he said.

"He's coming here later today," Tess told him quickly. "Does that help?"

"No."

"There's something else?"

"It's about your friend Henryk." Tyrone emphasized the word *friend*.

"Well, he's not coming here if that's your concern."

"That's not the concern. My concern is you."

"And why is that?"

"Because you can't just waste your life hanging in for some fantasy that may never happen."

"I don't understand."

She looked serene rather than puzzled. Tyrone was certain she knew exactly what he was getting at even though he was doing it badly.

He took a deep breath. "All right," he said. "You were attached to Henryk. For many reasons, he did not wish to entangle you, but it is obvious he cares. And then a young man comes along who also cares for you. Cares for you deeply. Take the opportunity. Don't waste it. We don't get many chances like that."

"Do you know how we met Henryk?" she asked.

"Are you changing the subject on me?"

"No, I'm not."

"Very well. You never told me. You said your mother met him, 'around,' is how I think you put it."

"It was Juan Carlos who met him. They met in a pool hall. Henryk used to play. I don't know if he still does. He was very good, I am told. Juan Carlos was — let me see — eighteen, and I was twelve and Henryk brought him home one night and my mother started to scream and there was all this commotion and my mother kept yelling, *Dios, Madre de Dios, que hacemos*, which means, 'Mother of God what are we going to do?' And I was screaming, 'What is wrong, why won't you tell me what's wrong?' and nobody would tell me. And then I touched Juan Carlos's face and it was all wet and slick and he was moaning and moaning something about my eye, my eye, and then I knew it was something very bad and I thought, two of us will be blind, how will my mother manage, what will she do? And then Henryk picked up Juan Carlos and said, 'I am taking him to the hospital,' and my mother was screaming, 'No, no, we cannot,' and Henryk must have guessed we were illegal because he said, just leave it to me, and he put Juan Carlos, who was almost dead with fright, on the back of his motorcycle. He rode — even then — and took him to the hospital and he must have known someone or something or maybe he just knew a private doctor, I don't know because we didn't go with him, and when he came back Juan Carlos wore this bandage on his head and Henryk never left us. And he never left us even after my mother died. Well, he left us, to sleep, you understand, but he was always back for a few hours every day."

She stopped and took a breath.

Tyrone nodded and then realized she was waiting. "I see," he said carefully, clearing his throat and gulping down half a glass of water.

"You wonder what this is all about? I'll tell you. It was then I realized, right then, I should never have children. How could I protect them? How could I know if something was wrong? What if they didn't say anything? What could I do for them when they most needed me? There was no hope. I was never going to have them, don't you see?"

"No," Tyrone said.

"What do you think this is all about?" she yelled at him. "Are you blind as well?"

He felt helpless, couldn't figure out how to placate her.

It was Bea who stepped in. *"Guapa,"* Bea said quietly. *"Tienes que ver su cara.* He really doesn't know."

"What do you think a young man like Rafe wants above all?" Tess said sharply.

"You," Tyrone said.

For once she appeared utterly annoyed with him. "Children," she said. "Think about it. Didn't he mention it to you? His mother and everything?"

"I'm sure you can work it out," he said, with a dim recollection of the conversation with the resident. But it had been such an idle observation Tyrone hadn't paid attention.

Tess shook her head. "No," she said. "Today I am going to end it once and for all."

"So you're going to stick with Henryk because he's safe? Maybe underwent a vasectomy? I didn't think you were someone so desperate to escape from life."

"It's nothing to do with Henryk. What do you know about it? Do you have children? Do you even know what you're talking about?"

And that was when he almost gave up. He had no answer, not a word.

He said, "Not everything has to be orderly with all *i*'s dotted and *t*'s crossed. What are you afraid of? Be young and free for once and damn the consequences. Look how you've managed so far. Don't be afraid. Don't throw everything away."

"Oye, guapa. Te dice la verdad," Bea said, as she watched Tyrone.

He got the gist that she was saying he was telling the truth and was on his side.

Tess kept her head down. He could see two tears slowly moving down her cheeks. She put her hands on the table, palms up.

363

"Just listen to this," he said urgently. "You must see that a twelve-year-old is not always in the same position to judge as when she is older. You —"

"Shut up for a minute," she interrupted.

Something softened in her face. The contrast made him realize how many subtle clues he was never in the habit of noticing.

"All right, now *what?*" he said.

She looked almost at peace. "I'm thinking. Maybe I can think some more. Maybe there is something in what you say. Maybe I am not obligated to make any decision just yet."

He said nothing.

"It bothers you?" Tess asked.

"I would have to say it does," he said. "It makes me impatient. You keep compromising. Why?"

"Why not?" She waited.

"I wish I had the answers. It feels wrong. You're young. Life is messy and hedging your bets doesn't make it neat. You just get older and still afraid to make decisions."

"Ah," Tess said, pursing her red mouth, undergoing that lightning change from darkness to light he envied. "What do you think, Bea? He has become an armchair philosopher. How disappointing. Do you think he's talking about himself?"

Beatrix smiled at him, put her finger to her lips, and nodded her head. To his surprise, he found both the gesture and her smile endearing.

"Maybe," Bea said out loud. "I think perhaps it's rather good."

He could hear water dripping in the sink to his right; he could hear Bea's indrawn breath. He could feel his own yearning and disappointment and at the same time he felt exhilarated at every decision he had recently made. Every unwitting turn that led him here, to these people. Maybe a life he could never have imagined was opening to him. Maybe the possibilities were still there.

He turned to Bea, pushing the faint and irritating memory of Roxanne far, far away. "I would be happy to discuss it further with you."

Tess burst out laughing. "Careful, he doesn't have a phone."

"I will get one!"

"No, Lawrence." Tess put a hand out. "Don't give in to the ordinary life just yet."

She was smiling.

"All right," he said.

"Remember when we first talked? You sounded like you hardly believed the chances you took. And now you sound different. Did you really know what decisions you were going to make before you made them?"

"Point taken," he said. "Remember to take your own advice."

She seemed expectant now. Even though he realized she was probably holding something back, he wondered if this time she even knew what it was. Maybe she was waiting for some signal. Perhaps something in Rafe's voice would tip the scales. And he hoped it would happen. When he remembered them walking together, the way they leaned towards each other, he couldn't imagine Rafe being willing to give her up.

He thought, *there is hope for us after all*, and turned to Bea with a small mocking bow. "Tess is right. Both about my life and hers. Will you allow me to check up on her from my special communications office located outside a variety store?"

"You have a computer?" Bea asked.

"Yes, that too."

"How about if I give you my e-mail?"

He focused in on her for a long second, just as he had focused in on Tess. The clean, smooth hair, the grace, the understated intelligence, the breasts rising from underneath the soft material of her dress.

"Ah," he said. "Another of life's curves. But of course."

[45] Walls of Jericho

At home, Tyrone walked between the buffet containing the maps of Mexico and the bay window in the nook with the maps of Milton and environs and found no place to stop. Throwing on his now familiar Hudson's Bay jacket, he climbed into Sid Katz's car and drove to his favorite phone booth outside the variety store.

"Would you like your car back?" he said, as soon as the assistant transferred him to Katz's line. He figured it would do him good to have the bike once again, it would shake him out of his lethargy and force him to keep moving even if it was only to Henryk's place and back. Sid, it appeared, was not in the same hurry to trade. It was like trying to rip a favorite toy from a child. "Are you sure? It's not very good weather right now," Tyrone tried one last time.

"Extremely sure," Katz said briskly. "I'm thinking of switching fields."

"Why don't you try representing motorcycle riders?" Tyrone said sarcastically.

"How did you know?" Katz's voice boomed so loudly Tyrone had to hold the receiver away from his ear.

Outside the booth, a miserable young kid with red ears, wearing a bomber jacket, was scuffing his unlaced sneakers on the cold ground, waiting his turn. Tyrone glanced at his watch. It was nine o'clock in the morning. The kid probably wanted to call his school pretending to be sick or to explain his delinquency. Maybe his parents had grounded him and taken away his cell. Let him wait. He was already missing the morning class anyway.

"How is Alison?" Tyrone asked abruptly, turning his focus back to Katz.

"I don't know," Katz replied glumly. "How is Callie?"

"Fine, fine," Tyrone said, not wanting to admit he had no idea. "What do you mean you don't know about Alison?"

"She's with her mother in Toronto."

"Why are you upset? I thought it was what you wanted."

"I didn't expect it. Who knows what those two are up to? Now about Callie —"

"Gotta go," Tyrone said hastily. "Someone's waiting for the phone. Talk to you next week?"

He hung up before Katz had a chance to reply.

The kid waiting for the phone looked just as glum on entering the booth as he'd looked outside. His face was covered in a sprinkling of pimples. "I made it short," Tyrone said to him with a wolfish smile. "I hope you have your excuses ready for playing hooky."

Keeping his head bent, the kid gave him the finger.

As he drove away from the phone booth, Tyrone wrestled with the decision that kept him awake on his sleepless nights. It broke into his thoughts at the most inopportune times in his waking moments. And yet, he did nothing, kept postponing and postponing. Confront his brother? Show up with a lawyer? Get a court appointed DNA test? Start court proceedings? All these steps were on the agenda, but he didn't want to see Leah, especially not as his brother's wife, so he procrastinated and intruded into other people's affairs instead.

He stopped the car and pulled over, rehearsing what he would or wouldn't do or say and how it might all go down. The encounter with Beatrix had opened a window on his life and he wanted to be clear about the way forward.

And there was Audrey's story. It affected him. Made him think how little anyone knew of what was in store and how very unpredictable and short life could be. Was that a reason to forgive his brother? And what about Leah? How could he ever forgive or face her again? She had been his and now she was not, unforgivably not. He had loved his brother. It was the two of them, the Tyrone boys, together for so long. He hit the steering wheel, his anger fierce, convinced once more he wanted nothing to do with either of them. He couldn't bear the thought of seeing them together.

And yet, and yet, it always came back to the young boy he suspected was his son. It all needed to be brought out into the open. He reached in his pocket for a tissue to wipe his face and found the two letters that were stuffed there instead.

Recklessly, before he gave himself a chance to think, he tore open the letter from Jessica, Spenser's daughter. He read it four times before he opened Spenser's.

He lost track of time, his head against the steering wheel.

Once he became aware of his surroundings again, he drove over to the liquor store and went straight to the aisle where they kept the bottles of whiskey. He wasn't looking for a single malt or anything aromatic with a complex finish to engage the mouth feel, all those descriptions connoisseurs use to show their membership in a rarified club. Any three bottles of cheap blended booze were going to do just fine.

In his kitchen, he removed a juice glass from the cabinet. Any other glassware suitable for alcoholic beverages was long gone. He uncapped one of the bottles and poured. Cheap or not, the liquid looked mellow. The true gold of the initiated. He sniffed it and went to the fridge to add some ice to make it more palatable. Ice should do it. How much Scotch could a juice glass hold anyway?

When he took his first sip he swilled it about with his tongue and felt its harsh, stinging warmth all the way down his throat to his stomach. It was terrible stuff. He should have gone for a good single malt on the first bottle at least. The second sip was no better. He shuddered. The third sip was still unexceptional. He wanted to get to that familiar oblivion where nothing mattered as fast as possible.

After he downed his sixth and seventh juice glasses, it was impossible to tell what he was drinking. He decided he would drive up to Barrie and punch out his brother. He took another shot. No. No. He would walk in on his brother after supper, after Jessica went to bed, and while he held his brother by the throat, Spenser would explain to him why he fucking well had to marry Leah — Leah, the only woman Tyrone loved and desired — never mind that she left him. It wasn't how things were supposed to work. Family should be more than just lip service. Brothers weren't supposed to marry their brother's wives unless they were already widows. It was right there in the Torah. He drained the glass and poured another. He would drive up to Barrie right away. Luckily, the car was just outside. Something he should have done long ago. It wasn't enough Spenser had married Leah, he had also adopted her son — Tyrone's son if it came right down to it. Spenser not only stole his wife, he stole his son.

And now Leah was dead.

Spenser had the nerve to send him those thoughtless, ugly words about a brain tumor and how devastated they all were. And would he come to the funeral? Funeral? There might not have been a funeral if she hadn't married Spenser and was where she rightfully belonged. Spenser's note was carefully and devastatingly neutral, devoid of everything but the bare facts. In his inebriated state, Tyrone chose to see that Spenser was insinuating that he, Tyrone, was at fault and Spenser had done nothing wrong.

He opened the kitchen door and stumbled out into the night. "Spenser, you bastard!" he roared. "Come and face it. I'll get you for this."

It started to snow. Large flakes blinded him and melted on his shirt. He brought the bottle to his mouth and took another swig. He saw Leah bending down in the immense night. She was dead. Dead. Dead. He cursed the trees. And yet here she was right there in front of him, dark and beautiful. More beautiful than he remembered, and more desirable.

"You know everything," she whispered reaching for him as he stared obsessively at her face.

"You've come back," he murmured, looking up into the falling snow. "Why did you ever leave?"

"You know everything, Lawrence," she whispered.

"I don't!" he yelled at the sky. "I don't know anything."

But of course, he did. He did. Was he speaking to himself without knowing it? Her words flowed inside his head and his heart. "The child you didn't want. Why do you think I left?"

"But now you're dead," he called out. "You're dead and I DID NOT KNOW."

"Where else was I to turn? I was sick. I didn't know how long I had. Who else was there?" Her voice filled his ears.

"You just didn't want to know," Leah said.

It was the last lucid thought he remembered under the falling snow.

He awoke with a vast headache to see a large woman with gleaming teeth bent over him. Her breath smelled a little stale and she looked concerned. He blinked his eyes rapidly, hoping to see Leah. When he opened them again, Audrey was still there.

"Audrey?" he said stupidly, putting a hand to his head. "Where am I?"

"Well thank God, you're back," she said dryly. "I was beginning to think I'd have to buy boxing gear."

"What?"

"You came stumbling over covered in snow and challenged me to a fight."

"Oh my God."

"Well, not God, exactly. You called me Spenser."

He saw that he was stretched full out on a twin bed in what looked to be a neat spare bedroom. There was killer light coming from two tall windows directly to his right. The frilly white curtains on either side of the windows did nothing to protect him from the brightness. He raised his head slowly and carefully and looked down. His shirt was missing. Every movement, no matter how small, made him feel nauseous. He dropped his head back on the pillow and closed his eyes.

"After the challenge, you fell down and threw up," Audrey said with no compassion.

"I am truly sorry," he said. "You have no idea —"

"Oh, I have some idea," she said. "You called me plenty of names and spilled your guts."

Callie flew into the room. "Audey," she chirped, "you said if we were lucky he die. He dead yet?" He felt sticky little fingers poking around his closed eyes.

"Gentle now," Audrey said. "But, no, not yet. Worse luck."

Tyrone was in no mood to be made fun of or poked at with sticky-fingered curiosity, especially not by the miniature spawn of a troubled Visigoth. He tried to sit up. The room spun and wobbled as the blood drained from his head. He didn't remember challenging Audrey but the memory of Leah was very clear and cold.

Holding his head in his hands, he wanted to cry. This seemed to be a season of tears. Instead he started to laugh, at fate, at how utterly unfair life was even though he suspected a great deal of the unfairness was of his own making. Gasping and coughing, dizzy and nauseous, not able to help himself, he laughed until Audrey began to look worried and he felt empty inside.

[46] GPS

In January, Tyrone discovered how to work the GPS in Katz's car. He programmed in Spenser's address in Barrie just to see what it would give him. It was not the route he himself might have taken. There were a few back streets he knew that made the ride shorter because traffic could be avoided.

Once he satisfied himself the thing worked, he lost interest and sat in the kitchen nook staring at his computer screen. After resurrecting his e-mail address from an account he once used, he wrote Beatrix a short note. She wrote a brief note back and there it rested. He found that after his drunken experience with the ghostly Leah, his heart wasn't up to much feeling.

There were mornings when, if he hadn't gotten so used to rising with the dawn, the feral cat and the few shivering birds who sheltered in the barn over the winter, he might not have gotten up at all. By some psychic instinct, Sheba would come scratching at his door on those mornings and he would feel obliged to let her in. Otherwise she spent her time sprawled over at Audrey's, letting Callie play horsey on her strong back.

Callie was at a stage where she wouldn't go anywhere without her, so dog and child and Cats, whenever she arrived on weekends, would wander over to bother him. He pretended to grumble, but he knew it kept him sane. He figured they must like his grumpy humor. He was sure he meant every crotchety word, although they appeared to think it was meant to amuse them.

He took out a legal pad and started a grocery list for their coming visit, opened his bottom desk drawer to its fullest extent to search for another pen, ejected the feral cat and immediately jabbed his fingers on something sharp. It wasn't until he ditched most of the drawer's contents onto the floor that he found the creased photo of Roxanne he had left there, strangely loath to throw it away. From what he remembered of the bike and how the photo was wedged, he surmised she might even have done it deliberately for reasons of her own.

He snuck a glance at her photo nevertheless. He remembered her bra strap carelessly showing under her tank top and how strong and smooth her arms were, strong enough to at least roll the bike away when he was thrown. He tossed her back in the drawer and bent down to the floor for the pencils, pens, writing pads, push pins and candle ends lying there. He piled everything on top of her and shut the drawer.

But something was bothering him. First Roxanne, and then Bea, coming at him, unsettling him, and just when he thought he was recovering, he discovered Leah was in the way. His memories and his grief over Leah. He'd known colleagues who divorced their wives and jumped into a relationship right away. It rarely ended well. The wiser ones took their time. It never occurred to him that he was in the same boat until his ill-fated marriage to Irene. Leah was right. There were so many things he hadn't wanted to know.

And so, feeling guilty at the thought of moving forward, he might have hung on to his indecisions for years if one bright morning towards the second week of February Henryk hadn't rolled in on his motorbike. The biker was on the great touring crotch-rocket model with full fairings and mud guards and hard cases attached at the back as if he were planning a long road trip. After an uncharacteristically mild spell, the roads were clear.

Tyrone had his coat on and was just about to make his way over to Audrey's. He watched Henryk through the mullioned panes of his living-room window. A sleek black Mercedes with flashy tire rims drove in close behind the biker.

For a moment he had a sense of déjà vu. But it couldn't possibly be Rafe and the stretch limo. And it couldn't be anyone else he knew. Unless she had suddenly switched cars, Karen Resnick owned a Japanese SUV. In fact, Juan Carlos and Karen, the most unlikely of couples, wanted to set up house and were busy, together, trying to help her difficult son. Henryk reported that BJ, a man of large chest and arms and precise words, when he was so inclined, got through to them, whatever he had said and however he said it. The thing BJ found most difficult, Henryk reported, was trying to dissuade Karen from contacting Paul Desroseau for parenting advice. And then, after letting Tyrone sit in appalled silence for what seemed a very long time, Henryk started to laugh.

"Very, very funny," Tyrone retorted somewhat put out that he was hearing everything second hand and that the bikers were gone without saying goodbye.

Now, as Tyrone watched, Henryk pulled off his helmet and gloves and started to head towards the house. The black Mercedes had followed the motorbike around the oak and stayed there with the driver's side facing the front door, all windows darkened and closed.

Tyrone opened up before Henryk had a chance to knock.

"Is that who I think it is?" Tyrone asked.

Henryk hit his gloves against his bare hand. "I am returning a favor," he said.

"A favor for whom?"

"You," Henryk said. "Who else?"

Spenser, a little heavier and better dressed than Tyrone remembered, got out quickly from the driver's side. Of the two of them he had always been prone to a little more flesh. He slowed down as he approached the door.

"Lawrence?" he called out. "I hope we can talk. Can we talk?"

He sounded hesitant as Tyrone remained silent. When Spenser came closer, Tyrone saw his brother's forehead was beaded with sweat. Spenser's face looked softer than he remembered. His hair, though, was darker, as if it recently became acquainted with a bottle of color formula, and his eyes were puffy.

Past the first shock, in spite of Spenser's apparent anxiety, what welled up in the former professor were the bad feelings that had stayed with him, especially resentment and blame. This was the brother who had betrayed him in the worst possible way. And now he wanted to talk? It was way too late. He bunched his fists, ready to let loose a barrage of angry words. Then he remembered Leah, or perhaps it was that she refused to let him forget. It was true that while in the past he knew everything at some level, especially when he was drinking, now he couldn't pretend he hadn't grasped it all when he was sober.

"What do you want, Spenser?" he asked in a hoarse voice.

Spenser raised his arms and then dropped them. The brothers stared at each other.

"Before you close the door," Spenser said quickly. "There's someone here I want you to meet."

In the past, Tyrone would have snapped, "Get out of here, I'm not interested." Now he watched Spenser's back and held himself rigid.

Spenser opened the rear passenger door of the car and leaned in, talking to the occupant. The back flap of his coat gaped. When he came away from the car he held a little boy by the hand. The child was perhaps four or five, with dark hair and Leah's dark eyes.

"This is Adam Lawrence Tyrone," Spenser said carefully, leading the boy up to the door. The child stared at the ground, taking fast, curious peeks up at Tyrone. He looked happy and confident and the former professor suppressed the thought that, as a single father, Spenser was taking good care of him.

"Adam, say hello to your Uncle Lawrence," Spenser said.

A tiny quick smile and another oblique glance upwards, but the child remained silent.

Spenser, a little edgy, looked over to Tyrone, as if expecting him to understand how to handle strange children in a nanosecond.

Swallowing his annoyance, Tyrone tried to calm himself.

"Hello," he said.

The boy continued to look at the ground while hanging on to Spenser's hand. Tyrone's raw instinct was to go back into the house and slam the door, avoid being gutted by the emotional turmoil he was feeling and trying to suppress. Why should he be the one to make all the effort? Spenser and Leah were both at fault that he didn't even know his own son. But a faint little voice was now in his head. The smarmy little badger in the book his niece had so loved. *Do you want to be right or do you want to be friends?*

"I have something for you," he said, clearing his throat. It just about killed him. Nevertheless, feelings other than anger threatened to overwhelm him and he was unable to turn away.

"What?" the little boy spoke in a deeper voice than expected and raised his eyebrows in such a familiar gesture it was as if Tyrone was looking in a mirror.

"I've been saving a whole bunch of trucks and cars for you, just for you, for a very long time," Tyrone said.

The boy looked up at Spenser and then at Tyrone and laughed. A high pitched, delighted childish laugh. He looked happy and carefree. Whatever it meant to him to lose his mother seemed to have lifted in that moment.

"You're funny," he said.

After everyone left, Tyrone sat at the kitchen nook in front of his computer screen, drinking coffee and staring out the window.

The house was too quiet after the events of the day. Henryk was back with his bikes, Spenser and Adam were in Barrie and Tyrone had promised he would show up for Jessica's bat mitzvah in Sid Katz's car. Reason enough, Tyrone convinced himself not to give Sid his car back until spring.

Spring was when the ground was more forgiving and less slippery and it was easier to take long journeys up to Barrie on a bike.

He promised Adam they would definitely and positively and beyond a doubt cross my heart and hope to die go riding as long as they only did it in empty parking lots and Adam wore a helmet and protective clothing.

Adam left, clutching a few toy trucks and cars he picked out from the assortment, enumerating everything he would need. "For an uncle ride," he called it impishly, in his deep little child's voice, and Tyrone smiled and smiled in spite of himself, although his throat seized whenever he tried to talk to Spenser. Still, the significance of Adam's second name was not lost on him.

He pecked away at his computer keyboard, composing his next e-mail to Bea. Beatrix, he called her, not yet ready to face the fact that her nickname and Leah's only differed by two letters. He was willing to take a chance, see where the river took him. He had, nonetheless, once more reached into his desk drawer and carefully rooted around. He didn't question what was driving him, just followed an impulse. When he at last found it, he took the creased picture of Roxanne out again, smoothed it, and, feeling defiant, propped it up at the back corner of his desk. He thought he would keep it there to remind him that if it weren't for her his life might have been poorer, or very different at any rate. He felt he needed reminders like it in order to keep perspective.

"Do you believe in coincidence?" he asked her photo. She didn't answer. All he could think of was that truth really *was* stranger than fiction. He could never have predicted or planned the domino effect that brought him to this point in his life.

The night outside was brilliant, one of those nights he remembered from a long time ago when life was full of possibilities.

That afternoon, under a winter sun, he had walked in his snow-covered fields and orchards with Adam. Together, but mostly at Adam's prodding, they decided the wild bees needed more shelter. Adam even found an old wooden crate. He dragged it over to the snow-covered hive Tyrone pointed out to him. Tyrone had to keep telling him not to step too close but Adam, too excited to listen, had an attention span of about five seconds. In the end, Tyrone was charged with finding out how best to use the crate to shelter the bees for the rest of the winter.

"I have a book," Tyrone said, trying hard not to keep studying the little boy, his son. "It's all about bees. Would you like to see it?"

He was encouraged by Adam's enthusiasm as the boy flipped the pages of the well-worn library book, pointed and asked questions.

"That's a honey bee and that's a bumble bee," Tyrone said as Adam traced their outline. "I'm thinking of getting some hives for honey bees, would you like that?"

"Will they hurt me?" Adam asked as if belatedly remembering Tyrone's prior warnings.

"No, no," Tyrone said. "We will have special clothes. Do you like honey?"

"Yes!" Adam shouted and got up, spreading his arms and zooming around like a bee.

Tyrone reminded himself he had a lot to learn about children.

This time, he swore, everything would be different. Hadn't the GPS of his journey led him directly to this point? Directly to Adam and perhaps a different journey?

Not daring to name what could be, he was afraid to hope for second chances.

He decided to think of it as an ongoing passage, started ironically enough by his wish for Spanish and motorcycle-riding lessons so he could run away to Mexico. At this point, Mexico had turned into a metaphor, and, at the same time, he was beginning to forgive the journey leading him to it.

He saw how Tess's fear about trying to face things when her basic instinct was to turn away mirrored his own. Now that Henryk was stepping back, it seemed Rafe was more hopeful. Fate and time were powerful forces. He would wait and see what came next in his own life without turning away. And he would make sure Adam was always a part of his life. And perhaps, sometime in the future, Spenser as well.

It was enough for now.

Acknowledgements

To my first readers – Sandra Shuman, Susan Szeyffert Gillett, Joanna Yuke and Michael Golvach – thank you for your comments and your encouragement. I truly appreciated the time you took to read the manuscript and to give me your feedback. The Lobsters writing group – all your comments were very helpful – I wish I could have had time to share more.

Shannon Whibbs, thank you for your editing comments. Judith Shutz, friend and editor extraordinaire – thank you for picking up any discrepancies, inconsistencies and everything else I may have missed. And a big thank you to wonder woman, Ruth Seeley, who *gets* it and makes it better. All errors that remain are unfortunately mine – there's no one left to blame.

A heartfelt and grateful thank you also to my advanced readers for your comments and suggestions: Grace Cale, Sandra Shuman, Paulette Lister and Michael Eben.

Joel Friedlander, Tracy Atkins and company, thank you for converting the finished files into a book and eBook. It's always so daunting to know what to do when one first starts on this path.

Jesse Krieger, Kristen Wise and team, thank you for overseeing all the many steps and plans required to launch the book into the future. I appreciate your patience, help and input greatly.

I look forward to what the future holds.

A. K. Blackman

On an added note, I have taken liberties with the Osgoode Hall Law Faculty building layout and room arrangement that readers who are familiar with the structure will notice. I used my imagination to envision an office and lecture room layout to fit the story. No rooms were harmed or defaced in this alternate arrangement.

CPSIA information can be obtained
at www.ICGtesting.com
Printed in the USA
LVHW012024071118
596367LV00003B/3